W9-CID-952

WRECKER

Also by Carl Hiaasen

Carl Hiaasen

WRECKER

ALFRED A. KNOPF 🐎 NEW YORK

THIS IS A BORZOI BOOK PUBLISHED BY ALFRED A. KNOPF

Text copyright © 2023 by Carl Hiaasen
Jacket art copyright © 2023 by Chris King
Map art copyright © 2023 by John S. Dykes

All rights reserved. Published in the United States by Alfred A. Knopf,
an imprint of Random House Children's Books, a division of Penguin
Random House LLC, New York.

Knopf, Borzoi Books, and the colophon are registered trademarks of
Penguin Random House LLC.

Visit us on the Web! rhcbooks.com

Educators and librarians, for a variety of teaching tools, visit us at
RHTeachersLibrarians.com

Library of Congress Cataloging-in-Publication Data
Names: Hiaasen, Carl, author.
Title: Wrecker / Carl Hiaasen.
Description: First edition. | New York : Alfred A. Knopf, [2023] | Audience: Ages
10 and up. | Summary: When fifteen-year-old Valdez Jones VIII, a.k.a. Wrecker,
unwittingly becomes entangled with a group of smugglers and grave robbers, he must
deep-dive into their shady dealings in order to escape their twisted net.
Identifiers: LCCN 2022026176 (print) | LCCN 2022026177 (ebook) |
ISBN 978-0-593-37628-7 (hardcover) | ISBN 978-0-593-37629-4 (library binding) |
ISBN 978-0-593-37631-7 (trade paperback) | ISBN 978-0-593-37630-0 (ebook) |
ISBN 978-0-593-70538-4 (international paperback)
Subjects: CYAC: Smuggling—Fiction. | Grave robbing—Fiction. |
Boats and boating—Fiction. | Key West (Fla.)—Fiction.
Classification: LCC PZ7.H493 Wr 2023 (print) | LCC PZ7.H493 (ebook) |
DDC [Fic]—dc23

The text of this book is set in 12-point Goudy Old Style.
Jacket title lettering by Mike Burroughs
Interior design by Cathy Bobak

Printed in the United States of America
10 9 8 7 6 5 4 3 2 1
First Edition

Random House Children's Books supports the First Amendment
and celebrates the right to read.

Penguin Random House LLC supports copyright. Copyright fuels creativity,
encourages diverse voices, promotes free speech, and creates a vibrant culture.
Thank you for buying an authorized edition of this book and for complying with
copyright laws by not reproducing, scanning, or distributing any part in any form
without permission. You are supporting writers and allowing Penguin Random
House to publish books for every reader.

This novel is a work of fiction. Most of the names, characters, and incidents are either the product of the author's imagination or used fictitiously. However, the shocking story of what happened to Manuel Cabeza is true and accurately recounted. So are the details of named shipwrecks and the lives of certain figures in the history of Key West. In addition, the island's bold graveyard iguanas are very real, though difficult to capture.

For the miraculous Katie

THE BOAR

FRONT STREET DOCK

MALLORY SQUARE

EATON STREET BAKERY

FRONT ST

AQUARIUM

GREENE ST

SHIPWRECK MUSEUM

EATON ST

MARGARET ST

FRANCES ST

WHITE ST

FLEMING ST

LIBRARY

IGUANA TREE

ANGELA ST

KEY WEST CEMETERY

FAUSTO'S GROCERY

ELIZABETH ST

SOUTHARD ST

WHITEHEAD ST

DUVAL ST

SIMONTON ST

OLIVIA ST

TRUMAN AVE

PETRONIA ST

FORT ST

SOUTH ST

SOUTHERNMOST POINT OF CONTINENTAL U.S.

ONE

Wrecker rides a heavy swell through the Northwest Channel. Halfway across he's already thinking about the return trip and hoping the wind doesn't kick up. Broccoli soup probably wasn't the smartest idea for lunch.

But fishing is good on the patch reef. Wrecker fills the cooler with yellowtails and mangrove snappers. Shrimp-pink clouds along the horizon promise another hour of daylight, plenty of time to get back to Key West.

As he pulls up the anchor, he hears another boat—a high-powered outboard, judging from the sound. His eyes track a silver rooster tail of spray, recklessly wide of the navigation markers.

Boneheads, he thinks.

With a roar, the outboard's props slam into a shoal. The monster engines grind to a stop, and agitated voices rise across the water. Wrecker could pretend he's out of earshot, but the code of the sea says you don't leave fellow mariners stranded. So he motors the half mile or so to the shallow flat where the speedboat is mired.

It's a sleek forty-footer, maybe forty-two, with grape-purple glitter wrap, twin lightning bolts painted along the pointy bow, and four mammoth Yamaha 300s mounted on the stern.

Pure Miami, thinks Wrecker. Twelve hundred horses, stuck in the mud.

He's never seen this boat before. The three men aboard are waving him closer. He eases his skiff to the edge of the flat and eyes the ugly trench gouged by the wayward craft, which rests tilted to one side in a cloud of roiled silt.

One of the guys—stocky, shirtless, thick gray hair, and a silver mustache—tries throwing a rope to Wrecker.

"Can you tow us off the flat, kid?" he calls out. "We'll pay you good money."

The rope splashes a few yards shy of Wrecker's skiff. The man hauls it in and makes another throw that also lands short.

"My boat's not big enough to move yours," Wrecker says extra loud, so that they hear him over the wind.

"Aw, come on, dude."

First he was "kid," now he's "dude." Wrecker guesses "bro" will be next.

He gestures at his motor, an old Evinrude 40. "That's all I got for power. You better call Sea Tug."

The man consults with his companions. Wrecker suspects they don't want to ask the Sea Tug company for help because the tow captain would be required by law to notify the Coast Guard what happened. Since the Florida Keys are a national marine sanctuary, the damage caused by the grounding could cost the speedboat's owner big bucks.

Wrecker is careful to keep his skiff clear of the shallows.

"Is the tide coming in or out?" Silver Mustache yells.

"Rising," Wrecker calls back.

"How long till it's deep enough for us to float off?"

Wrecker says, "Three hours, maybe four."

The man curses before huddling again with his friends. Wrecker can't see their faces or hear what they're saying. There's no name painted on the go-fast, which is weird. Most guys put colorful names on their speedboats, unless they're professional offshore racers.

And professional racers usually don't run aground.

"I gotta go," Wrecker tells the men, "before it gets dark."

"Yo, hang on." Silver Mustache lobs something underhand into Wrecker's skiff.

It's a half-empty beer can with a wad of cash folded into the pop-tab opening.

Is this a trap? Wrecker thinks.

The towrope comes flying again. This time Wrecker catches it and ties it to a steel eye on his transom. Silver Mustache knots the other end to the bow of the no-name go-fast.

Wrecker shifts the Evinrude into gear and guns it—nothing happens but noise, smoke, and churning bubbles. The purple speedboat, which weighs ten times more than Wrecker's skiff, doesn't budge an inch. Wrecker isn't surprised. He twists the tiller handle back to the neutral position.

"I told you!" he shouts to the men. "Your boat's too heavy."

"Try again," Silver Mustache barks. "Come on, bro!"

Wrecker shakes his head. "I don't wanna blow up my motor."

He unhitches the speedboat's towrope and lets the current sweep it clear of his propeller.

"So, three hours and we can get outta here?" Silver Mustache asks.

"Maybe four. Depends on if the wind switches." Wrecker cocks his arm to toss back the beer can crammed with cash.

"No, keep it!" Silver Mustache shouts.

"For what? I didn't do anything."

"You tried."

"Big deal," says Wrecker.

"Keep the money. Seriously," Silver Mustache tells him. "But, yo, just remember: you never saw us, okay, 'cause we were never here. Got it?"

Wrecker nods uneasily. One of the other guys on the speedboat says something to Silver Mustache, who scowls and tells him to shut the bleep up. Wrecker is pretty good at reading lips.

"What's your name, kid?" Silver Mustache asks.

"Charles."

"Charles what?"

"Good luck with the tide." Wrecker twists the throttle out of neutral and aims his skiff across the channel, toward Key West.

The ride back isn't rough, though the sun is down by the time he reaches the dock. Fortunately, there's a lightbulb that stays on all night over the fish table. Wrecker quickly sharpens his knife and starts cleaning his catch, tossing the heads, bones, and guts in the water, where the jacks and baby tarpon are waiting. A stray cat watches the feeding frenzy from on top of a wooden piling.

Afterward, Wrecker seals the fillets in sandwich bags and rinses down his fishing rods with fresh water. Before getting on his bike, he pulls the soggy cash out of the beer can and counts it. Then, just to be sure, he counts it again.

What the bleep? he thinks.

He'd lied to the men about his name. It's not Charles. He's not sure where he came up with that one. Charles Barkley? Charles Darwin?

His real name is Valdez Jones.

Actually, Valdez Jones VIII.

He calls himself Wrecker because his great-great-great-great-great-grandfather salvaged shipwrecks for a living. So did his great-great-great-great-grandfather and his great-great-great-grandfather. Unluckily, his great-great-grandfather was born too late for the wrecking trade—by then there were lighthouses along the reefs and the ships were powered by steam, no longer at the mercy of the wind—so he smuggled rum and pineapples from Havana to Key West on motor yachts.

The bootlegger's only son—Wrecker's great-grandfather—owned a head boat called the *Maiden of Matecumbe*, which took platoons of sun-seeking northerners fishing for groupers and amberjacks on the reefs. The fishing captain's only son, Wrecker's grandfather, grew up in Key West but was prone to seasickness and seldom ventured out on the water; instead, he drove tourists around town on the Conch Train and chain-smoked himself to death at age fifty-two.

And *his* only son, who is Wrecker's dad, played guitar, sang in the bars on Duval Street, and told anyone who'd listen that he was destined to become the next Jimmy Buffett. One day he packed a suitcase and moved to Nashville, where he changed his name to Austin Breakwater and basically lost connection to the family. Wrecker was barely three years old on the morning that

Valdez Jones VII drove away; he has no strong memories of the man, good or bad, only a few photos.

Later that night, before leaving for the cemetery, Wrecker tells his stepsister, Suzanne, about the grape-purple speedboat.

"Well, that's ironic," she says.

"What do you mean?"

"You call yourself Wrecker, even though you're not one—and tonight you find a boat crashed on a reef, just like in the olden times."

"They didn't hit a reef. They ran up on the flats," he says. "And the only reason I'm not a wrecker is because that job doesn't exist anymore."

Suzanne rolls her eyes. "You're missing the point."

Wrecker inserts a pair of new batteries into his flashlight, which is small enough to carry in a pocket.

His stepsister says, "What do you think those jokers were doing out there?"

"Partying, I guess. Probably drank too much and got lost." Wrecker doesn't tell her about the cash in the beer can, or why they gave it to him. The money has already been hidden.

"What time will you be home?" Suzanne asks.

It's not really my home, Wrecker thinks. But it's nice of her to say that. For more than a year he's been living at her house on Elizabeth Street.

"Not too late," he says.

"Just be careful."

"Always, sis."

The old Key West cemetery is a weirdly popular tourist attraction. It's only nineteen acres, but as many as one hundred thousand souls are laid to rest there—if you happen to believe in souls. Wrecker's not sure he does. The graveyard was hastily created in 1847, after the city's original cemetery got flooded by a ferocious hurricane, scattering waterlogged coffins all over the island.

Solares Hill, the highest point on the island, was chosen to be the new burial site. Some of the dead are buried underground, and some lie in elevated tombs or family vaults. At night the cemetery gate is locked.

Wrecker leans his bicycle against a tree and walks along Frances Street to the lavender house. The ladder he always borrows is lying right where he left it. He doesn't know who lives in the house, but the people always go to bed early; Wrecker never sees any lights on.

The ladder is necessary to avoid the sharp points on the cemetery's wrought-iron fence. Once Wrecker tried to scale it by hand and snagged a belt loop on one of the spear-like shafts, literally yanking off his pants. Fortunately, nobody was around to witness him running in his boxer shorts among the tombstones.

Coiled on the back wall of the lavender house is the garden hose that Wrecker always uses. He turns on the water and walks the hose across the street. He props the ladder against the fence and climbs up. Balancing on the crossbars, he lifts the ladder to the other side and hops down.

The grave of Sarah Chillingwood is only a few steps away. She was born on March 15, 1949, and died on March 15, 1978, her twenty-ninth birthday. Wrecker has no idea what happened to her, though who wouldn't be curious?

An old British man who lives on Pearl Street pays Wrecker the ridiculous sum of fifty dollars a week to take care of the young woman's marker. Wrecker doesn't even know the old man's name. One day he approached Wrecker in the checkout line at CVS and said he was looking for someone who wasn't afraid of working in a graveyard. At first Wrecker thought the man was nuts, or maybe some kind of predator, until he stopped him again in the parking lot and handed him a map of the cemetery, with Sarah's burial site marked with a wiggly X. There were tears in his eyes when he talked about the mess he'd found that morning.

The problem is iguanas, which invaded South Florida a long time ago. The gnarly green lizards love to sun themselves on the stone markers in the cemetery, and they're not bashful about where they poop (which is why Wrecker requires a hose). Chickens also roam the cemetery and disrespectfully deposit their droppings on the departed.

Because the man on Pearl Street visits Sarah Chillingwood's grave almost every morning, Wrecker comes to do the poop-cleaning at night, after the chickens are roosting in the trees and the iguanas have retreated into the crevices beneath the broken grave vaults.

Sarah Chillingwood's flat head marker is made of smooth gray marble. Etched in smaller letters beneath her name are these words: THE RUMOR WAS TRUE.

Wrecker wouldn't feel right asking the old man for the story behind the inscription. Many of the memorial stones have unusual epitaphs, which is a big reason tourists are drawn to the cemetery. A top attraction is the grave marker of a woman named Pearl Roberts, which says: I TOLD YOU I WAS SICK.

Mrs. Roberts was only fifty when she died. Wrecker doesn't know her story, but obviously she had a sense of humor. Maybe young Sarah Chillingwood did, too.

He grimaces as he sprays away the foul brown chunks that the iguanas contributed during another lazy day of basking. Still, if he's being honest, there are worse jobs that a teenager could have. And fifty dollars cash? Seriously.

Wrecker hears a sound that doesn't belong. He turns off the flashlight and kneels to conceal himself among the tombs.

Something is moving in the cemetery, something larger than a rooster or a lizard. Wrecker pinches the borrowed hose to cut the flow of water splashing on the marble. He got busted here once—some guy walking a pit bull saw him go over the fence and dialed the cops, who grabbed him on his way out. At the police station they let him call his stepsister, who went to the house on Pearl Street and woke up the old British man, who came downtown and confirmed Wrecker's story about why he was at Sarah Chillingwood's burial plot.

The cops let him go but warned him not to come back at night or he'd get charged with trespassing. Whatever. They weren't interested to hear about the iguanas lurking under the cracked tombs, or why the best time to clean a headstone is after dark.

Wrecker listens for footsteps in the graveyard and considers making a run for the ladder. Mosquitoes are draining his arms, but slapping them would make noise, so he lets them fill up on his blood.

What's that sound? Wrecker peers into the moonless night.

Maybe it's a tomcat moaning, or a dog whining. . . .

Or a person crying.

Wrecker puts down the hose and silently creeps through the acres of dead, following the sorrowful sound toward the Olivia Street side of the cemetery. There he spots a figure standing in front of a simple grave.

It's a girl, weeping. She looks about the same age as he is. Her head is bowed, and her shoulders are shaking. Her long hair is glossy black and straight.

Wrecker crouches in the shadows. After a while the

mysterious mourner grows quiet. She lights a candle and holds it above the stone marker. With her other hand she's arranging some roses—red, white, pink—in a Mason jar.

Wrecker feels like he's spying. He doesn't belong at this place in this moment, a stranger's private grief. He wants to run away, but what if she hears him and gets scared? Or calls the police?

Unexpectedly, the girl begins to sing.

El dolor nunca tuvo la intención de quedarse
Pero un dolor tan profundo dura años
La tragedia, la vergüenza
Los corazones llorosos deben preguntarse por qué
Y espero que los arcoíris iluminen el cielo

Wrecker doesn't know much Spanish, but the melody is sad and the girl's voice wavers with emotion. Silently he slips away, weaving between the tombstones.

Using the flashlight would give away his position, so he runs in the dark. Many of the old gravesites are crumbled and caved, creating an eerie obstacle course. Twice he stumbles hard, and the third time he goes down—landing, luckily, on a soft patch of grass in a neat family plot. Behind him is the unmistakable sound of chasing footsteps.

He gets up and sprints to the ladder. He's safely on

the other side of the cemetery fence when a girl's voice calls out:

"Wait! Who are you?"

"Sorry for your loss!" Wrecker calls back, and disappears down Frances Street.

TWO

He wakes up before dawn and returns to the cemetery.
The ladder is still propped against the fence. He carries
it to the lavender house while dragging the hose, which
is still running. As he turns off the spigot, he thinks
about the jaw-dropping water bill that's going to land in
the mailbox of whoever lives there. There's no way for
Wrecker to pay them back without revealing his secret
graveyard routine.

When he gets back to his stepsister's house, he
smells bacon frying and realizes he's got to invent a
story explaining why he was gone when she woke up.

She rolls out of the kitchen saying, "Tell me something priceless."

"Uh, good morning?"

"You're just now getting home? Did the cops catch
you again?"

"No way," Wrecker says.

Except for the old man who pays him, Suzanne is
the only person who knows that he still sneaks into the
cemetery after hours.

"Were you seriously in the graveyard all night?" she asks.

"No, I got up early to go find something I left there."

"Is your homework done? Let me guess: slipped your mind."

"I'll finish it right now," Wrecker says.

He doesn't mind doing his classes online. His two closest friends moved away during the early months of the lockdown—their parents got laid off from work—and there really isn't anyone else Wrecker wants to hang out with when the school reopens. Besides, sitting for hours in classrooms makes him restless, especially when the weather's nice outside. In that way, the pandemic feels almost liberating—once his virtual classes end for the day, he can shut his laptop and be out on the water in minutes.

He stays away from social media, a freakish choice for someone his age, but it gives him plenty of time to do his homework.

"Algebra and history are all I've got left," he tells his stepsister. "Anyhow, I thought you'd still be in bed."

"I'm taking your mother to Lauderdale for her operation."

"What now?" Wrecker asks.

"She doesn't like her chin anymore."

"That's ridiculous. Last time it was her cheeks."

"No, her nose," Suzanne says. "Hey, she's not the

one paying for it. Dad says 'Yes, my little honey bear' to everything."

Wrecker's mother and stepfather own a remodeled two-story Conch house on Fleming Street. Wrecker stayed there for a while. It wasn't an ideal situation— his stepfather's words—so Wrecker has moved in with Suzanne.

Temporarily.

She fixes him a plate of scrambled eggs, bacon, and cauliflower grits, which taste way better than they sound.

"So, what was it you forgot last night at the cemetery?" she asks.

Wrecker doesn't want to talk about the weeping girl, about how he fled, leaving a ladder standing and a hose running.

"My wallet," he says.

"Liar. Since when do *you* have a wallet?"

"See?" Wrecker says, and pulls out a fake-crocodile billfold. He bought it because the British guy on Pearl Street said anybody making as much money as he was paying Wrecker ought to have something classy to carry it in.

But the wad of cash from Silver Mustache isn't in the wallet. It's hidden in the toe of the oldest, nastiest sneaker Wrecker owns.

"Here's a question," says Suzanne. "Does Sarah ever talk to you?"

"Dead Sarah?"

"You hear lots of stories about that graveyard."

Wrecker smiles and shakes his head. "I don't believe in ghosts. You know that."

"Spirits, either?"

"What's the difference?"

"Some people who visit Gettysburg say you can hear the cries of wounded soldiers at night."

"After how many beers?" Wrecker says.

"Civil War tourists don't drink like Key West tourists. Anyway, it's bad karma to joke about things like that."

"No, sis, Sarah doesn't 'talk' to me. I never hear voices in the cemetery."

Except the one last night, Wrecker thinks, *and it definitely didn't belong to a ghost.*

He finishes his homework four minutes before the start of virtual school. Another good thing about Zoom classes is the chill dress code, which is basically anything more than underwear. Wrecker favors old T-shirts, board shorts, and no shoes. His teachers can only see him from the waist up on their laptops. Suzanne's cat, a half-blind female Siamese, is usually dozing on his lap. Suzanne calls her the Deacon.

Today, instead of taking the boat out after classes, Wrecker rides his bike back to the cemetery. He can't stop thinking about the black-haired singer, and he's hoping she left some clues.

At the entry gate looms a gaggle of tourists armed with maps and Yeti tumblers. Wrecker breezes past and goes to the section where Sarah Chillingwood is buried. Sunning on her marker are two young iguanas and a brown curly-tailed lizard. Wrecker chases them off before they can unload.

Then he starts retracing his path from last night, searching for an upright rounded tombstone with fresh red, white, and pink roses. It shouldn't be hard to find because most visitors leave silk or plastic flowers, which don't wilt and rot away like real ones.

The cemetery is laid out like a miniature town, with roads numbered up to Eighth Avenue going one direction. Laurel, Violet, and Clara Streets run the opposite way. The more recent graves stand out because they look smooth and polished; many of the older markers are fractured and sun-bleached, crooked as a witch's teeth. On some of the stones, the names of the dead have been sanded away by time and weather. The sight of those worn-down markers always makes Wrecker think there are no family members who visit, or who've got enough money to pay for new engravings.

Following inside the fence line along Olivia Street, he moves from one gravesite to another until finally, in an out-of-the-way spot, he spies an overturned jar and a clump of chewed-up green stems.

Iguanas do love to eat flowers.

Buried in the plot is a man named Manuel Cabeza. The small upright headstone says his nickname was "El Isleño," and he served as an army private in World War I. He was born on June 17, 1887, and died at age thirty-four on December 25, 1921, on Christmas Day.

Wrecker rights the empty jar. He can't tell if the gnawed stems once held roses, so he's not a hundred percent certain that this is where he saw the crying girl. Also, she's way too young to have known Manuel Cabeza, so why would she have been singing sad songs for him?

He reaches out to touch a glossy smudge on the tombstone. It's a hardened drop of fresh candle wax.

And that's how he knows he's at the right grave.

Suzanne isn't back from Fort Lauderdale yet, so Wrecker feeds the cat and fries a burger for dinner. After dark he rides his bike to the end of Front Street, where he docks his skiff. It rained earlier and he wants to make sure the bilge pump is working. On board he keeps an empty plastic milk jug with the bottom sliced off for bailing water, just in case.

The skiff is wet but floating high; the little pump did its job. Farther down the bight, where the super-sized boats are docked, somebody is throwing a loud party on a yacht. A live band on the upper deck is playing reggae music, or attempting to.

Wrecker hears a splash, and the crowd laughs—some fool either jumped overboard, or fell. One of the crew members throws a rope and drags him in. The yacht is lit up like a shopping mall. Wrecker can smell cigarette smoke and marijuana.

A sleek boat with four huge engines idles into the slip beside the yacht. The pointed hull is painted a dark color, possibly purple. Wrecker backs away from the dock lights, into a shadow.

Three heavyset figures step off the speedboat and join the yacht party. Wrecker is too far away to see the details of their faces, but he's almost certain that the men are Silver Mustache and his friends. For a moment he considers hurrying back to Suzanne's house to get the wad of cash and return it to them. Maybe that would break the guilty connection he feels, knowing he was overpaid, not for trying to help them at sea, but rather to buy his silence.

But what if giving back their money made them think that he *wasn't* going to keep quiet, that he was a threat to whatever sketchy deals they're doing?

Wrecker rides away on his bike. He wonders if it took the men all this time—a whole day—to float their grounded speedboat off the flats. That wouldn't make sense, unless the hull had been loaded with something heavy.

Key West has always been a popular hangout for smugglers, and it wouldn't be shocking to learn that

Silver Mustache and his crew are moving some type of illegal cargo. Wrecker wishes they'd go back to Miami or wherever they came from, so he wouldn't have to worry about running into them on the island.

By the time he arrives at the cemetery, the rain is falling hard again. There's no reason for Wrecker to stay; the squall is doing his job for him, washing the iguana poop from Sarah Chillingwood's stone.

Yet he doesn't leave. He grabs the ladder from the house on Frances Street and goes over the fence. Right away he realizes he doesn't have his flashlight. Slowly he cat-steps through the dark rows of tombs toward the grave of Manuel Cabeza, where he posts up behind a nearby vault to wait for the black-haired girl who brought the flowers.

How'd she get in here last night? he wonders.

His clothes are sopping. Hard-blown raindrops sting his cheeks and forehead. Usually he doesn't mind this kind of weather, but tonight he wishes for it to pass quickly. The mourning girl probably won't come out in a gusty downpour. Most normal people wouldn't.

Wrecker's phone starts vibrating in the back pocket of his board shorts. His stepsister is calling.

I'm ok, he texts. Waiting for rain to quit

u with Sarah? she asks.

Course

Hmwrk?!?

Tomorrow's Saturday, Wrecker types.

A rain puddle is forming where he sits, dripping like one of the graveyard statues. Another hour drags by. Nobody comes. The cemetery is as quiet as, well, a cemetery.

Eventually the sky clears, and the Cuban frogs start to chirp. Wrecker's drenched T-shirt is sticking to his skin, and the ruthless mosquitoes have found him. At midnight he surrenders. He scales the fence, returns the ladder to the lavender house, and rides away on shining, half-flooded streets.

His stepsister is still up, watching reruns of *That '70s Show.*

"How's Mom?" Wrecker asks after changing into dry clothes.

"Well, she's finally wearing a mask."

"It's about time."

"But only to cover the stitches in her chin," Suzanne says. "She got a plastic implant."

Wrecker sits down on the other end of the couch. "What for?"

"Because she wants to look like Reese Witherspoon. You know, the actress."

"This Reese person has a chin worth copying?"

"It's pretty darn cute," says Suzanne. "But honestly? Carole's dreaming."

"What does Roger think?"

"He's not overjoyed. He thought she was getting a Christina Applegate."

"Now you lost me," Wrecker sighs.

"Go see your mom tomorrow, Valdez."

"Sure."

"After you put up those flyers for me. The staple gun's on the counter. Also tape, if you need it."

"First thing in the morning," he promises.

Wrecker's stepsister volunteers with a group that's trying to stop giant cruise ships from returning to Key West. Before the COVID lockdown, three or four of the ocean liners would arrive every day, unloading thousands and thousands of tourists. They stalked through Old Town like an army of loudly dressed zombies, loading up on rum drinks and cheap T-shirts.

Over the years the huge ships churned up so much silt that it smothered fragile coral reefs and practically ruined the harbor fishing. It's why Wrecker's best snapper holes are miles from the island.

But soon after the pandemic shut down the cruise docks, he noticed that the water around the Port of Key West began to clean up. Now it's almost as clear and rich with sea life as it was forty years ago—at least that's what the old-timers say.

As a result, the town voted to limit the size of incoming passenger liners in the future. Naturally the cruise industry hired a battalion of lawyers and lobbyists to get the referendum thrown out. Wrecker is happy to help Suzanne by posting her flyers—"Fight for Safer, Smaller Ships!"—on the utility poles along Truman Avenue and Simonton Street. The name of her group is the Friends of Blue Waters.

"I'm off to bed," she says.

He rises to help her into the wheelchair. It's a reflex he can't shake. His stepsister, as always, says, "Sit your butt down. I got this."

The accident happened a few years ago, before her dad married Wrecker's mom. One night Suzanne was standing on a street corner in Miami Beach, waiting for a taxi, when a drunk driver swerved off the road and hit her. The guy was a pro ballplayer, so he didn't go to jail for even a night. His insurance company paid Suzanne's medical bills, plus a ton of money because she couldn't use her legs anymore. She banked some of the payout and spent the rest on a small house in Key West, her favorite place in the world. Her father would fly down from Atlanta to see her every other weekend, and on one of those visits he met Wrecker's mother, who was Suzanne's rehab therapist at the time.

And the rest is whatever it is, Roger being Roger.

Wrecker's mom doesn't need a job anymore, and Suzanne spends her days crusading for civic causes. She is currently single, having dumped the most recent boyfriend because of "ghastly" political differences.

"Why don't you get one with a motor?" Wrecker asks, referring to her wheelchair.

"Because I happen to enjoy the exercise," Suzanne says. "Good night, Valdez." She spins around and rolls on down the hall.

"Night, sis."

"Turn off the lights, please."

Wrecker makes a bologna-and-avocado sandwich, goes to his room, and locks the door. He takes the dirty sneaker from beneath the bed, removes the cash, and counts it—not because he's worried that Suzanne might have found the money, but because he can still hardly believe how much is there.

Ten fifty-dollar bills. They smell like the beer can that Silver Mustache tossed into his skiff, but they still add up to five hundred bucks.

Wrecker has no idea how to spend it. He's not even sure he can do that without feeling like a criminal. After cramming the cash back in the sneaker, he sits down with his laptop and googles five words: Key West cemetery Manuel Cabeza.

An hour later, Wrecker lies down in bed and turns off the light. He doesn't sleep the whole night, but he actually feels relieved to stay awake.

Because the story of what happened to Manuel Cabeza would have given him nightmares.

THREE

Wrecker's great-great-great-great-great-grandfather, the first Valdez Jones, was a Black diver who worked on ship-salvaging crews based in the Bahamas. In 1824 he was aboard a sloop named *Whim*, sailing off the coast of mainland Florida, when a pirate boat gave chase. The wreckers abandoned their ship, which was sunk and looted by the raiders. Valdez Jones and the rest of the crew escaped, eventually making their way down to Key West.

Swimming inside a foundered vessel was one of the most dangerous jobs in the wrecking trade. There were no dive suits or scuba tanks, so men like Valdez Jones had to hold their breath for long periods while descending into broken hulls and attaching ropes or chains to the cargo—from five-hundred-pound cotton bales to oxcarts. The dark water inside sunken vessels was usually toxic from coal oil, paint, lampblack, and other harsh chemicals, so the divers often got sick. Because of their skill and physical endurance, they were considered among the most valuable members of any crew.

After eluding the pirate attack, the first Valdez Jones returned to Andros Island and signed on with another wrecking sloop that made regular crossings to the reefs of the Keys. When the U.S. government passed a law meant to stop Bahamian vessels from salvaging in Florida waters, Valdez Jones and his wife packed up, moved to Key West, and became American citizens. That makes Wrecker a seventh-generation Conch, which is what people with deep roots on the island are called.

He learned about the seafaring side of his family from records at the public library and the federal courthouse, where captains filed their claims to be paid for the goods they recovered from shipwrecks. It had made Wrecker proud to see the names of three generations of Valdez Joneses on the crew lists. He sometimes wonders if his own father, Valdez Jones VII, ever thinks about the line of daring seamen who carried his name.

"Maybe he could write a song about it," says Wrecker's mother, a cold joke.

She's still bitter about the way Wrecker's dad struck out for Nashville, leaving a wife and child behind. She had waited almost three years before filing for divorce.

"Didn't he ever talk about the early Joneses?" Wrecker asks.

"I remember him saying they were sailors."

"Well, they were more than sailors."

"Mainly what he talked about," says Wrecker's

mother, "was himself. How rich and famous he was going to be."

They're sitting on the pool deck behind the house where Wrecker's stepfather and mother live—Roger and Carole Dungler, the former Carole Davenport Jones.

Usually she prefers the front porch, but on this morning the street is busy and brightly lit by the sun. She doesn't want anyone to see her face, puffy and bandaged.

Wrecker has nothing bad to say about his mom. He loves her. After his father left, she worked hard to hold things together. They weren't as close as some mothers and sons, but they didn't fight. He'd always liked being outdoors, on his own, and she wasn't the outdoor type. Still isn't. And, except for golfing, neither is Roger. Considering their mutual lack of interest in fishing or sailing, Wrecker often wonders why the Dunglers stay in the Keys; they could afford to live anywhere.

Roger never understood how a kid Wrecker's age could spend so much time alone on the water. He constantly pushed his stepson to try out for football, or run track, or sign up for the community baseball league. There were many discussions that never quite got as loud as full-on arguments. Often they ended like this:

Roger: "Organized sports would teach you how to be a team player, Valdez."

Wrecker: "No offense, Roger, but I don't *want* to be a team player. I want to be my own team."

The mood in the house sometimes got tense when Wrecker returned from fishing, which was usually after dark. Roger believed in early dinners, all hands on deck. Wrecker believed in watching the sun go down flame-red over the Gulf. His mother wasn't overjoyed when he and Roger agreed he should move out of the house, but she didn't make a scene. It seemed like she knew he'd be all right.

Today they'd gotten on the subject of his missing father's ancestors when his mom had remarked for the thousandth time that she wasn't fond of the nickname "Wrecker." And he had told her, for the thousandth time, that she could call him Valdez or Number Eight, or whatever the heck she wanted.

"Those old wreckers were nothing but bandits," she'd said.

"Not true. They rescued lots of sailors from sinking ships."

"They hung lamps to trick the captains into crashing on the rocks!"

"Bull," Wrecker had said sharply. He'd heard the story before—everybody in Key West had. It was one of many colorful island yarns.

"Mom, I looked at the shipwreck files in court. There were literally zero cases like that."

She'd snorted, flicked a hand in the air, and told him to get her some Tylenols, which he did.

"How bad does your chin hurt?" he asks now.

"Feels like I got socked by Joe Frazier."

"Who's that?"

"Ha, never mind," Wrecker's mother says. "I won't be leaving the house for a while. I can't be seen like this."

"Just wear your mask."

"I can't. It snags on the stitches."

Really, Mom? Wrecker thinks.

He says, "The bougainvilleas smell nice today."

She shakes her head. "My nose is all stuffed up because of the surgery. If there was a dead skunk in the room, I wouldn't know it."

But they didn't operate on your nose, Wrecker muses. *That was last time.*

"How come you don't care about *my* side of the family, the Davenports?" his mother asks.

"I do care, Mom."

The Davenport tree includes a dentist (Wrecker's grandmother), a Ford salesman, a registered nurse, a tax accountant, an army lieutenant, and several generations of Iowa corn farmers—interesting enough, although not as dramatic as shipwreck hunters on the wild sea.

"Sorry my people were so boring," she mutters.

"I'm sure they weren't. Tell me more about them," says Wrecker, knowing she'll drop the subject. His mother doesn't have stories because she's never shown any curiosity about her own ancestors. Some people are like that.

"It's such a calm, pretty day—why aren't you out on your boat?" she asks.

"Gotta go to the library."

"Homework on a Saturday? *You?*"

"Where's Roger, Mom?"

"Playing golf with Mr. Riggins, the city commissioner. What have you got there?"

"Staple gun and a roll of tape," Wrecker says. "I put up some flyers for Suzanne."

"She's an agitator. There's always something new to protest about. What kind of fish did you bring me?"

"Yellowtail."

"By the way, what was the expiration date on that Tylenol? I don't think it's working."

Wrecker would like his mother to be living a happy life, but she wasn't blessed with a sunny, upbeat personality. Roger's not a barrel of laughs, either, but sometimes Wrecker can't help feeling sorry for the guy. Suzanne's private nickname for Wrecker's mother is "Princess High Maintenance."

Due to a series of cosmetic surgeries, she barely resembles the woman standing next to Wrecker's father in the pictures that are saved on Wrecker's phone. It's not that she isn't pretty; she's just completely different, except for the eyes.

Wrecker stands up to go.

"Valdez, did you bring enough fish for Roger, too?"

"Yeah, but not for the commissioner. He can go catch his own."

"That's cold," his mother says, not meaning it.

Wrecker blows her a kiss and leaves through the back gate.

From a book of Florida Keys history in the county library:

Manuel Cabeza was known as "El Isleño," the Islander, because his family's Spanish roots were in the Canary Islands. Born in Key West, he signed up with the army when World War I broke out. He returned home with combat medals for heroic service on the front lines in France.

On the island, Cabeza ran a lively coffee shop and gathering spot called the Red Rooster on Thomas Street. He got a reputation as a tough character during a time in the town's history when it paid to be tough. In those years, Key West was a place where it was easy to find bootleg booze, gambling houses, or a fistfight, if that's what you were looking for.

Cabeza fell in love with a breathtaking woman named Angela, who was said to be from New Orleans, and before long she moved into his second-floor apartment on Petronia Street. The romance angered some people on the island because Angela was of mixed racial background. "Mulatto" was the term commonly used at the time.

One night, the Islander was dragged from his shop by six

or seven men wearing the white hoods of the Ku Klux Klan. Fighting every step of the way, Cabeza managed to unmask two of his captors, whom he recognized.

Outnumbered, El Isleño was beaten with baseball bats, tied up, and taken to a wooded part of the island. There he was whipped, covered with tar and feathers, and ordered to leave town for the so-called crime of "living with a Negro woman."

The fiery Cabeza was badly injured but determined to take revenge. The next day, Christmas Eve, he grabbed his army revolver, flagged down a taxi, and went hunting for the men who'd attacked him.

One of them was William Decker, the owner of a cigar factory, who was rumored to be romantically interested in Angela. Cabeza spotted Decker in his car on Duval Street and shot him dead at the wheel.

Later that day, a mob surrounded the building where Cabeza had taken refuge. Gunfire was exchanged until the sheriff arrived, promising protection to the Islander if he surrendered peacefully. Half a dozen U.S. Marines escorted him to the county jail, but an hour past midnight the sheriff told them all to go home.

It wasn't long before fifteen men in white hoods walked into the unguarded building, beat Cabeza with blackjacks, and shot him. Then they tied him to the bumper of a car and dragged him down to a spot near a trolley station on a county road, where he was hanged from a telegraph pole and shot again.

That was the gruesome sight that greeted Key West on

Christmas morning, 1921. No one was ever arrested for the lynching, and a grand jury of white residents basically said that Manuel Cabeza had it coming. Later, a secret voodoo curse was blamed for the untimely deaths of the sheriff and several of the Klansmen who'd participated in the killing of the Islander. Local lore said it was Angela herself who placed the curse upon the conspirators, and the whole island.

Yet another curse supposedly came from Cabeza's father. A local writer described the heartbroken man kneeling at El Isleño's grave, praying that "those responsible for my son's death die a thousand times more painful death."

Almost ninety-nine years after Manuel Cabeza was murdered by the Ku Klux Klan, the City of Key West honored his memory by placing an official military headstone on his long-neglected burial site in the old cemetery. The ceremony was attended by his elderly niece. No one is certain what happened to Angela.

This is the fourth account of Manuel Cabeza's death that Wrecker has found. Although some of the details differed in small ways, the brutal outcome remained the same. One newspaper reported that the Islander was hanged from a palm tree, not a utility pole, though that wouldn't have changed the chilling message being sent.

The power of the Ku Klux Klan peaked during the 1920s in Key West. Among its members were the police chief, county sheriff, fire chief, tax collector, at least one judge, and many well-known businessmen. Wrecker feels sickened and dazed to think that a gang so hateful and ruthless once ruled one of the most famously laid-back towns in America.

Obviously it wasn't so laid-back a hundred years ago. Nor was El Isleño the first—or the last—to be tarred, feathered, and tortured by marauding Klansmen on the island.

After returning the book to the shelf, Wrecker heads for the cemetery. Ironically, he finds himself on Angela Street, though it was called that long before the events of 1921. Anyway, town leaders would never have named a road after a mixed-race common-law wife of a man who was lynched as an outlaw.

Wrecker is hoping to cross paths with the black-haired girl at the graveyard. He's curious about her connection to Manuel Cabeza—is she a great-great-great-granddaughter? Did El Isleño and Angela even have any children?

Riding up to the gate, Wrecker sees a line of three black cars waiting to enter. One is a long hearse with a casket visible through the back window. Wrecker wonders who's getting buried today—not that he would necessarily know the person, but Key West is still a small community. The cemetery has at least three times as many dead people as there are living ones on the island.

Wrecker could easily slip past the cortege of black cars, but he wouldn't feel right snooping around the cemetery during a family funeral. Besides, it's a long shot that the mystery singer will show up with other mourners around. Wrecker doesn't even know if she's still in town.

He turns his bike around and rides home to get his fishing rods. An hour later he's out of sight of the harbor, his skiff drifting along one of his favorite coral ledges. Most of the snappers he's catching are too small, so he tosses them back. When he runs out of bait, he stows his tackle and sits back to watch red-throated frigate birds hassle the gulls. Every so often a loggerhead turtle as wide as a boulder pops up in the waves and takes a raspy breath.

The afternoon slides along in a lazing, timeless way, nudged by the soft breeze. Wrecker is half dozing when he hears the grape-purple powerboat. This time it's speeding down the middle of the channel, safely clear of the flats. The men must have put new propellers on the motors after their accident, because the boat is moving as fast as before, maybe faster.

Silver Mustache is standing beside the driver, studying Wrecker's skiff through binoculars. Wrecker can't think of anything else to do except wave.

Nobody waves back.

Wrecker waits until the speedboat is a dot in the distance before pulling his anchor.

FOUR

The next morning, Wrecker goes to the house on Pearl Street to collect his fifty dollars. Usually the old man leaves the money in an envelope under the doormat, but it's not there. Wrecker knocks.

"Come in, come in!" the man shouts.

Wrecker has never set foot inside the place. He masks up before opening the door. The house smells like fried sausage and mothballs. Framed family photographs and paintings of tropical beaches cover the Dade pine walls. An antique typewriter sits beside a stack of blank paper on an antique writing desk. Some old-timey love ballad is coming from scratchy speakers on a bookshelf.

The old man is sprawled on the floor of the kitchen, his pale legs tangled.

"Look what I've done. Help me up, please."

"Are you hurt?" Wrecker asks.

"Landed flush on my butt." The man laughs. "But that's what butts are for, eh?"

Wrecker lifts him into a straight-backed chair at the

table. The old man takes the envelope from a pocket and gives it to Wrecker, who puts the cash in his fake-crocodile wallet.

"I'm not drunk—I just lost my balance," the old man says stoutly. "I haven't had a beer in five years! My hips are shot, that's all. I'm as sober as a pope!"

Wrecker hands him a walking cane that's propped in the corner.

But the old man points up to a picture of a young blond woman, not quite smiling, on the White Street Pier. She's wearing a polka-dotted sundress and a royal-blue baseball cap.

"That's Sarah," he says. "My sister."

There are several other photos of her, too. One was taken when she was a toddler. A taller boy is standing beside her on a rocky cliff above a metal-gray, wind-swept ocean. Both children are bundled for the cold—scarves, caps, woolen sweaters.

"The two of us," the old man says, closing his pale blue eyes.

Wrecker is searching for a gentle way to ask how Sarah died. Her brother doesn't wait for the question.

"She'd met a man and moved here to marry him," he says. "The whole family flew over as a surprise for her twenty-ninth birthday, but when we arrived, she looked like she'd been crying."

"Did she say why?"

"We learned the truth after she passed. Everyone

went home to Belfast except me. That was, what? Forty-three years ago."

"I thought you were from England," Wrecker says.

"Good God, no! Northern Ireland!"

"And you never wanted to move back?"

"Oh, I'll go someday," says the old man. "For now, it's right that I stay here and take care of my sister. She loved this island. I do, too."

Wrecker swallows hard before asking: "What happened?"

"Sarah drowned. Pass me that cup of tea, please."

"It's cold."

Wrecker unsteadily pours the man a new cup from the hot teapot. He's mad at himself for asking too many personal questions. "I'd better be going," he says.

"Would you mind letting yourself out? I'm still a bit wobbly."

"Is there anyone I can call to come help?"

"Nobody," says the old man. "Sarah jumped off a boat, to finish the story. It wasn't an accident. Our family went on a sunset sail. The sky was perfect that day, perfect for her birthday."

His face is raw with grief, as if the tragedy had happened yesterday.

Helplessly, Wrecker says, "I'm sorry, Mr. Chillingwood."

"My name's Riley, son. So was Sarah's until she married Johnny. That gobshite was the reason she jumped—he broke her heart. I dived in after her, but she kicked me away and swam out of sight. All because worthless Johnny Chillingwood didn't love her anymore."

Mr. Riley's breathing is choppy and strained. "The Coast Guard found her, but it took a while."

Wrecker feels terrible for stirring up such painful memories.

But the old man goes on: "Her gravestone was supposed to say 'Sarah Riley,' but Johnny being her legal husband, he made them put 'Chillingwood' as her last name. He wanted the whole town to think he still loved her, but everybody at the funeral knew the score."

"What about the other words on her stone?" Wrecker asks.

" 'The rumor was true'? That was my idea. I waited until the rest of the family was home in Ireland before I called the mason back to the cemetery."

"Can you tell me the rumor?"

"That Johnny was running around on Sarah. He had a girlfriend." Mr. Riley's voice is biting and bitter. He takes another sip of tea. "This woman, she worked part-time at the sandal factory and danced for money at the downtown bars at night. Can you imagine my sister's shame? The heartache? Of course she'd heard the gossip and kept asking Johnny for the truth. Finally he came out and demanded a divorce. The next afternoon is when she drowned herself."

The old man coughs as he rises, gripping the sides of the table. "Johnny's in the graveyard, too, but the name got chipped off his stone. Are any of your people resting there, son?"

"No, their ashes were scattered in the Atlantic," says Wrecker. "Even my father's father, and he never owned a boat. He'd get seasick in a bathtub, my grandma used to say."

Mr. Riley smiles. "How much of your family's still here?"

"Only my mom, her husband, and my stepsister."

Wrecker knows that if he had the resources to trace every branch of his family, he'd discover scores of other relatives that descended from the original Valdez Jones. Those who had been born in Key West hadn't stayed; not everyone is cut out for island life, or island wages. Less than a week after Valdez Jones VI died, Wrecker's grandmother packed up and moved to De-Funiak Springs for the remainder of her years. Wrecker had second or third cousins who lived up the highway in Tavernier, but he hadn't seen them since they were all in diapers.

"Do you have Caribbean roots?" Mr. Riley asks curiously.

"The Bahamas. On my father's side."

"Yes, I can see it in your face."

"They were wreckers."

"Hard, dangerous work," Mr. Riley says. "I understand why you're so proud."

Wrecker wasn't conscious of showing it. The old man asks if he spends much time on the water.

"I've got my own boat," Wrecker says. "So, yes."

"I envy you." Mr. Riley taps his cane thoughtfully. "I used to travel a lot for business, but there was no true solitude on most of those trips. Nothing like the quiet grace of an empty blue sea."

"Yes, sir. I'm lucky to have that."

"Well, you're doing a fine job watching over Sarah. I'll visit her tomorrow."

"Try to go before it gets too hot," Wrecker says.

"The look in your eyes tells me you've got more questions."

"Just one."

"You're wondering how Johnny Chillingwood met his Maker."

"I know it's none of my business."

"Snakebite," Mr. Riley says. "Big diamondback nailed him in the woods on Little Torch Key. By then he was that other woman's problem, the table dancer. Our poor Sarah was long gone."

"What was Johnny doing up on Little Torch?" Wrecker asks.

"Hunting those little deer," Mr. Riley says.

"No way. That's totally against the law."

"You think he cared? Ha!"

It makes Wrecker angry, even though the man's dead and gone. The dog-sized Florida Key deer are an endangered species, and practically tame.

"Johnny was a poacher, among other crooked pursuits," Mr. Riley continues. "The snake that got him was nigh seven feet long, yet it never once rattled its tail. That's what Johnny said before he died. He didn't have a chance to run. You believe in karma, son?"

"Is that like payback?"

Mr. Riley chuckles grimly. "A cosmic version, yes."

"Tell me what happened to the name on Johnny's gravestone."

"Hard to know for sure." The old man winks. "Hailstorm?"

"Why not," Wrecker says.

"They skinned that big diamondback. You want to see it?"

"Maybe next time."

"I got it pegged to a wall."

"Thanks again for the money, Mr. Riley. I hope you feel better soon."

"Son, that's not up to me."

Wrecker wants to see where the Ku Klux Klan hanged the Islander, Manuel Cabeza, but the precise location is not marked. The county road is now Flagler Avenue, and the telegraph pole would have been cut down and replaced long ago. Still, Wrecker can picture the brutal ceremony: the killers illuminated by the headlights of their cars; El Isleño lifeless at the end of the rope; the muzzle flashes of gunshots; the husky profane jeering.

What kind of man would be part of that? Wrecker wonders.

His great-great-grandfather, the rumrunner, would have been twenty-three or twenty-four at that time. And like other Blacks on the island, he would have stayed off the streets—at home with his doors locked—while the convoy of Klansmen roared through Old Town.

Wrecker's father and grandfather both married women who were white. Had the men been born in an earlier time, they might have been lynched for it. That's what Wrecker is thinking as he pedals away, a chill running down his neck.

On the way home he stops at a sprawling leafless banyan on the corner of Southard and Margaret, not far from the cemetery. It's called the Iguana Tree because the island's gnarliest old lizards bask high in the branches. Wrecker spots a regal five-footer—scarred and spike-headed—indifferently staring down at the passing tourists. They've got no clue that they're being watched by a major reptile; its rust-colored head and long sinewy tail blend in perfectly with the bark of the tree.

"Yo, Wreck!"

It's a girl he knows from school, cruising down the middle of Southard on an electric skateboard.

"Hi, Willi," he says with a self-conscious wave.

She performs a slick U-turn and jumps the curb, spooking two roosters and a hen with three chicks. She rolls to a stop beside Wrecker and his bicycle. Her skate uniform is flip-flops, a gray hoodie, and white cutoff jeans. She smells good, like lilac. In sixth grade Wrecker had a crush on a girl who wore the same perfume. She moved to Boca Raton.

"Does he have a name?" Willi asks, pointing at the iguana in the tree.

"He doesn't need one."

"How about 'Ichabod'? He looks like a wise old Ichabod."

"I guess he does." Wrecker is more shy than usual around Willi, and he's not sure why.

She has curly sun-streaked hair and wide eyes that are sea-foam green. Star soccer player and, of course, straight A's. Yet, amazingly, her boyfriend is as dumb as a mud fence. Wrecker has never made sense of it. Maybe the guy has the secret soul of a poet, or maybe Willi's just killing time until someone better comes along.

She puts an end to Wrecker's speculation by saying, "Clay and I broke up."

"Oh. Sorry."

"No, you're not."

Even though the lower part of her face is covered, Wrecker can tell she's smiling. "I like your mask," he says.

"It's a Maryland blue crab. My cousin in Baltimore made it. Yours is . . . ?"

"Fish scales. I dunno." Wrecker readjusts the gaiter he's wearing. He bought it for five bucks at a tackle shop. "It's supposed to be a tarpon," he says.

"You get the vaccine?"

"Oh yeah."

Willi takes off her mask. "Me too."

Wrecker tugs the tarpon gaiter down around his neck.

"I heard a story about you," Willi says. "Don't get mad, okay?"

"What'd ya hear?"

"That you've been hangin' out in the graveyard at night."

"Bull," says Wrecker.

"Clay said you use his uncle's ladder to climb the fence."

"Seriously?"

"His uncle lives on Frances Street," Willi says.

Wrecker wishes he'd left his face covered so that she couldn't see how busted he looks. He's dying to know if Clay's uncle said anything about the garden hose, but he can't bring it up without basically confessing.

"Tell Clay to come see me," he says to Willi.

"We're not together anymore, remember? Anyway, he's too chicken."

"He shouldn't be talking crap about someone he's scared of."

Willi shrugs. "His uncle drinks too much. That's between you and me. Stumbles around his house in the dark, bouncin' off the furniture."

"I better go," Wrecker says.

"Yo, check out Ichabod's hot date."

Grateful to hear the subject change, Wrecker looks up in the tree. The old spike-headed iguana has been joined on the same limb by a sleeker, brighter one.

Willi says, "Could be true love."

"Just what the island needs—more lizards."

"Yo, Wreck, I only told you what Clay's uncle said just in case."

"In case of what?"

"Case it was true, and maybe some night you wanted company at the graveyard. I don't freak out easy."

"Thanks, but—"

"Still got my number? I bet you do."

Willi's eyes are dancing as she hops on the skateboard. Wrecker wants to act cool and look the other way while she glides off, but he can't.

And of course she turns, glancing over one shoulder.

And catches him staring at her.

"What an idiot," he mutters, referring to himself.

* * *

The note on Suzanne's refrigerator says she went to a night rally for the Friends of Blue Waters near the cruise-ship docks. Wrecker heats a plate of spaghetti, inhales it, and bikes to Mallory Square. The gathering is larger than he expected—at least two hundred people.

Suzanne, who's handing out leaflets by the stage, seems happily surprised to see him. "Finally my little bro is getting politically involved!"

"Hey, who put up all those flyers around town?"

Onstage, a Mohawk-cut dude with an acoustic guitar starts playing a Bob Marley song. A jaunty cockatoo on his shoulder sings along. Meanwhile, people are dropping money in an old pickle jar, which is almost half-full.

LEGAL FUND, says the handwritten cardboard sign propped nearby.

Wrecker steps forward and pulls the roll from his pocket—ten fifty-dollar bills. Quickly he pushes the cash into the pickle jar. Suzanne sees him do it, though she's got no idea how much was in his hand. Wrecker knows she thinks it's his graveyard money.

She smiles warmly. "Thanks, Valdez. You're a good guy."

"Not exactly 'getting involved,' but maybe it'll help."

"Come on, man, show me some. I mean, right now."

They bump elbows. "Love you," his stepsister says. "Love you, too."

Fifteen minutes later, Wrecker is standing in the dark next to the iron fence around the cemetery, wondering where he's going to find another ladder and hose.

A cold front is moving through. The hard northeaster has kicked up, whipping through the rows of tombs, knocking down vases, scattering plastic flower petals. Wrecker wishes he had the all-weather jacket he keeps stowed on the skiff.

In a lull between gusts, a sound rises from the graveyard—a soft melody wavering like the call of a lonesome bird. Wrecker cups both ears to listen.

It's someone singing in Spanish.

He scrambles over the fence, shredding his sleeves on the spikes, and drops down among the graves.

FIVE

The battleship *Maine* exploded and sank in Havana Harbor on February 15, 1898, killing more than 260 American sailors. The U.S. government blamed Spain, which owned Cuba at the time, and war was declared. The cause of the harbor disaster has always been debated; some investigators believed the blast was sparked not by an enemy bomb but rather by coal accidentally catching fire inside the vessel's storage bunker.

Either way, a horrible tragedy. Ninety miles across the sea from where the *Maine* went down, a monument to those who perished stands as the tallest marker in the Key West cemetery. Its centerpiece is a copper statue of a sailor saluting with one hand and holding an upright oar with the other. Buried at the memorial are two dozen casualties of the battleship explosion along with several veterans of the ensuing Spanish-American War. There are also honored graves of American servicemen from other conflicts, including several Black Americans who served as sailors in the Civil War.

But on this night, the U.S.S. *Maine* monument is

also a safe hiding place. Wrecker is hunkered low near the feet of the copper sailor. The singing had stopped as soon as he landed on the other side of the cemetery fence. He'd run to the grave of Manuel Cabeza, but the long-haired girl wasn't there. No flowers, no candle.

Maybe what I heard was just a trick of the wind, Wrecker had thought as he darted for cover. *Or maybe . . .*

Nope. Not even maybe. The whole idea of ghosts was nonsense.

The *Maine* memorial is blocking the chilly gusts while Wrecker waits for the phantom singer to start again. The wind makes it hard to hear anything, except for the jetliners landing every few minutes at the airport.

Impatience sets in. There's still a job to do.

When the next plane comes roaring overhead, Wrecker gets up and dashes to the plot of Sarah Chillingwood. Glistening on the slab is a humongous iguana dump.

Lucky me, he thinks, standing there without a hose, or even a pail of water.

He drops to his knees, peels off his torn T-shirt, bunches it like a rag, and starts scrubbing. After he's done, he sits down at the other end of the grave marker. The marble is cold enough that he can feel it through the seat of his pants. His teeth start to chatter.

"Yo, kid!" a gruff voice shouts from the shadows.

Wrecker's breath snags in his throat. He sees a

broad figure garbed in dark clothes leaning against an old tomb. A match flares, followed by the foul whiff of a cigar.

Cops don't usually smoke on duty, but Wrecker isn't taking any chances.

"I'm on my way out," he calls to the other graveyard traveler, but the man begins walking toward him.

Wrecker jumps to his feet and kicks away his filthy T-shirt.

"Chill out, Charles," says the approaching prowler.

"What?"

"Remember me? Sure you do." The lava-orange glow of the cigar tip illuminates the features of the man's face, most notably a trimmed silver mustache.

"Bro, you must be freezing your butt off," he says.

"I'm okay." Wrecker's trying not to appear nervous, and failing.

Silver Mustache now stands only a few feet away, arms folded. He's not as tall as Wrecker, but he looks twice as heavy. He's wearing a long dark coat and, of all things, black leather gloves.

Possibly the only pair on the island, Wrecker thinks.

"So here lies the late Sarah Chillingwood," Silver Mustache says, shining a penlight on her stone. "How'd she go so young?"

"I don't know." Wrecker won't be sharing the private details of the dead woman's story.

"Aw, c'mon, Charlie. You come here every freakin'

night, and you don't even know how she croaked? Also: What rumor was true? Who puts that on a gravestone?"

"She's not my family," Wrecker says. "An old guy in town, he pays me to take care of the grave."

Silver Mustache grins through a cloud of smoke that the wind sweeps away. "So this isn't personal. You're a businessman, just like me."

"I don't ask questions."

"I didn't either when I was your age, but you'll learn. How much does the old man pay you to watch over her?"

"Fifty dollars a week," Wrecker replies.

Silver Mustache cackles. "You're an operator, Charlie."

"That's not my name."

"Fine. *Charles*, then."

"That's not it, either. I'll tell you mine if you tell me yours."

"Kid, there's no need for that."

"Exactly," says Wrecker. "FYI, Sarah was the old man's sister. I didn't ask for fifty bucks—that's what he offered. The iguanas around here, they crap all over the graves. It's gross."

Silver Mustache pinches the end of his cigar, snuffing the ember. Wrecker is grateful to be free of the burning stink, but now he's getting a full blast of the man's cologne.

Stifling a sneeze, Wrecker asks, "Who says I come here every night?"

"This island has lots of eyes, and lots of big mouths. Should I keep calling you Charles?"

"What do I call *you?*"

"A stranger. Officially, we don't know each other—never met, never will," says Silver Mustache. "Back to business: You wanna make another fifty a week?"

"I'm good."

"That's kind of insulting. What'd you do with the five hundred I tossed in your boat the other day? New Jordans? More fishing poles?"

Wrecker says, "I gave the money away. Every dollar."

"Yeah, I'm sure."

"They're, like, environmentalists. Trying to keep the harbor clean."

"What a crock."

"It's the truth," Wrecker says. "I don't care if you believe me or not."

"You wasted five hundred bucks on a bunch of snowflake tree huggers?"

"They're doing something good."

Silver Mustache wags a gloved finger. "You're not well, kid. Did your momma drop you on your head when you were a baby?"

Wrecker's afraid he might say something he'll regret. He looks up at the clear sky, sprayed with stars. His teeth are chattering again.

"It's c-c-cold, man," he murmurs.

"Take a walk with me."

It sounds like more of an order than an offer, but Wrecker rolls with it. He's curious to find out what Silver Mustache is doing in the cemetery. The man leads him through the Catholic section to a new granite crypt. It's only wide enough to hold a single coffin. Nothing has been engraved on the stone plaque above the mahogany door.

"Stonemason's driving down from Hialeah tomorrow," Silver Mustache explains, relighting his cigar. "The funeral was yesterday. You were here, bro. On your bike?"

"That's right."

"I was riding in the black hearse with the casket. You couldn't see me," Silver Mustache says.

Wrecker is wishing he had a long warm coat and gloves, too.

"Was this somebody in your f-f-family?" he asks with a shiver.

"Nah, just a friend. He was like a brother to me, though. Caught the corona and, boom, he was gone in forty-eight hours. Truly tragic."

The stars aren't bright enough for Wrecker to read the expression on the man's face.

"Your friend wasn't v-v-vaxed?"

"Obviously," Silver Mustache says. "I told him to get the shots, but he was stubborn as a donkey."

"D-d-did he live on the island?"

"Moved here not long ago. Fell crazy in love with the place. Who doesn't?"

"S-s-sure," Wrecker says.

"Anyway, I'll pay you to keep an eye on him."

"I can't take on any m-m-more work. I'm too b-b-busy with school."

"What's the big deal? When you're done with poor Sarah, cruise over this way and check on my friend. What's five minutes more if you're already standing in a bleepin' graveyard?"

"He'll be f-f-fine. There aren't as many iguanas in this part." Wrecker has no idea if that's true or not.

Silver Mustache says, "See that tree? It's fulla roosters and hens. All of us that came to the funeral, we had to clean our shoes after." He glances at the outrageous gold watch on his wrist. "Gotta go," he says. "Here, hold out your right hand."

"Why?"

"'Cause we're gonna shake on the deal. That's what businessmen like us do."

Not surprisingly, Silver Mustache's grip is strong. He folds something into the palm of Wrecker's hand.

"That's a fifty," he says, "with my number written on President Grant's sour mug. Call me right away if you come here and find anything wrong."

Like what? Wrecker thinks.

"My friend had some enemies, bad people. I need to know if this place gets . . . disrespected. You understand?"

"Yeah, I guess."

"Let's get outta here, dude," Silver Mustache says. "Your lips are turning blue."

They walk to the cemetery entrance, where the gate stands open. Wrecker doesn't know if Silver Mustache has a key, or broke the lock. A black sedan with tinted windows sits idling in the driveway.

"We'll be in touch," Silver Mustache says.

"I have a q-q-question."

"Fire away."

"Was there anyone else here tonight?"

"Here? In the graveyard?"

"I heard a girl singing, in Spanish," Wrecker says. "I know it sounds crazy."

Silver Mustache is smiling. He touches the music app on his phone, and a soft female voice rises over the humming wind.

"Celia Cruz," he says. "The Cuban queen of my playlist."

"That's the voice I heard."

"She wasn't a girl when she made that record, but she could sing like one. I was listening to her tonight while visiting my dead amigo. She was his favorite, too."

Wrecker feels foolish for allowing the notion of

a ghost to enter his mind. But tonight's serenade by Celia Cruz doesn't solve the mystery of the flesh-and-blood girl he saw with his own eyes weeping at Manuel Cabeza's grave.

"Need a ride?" Silver Mustache asks, pocketing his phone.

Wrecker shakes his head. "My b-b-bike's at the end of the b-b-block."

"When you goin' fishing again?"

"Soon as this c-c-cold front p-p-pushes through."

"So maybe I'll see you out on the water," Silver Mustache says. "But remember, you won't see me— even if you do."

"Yep. G-g-got it."

"And what I said about your mommy droppin' you on your gourd? That was just a joke, kid. I can see you're not dumb."

"I'm not," Wrecker says.

"Stay that way."

Then Silver Mustache slides into the back seat of the black sedan, which speeds off the wrong way up Angela Street.

SIX

Wrecker stands in the steaming shower until Suzanne bangs on the door and tells him to stop wasting water. A bowl of chicken-noodle soup is waiting when he walks into the kitchen.

"So let's hear about tonight's drama," Suzanne says.

"No drama. I tore my shirt off jumping the fence."

"Because the ladder . . . broke? Or what?"

"The ladder wasn't available," Wrecker says.

The hot soup tastes better than anything he could imagine.

"And naturally it didn't occur to you to take a jacket." Suzanne rolls her wheelchair over to the coffee-maker. "How about an espresso?"

"I'm good, sis. I didn't know the wind was going to be so cold."

"FYI, Dad tested positive today. He thinks he caught it at a poker game last week. Or trivia night at the lodge."

"Natural selection," says Wrecker.

"Don't go all Darwin on me."

"How sick is he?"

"Not bad. Runny nose, sore throat. I practically had to drag him to the health department for the test."

"Good thing you did," Wrecker says.

Roger has refused to get the vaccine. He says it's a government plot to inject microchip tracking devices in people's arms. And now he's got the virus.

"Your mother thinks she has a cough," Suzanne reports, "but she won't get tested. She's terrified of the swab."

"Seriously? She'll let a surgeon carve a fake chin on her face, but she's afraid to put a Q-tip up her nose."

"No comment."

"Well, on the plus side—"

"Stop, Valdez. I know what you're gonna say."

"—we're off the hook for dinner next Sunday. They'll be quarantined."

"That's mean," Suzanne says.

"You're thinking the same thing. Admit it."

"We're both going to hell."

"Doubtful." Wrecker refills his soup bowl. He doesn't dislike Roger, but family gatherings can still get uncomfortable.

"Dad never *told* you to move out of his house," Suzanne says.

Wrecker reminds her that the decision was mutual. "Best for everyone," he adds. "Mom was driving me nuts, anyway. Every weekend she'd make all these plans for me and Roger."

"She just wanted you to know what it was like to have a full-time father."

I'm not sure Roger signed up for that, Wrecker thinks.

"Sis, I won't be staying here forever. Promise."

"I honestly don't mind the company," Suzanne says. "Thanks for coming to the rally tonight, by the way. Can I ask how much money you dropped in the jar?"

Wrecker tells her twenty bucks; it sounds like an amount he could afford.

"You're a good soul, Valdez," she says. "Somebody gave us five hundred—ten fifties rolled together. You believe that?"

"Who was it?" Wrecker asks innocently.

"No clue. One of the volunteers actually thought it was you, which was pretty hilarious."

"Where would I get five hundred dollars?"

"Exactly. And if you had it, you wouldn't give it away."

"Definitely not!" Wrecker says.

Later, lying in bed, he wonders how he got tangled up with a character like Silver Mustache. He shouldn't have accepted the cash tonight in the graveyard, just as he shouldn't have kept the beer-can cash that afternoon in the skiff. It's not like he's hard up for money; he simply didn't have the spine to say no, which is almost worse.

Now he's basically on the payroll of a smuggler, mobster, whatever, who knows way more about him than he does about the guy. Even though Silver Mustache hasn't asked him to commit any actual crimes, it's probably only a matter of time.

On an impulse, Wrecker shoots a text to Willi:

Hey. U up?

Semi, she texts back.

Did Clay's uncle tell anyone else about u-know-what? Besides Clay, I mean

Five minutes pass. Ten. Fifteen. Wrecker assumes she's dozed off. Then his screen lights up:

Take me out on yr boat

??? he texts back.

Tomorrow after school

Too cold

Aww, poor baby. Bundle up

What about yr soccer practice?

Season's over, Willi says. We went to state again, FYI

Can't I just call u?

Nope, she says. See u @ the dock. 3pm

Wrecker stares helplessly at his phone. He'd traded numbers with Willi after a school basketball game, before the pandemic, and then he hadn't followed up on a couple of friendly messages she'd sent.

Nobody's fault but his. Being shy is no defense for being rude.

And this, he thinks, *is the price to be paid.*

He doesn't sleep very well, or very long.

In the summer of 1856, long before the invention of radar weather forecasts, South Florida was surprised by a fierce August hurricane. It battered a 137-foot merchant vessel called the *Isaac Allerton,* which foundered on Washerwoman Shoals and sank in thirty feet of water in Hawk Channel, not far from Key West. More than seventy ships participated for months in what would become the largest, longest salvage effort of the era. Because the wreck was so deep, only a portion of the cargo was brought up. Among the many free divers recruited for the operation was Wrecker's great-great-great-great-grandfather, Valdez Jones Jr. He was a young man at the time but had already learned the skills of his perilous trade from his father.

To Wrecker's everlasting pride, many items recovered from the cargo holds of the *Allerton* are displayed in the island's Shipwreck Museum at the end of Whitehead Street. Tickets normally cost eighteen bucks, but Wrecker goes there so often that the manager gave him a lifetime pass. One of his favorite spots is at the top of the six-story lookout tower, where he has come after virtual school to scope out the sea conditions before taking Willi on the boat.

The wind's still blowing hard from the northeast. Not good.

From the tall tower he can see much of the harbor and also the town, including the metal roof of the house on Fleming where his mother and stepfather live. It's an easy bike ride from the museum. When he arrives, he texts his mom from the sidewalk.

His mother appears on the second-floor deck and blows a kiss.

"How's Roger?" Wrecker calls up to her.

"Now it's fever and chills. He's isolating in your old bedroom."

"You really ought to get tested, Mom."

"He's also got diarrhea," she says. "I mean, like a fire hydrant."

Thanks for the visual, Wrecker thinks.

"Where's your mask?" he asks.

"My new chin needs to breathe!"

"Suzanne told me you had a cough."

His mother starts coughing at the mention of the word "cough."

"Allergies," she says. "Night-blooming jasmine."

"Did you ever sign up for your vaccine shots?"

"Ha! I'm not standing in any line looking the way I do."

Annoyed, Wrecker says, "Well, at least do a home test. It's simple."

"Oh, I'll be just fine. I'm gobbling my vitamin D's like Skittles."

Carole Davenport Dungler is dressed in a blazing-red scarf, long black sweater, and white slacks. She plants both hands on the wooden rail and leans forward so she won't have to stretch her face by speaking loudly. Wrecker notes that she's full-on Lady Gaga with her makeup, trying to hide the bruising and stitches from the cosmetic surgery. He doubts that her doctor would approve.

Also, she must have taken a bath in her favorite French perfume—Wrecker can smell it all the way from the sidewalk.

"Guess who finally made a record," she says.

"You're kidding."

"It's on that Spot Remover app."

"You mean Spotify," Wrecker says tightly. "Dad's really got a song out?"

"He most certainly does."

"What's it's called?"

"'Tequilaville Sunset,' by the one and only Austin Breakwater."

"Wait—'Tequilaville'? Like Margaritaville? That's a straight-up rip-off of Buffett."

"Truly lame," his mother agrees. "And I'm not just being mean-spirited. You know I love a good beach ballad."

"Whatever. I'll check it out. Meanwhile, please get tested."

"You're growing up to be a cranky nag, Valdez. Now, I'd better go look in on poor Rog."

"Tell him I asked about him."

"As you should," his mother says, disappearing through the door.

Wrecker puts in his buds and searches Spotify for his father's Nashville name. On the way to the dock, he listens to—and then replays—the new Austin Breakwater single. His mom's not wrong: the song is weak. Wrecker doesn't know whether to laugh at the man or feel sorry for him.

The waves are too high for crossing the Northwest Channel, so he ends up taking Willi to the calm side of Sunset Key, a big-money resort island not far from the main harbor. Her hair is tied in multiple braids, and she's dressed in sweatpants, the gray hoodie, a puffy down jacket, and what appears to be snow-skiing goggles.

"Aren't you freezing?" she asks.

"I've been warmer." Wrecker doesn't own any heavy clothes. He's wearing his all-weather boat jacket, a pair of jeans, and a frayed knit cap.

"What will we catch here, Wreck?"

"Mainly a sunburn. It's too rough to get out to my snapper holes."

Willi opens a tall thermos and pours coffee into two plastic mugs.

"By the way, this is *not* a move," she says. "Hot chocolate would have been a move."

"How come you didn't want to talk on the phone?" he asks.

"What a question. Isn't this more fun?" Willi takes off her goggles and wipes the salt spray from the mirrored lenses.

"Clay's uncle," Wrecker presses on. "How does he even know who I am?"

"He played guitar in a band with your dad, back in the day. At Sloppy Joe's, he said. He knows your mom, too, from when she was a physical therapist."

"Did he tell anyone besides Clay about me going to the cemetery?"

"Well, I would be glad to ask Clay, except he's ghosting me right now."

"Oh. Who dumped who?"

"Listen to *you*, Wreck. Cutting straight to the chase!"

"Sorry," he mumbles, embarrassed at his own nosiness. The coffee is so hot that it's practically flavorless. He drinks it anyway.

"Cold truth? He broke up with me," Willi says.

"Is it okay to ask what happened?"

"I'll save the gruesome details for tonight."

"Why? What's happening tonight?"

"Big graveyard date," she says. "Me and you."

"Uh-uh. No way."

"Whaa-aat? I'm not afraid of that place."

"How do you feel about the jail?" Wrecker says. "Because that's where we'll end up if we get caught."

Willi rolls her eyes. "Oh dear. The long arm of the law."

"I'm dead serious."

"My mom and dad both work late, so I can basically come and go when I want. I'll be at the cemetery fence tonight, Wreck, waiting for you—"

"No, Willi."

"With a ladder."

A yellow trimaran crammed with tourists glides past, one of the new "vaccination celebration" cruises. Wrecker wishes he was fishing alone somewhere, any-where, just a speck on the horizon.

"All right," he says to Willi.

"Time, please?"

"Eight-thirty. On the Angela Street side, not Frances."

"Duh. You think I want Clay's loser uncle spying on us?" She returns the coffee cups and empty thermos to her backpack. "I like this little boat," she says. "It fits your style."

"What style are you talking about?"

"Loners get a bad rep, and it's not fair. That's all I meant."

"I'm not a loner."

She fits the ski goggles back on. "Are you a religious person, Wreck?"

He stands up and starts hauling the anchor. The wet rope chills his fingers. He says, "I don't go to church much, if that's what you mean."

Willi turns her face toward the sun. "Yesterday some preacher on TikTok was saying Jesus is coming back any day. And what I was thinking—if he shows up first in Key West?—it'd be super-cool if he came speeding into the harbor on a Jet Ski."

"Jesus on a Jet Ski?"

"Why not."

"That happens, I'm all in," Wrecker says.

"Better than on some big fancy yacht, right? Image-wise, I mean."

"Surfing in on a kiteboard would rock it, too."

"That's the idea! Or maybe a parasail." Willi laughs and lightly claps her hands. "This is a good start for us, don't you think?"

Wrecker is aware that he's overmatched, and that's fine. He cranks the motor and points the skiff toward the chalk-colored skyline of Key West.

SEVEN

After dinner Suzanne can't find the dishwashing liquid, a major crisis. She tells Wrecker to get some at Fausto's.

"They closed at eight," he says.

"Then go to Publix."

"I can't. I've got to be at the cemetery in fifteen minutes."

"Why? Who's clocking you in? Not poor dead Sarah."

"Bad weather's coming," Wrecker says. Not true.

"I can't leave dirty dishes in the sink all night. Gross."

"Big front over the Gulf," he says. "Sorry, sis."

Once he's out the door, he feels guilty. Suzanne is such a neat freak that she'll probably wheel herself to the van and speed all the way to the supermarket.

At least she won't get wet, Wrecker thinks. *Not a cloud in the sky.*

Willi is waiting near the small dog park at the corner of Angela and Grinnell. She's wearing the same hoodie from the boat ride but has traded her sweatpants for jeans. When she spots Wrecker, she crosses the street shouldering a six-foot aluminum ladder, which she stands against the cemetery fence.

"You first," she says.

Wrecker scans in all directions to make sure nobody's in sight.

"Hurry up," Willi tells him.

"Where'd you get this ladder?"

"I stole it off a fire truck."

"No, really," Wrecker says.

"Really I borrowed it from a friend. Now would you please hurry?"

As soon as Wrecker is over the fence, he drops close to the ground. Above him, Willi balances on the top bar while pulling the ladder up behind her. After handing it down to Wrecker, she jumps the rest of the way.

The island night is beginning to cool, but the cemetery air feels warm from all the stone markers shedding the last heat of the day.

Willi notices the bulging pockets of Wrecker's jacket and asks what he brought.

"Dawn."

"What?"

"Dishwashing detergent. You know." He's also carrying a kitchen scrub sponge and a plastic bottle of water.

"You'll see why in a minute," he says to Willi.

"I'm starting to feel invested in this adventure, Wreck."

They zigzag through the rows of dead to the plot where Sarah Chillingwood lies. Willi reads the inscription and asks, "What was the rumor?"

Wrecker gives her a short summary of Sarah's sad story while he squirts dish soap on the iguana mess and starts scrubbing the stone. Willi watches wordlessly until he's done.

"This is way easier with a hose," Wrecker says, rinsing the marble with the bottled water.

"What is it that connects you to this person?" Willi asks.

"Fifty bucks a week."

"There's got to be something else."

"Her brother pays me to do it. He's old now and all alone."

"Well, let's make up a better story," Willi says. "What if your grandpa was the one who found Sarah's body and asked you to keep watch over her for eternity?"

Wrecker dries his hands on his pants. "The Coast Guard is who found her body," he says. "And I don't remember my grandfather—he died when I was a baby. Also, he wasn't even a diver—"

"Whoa, Wreck, it's only supposed to be a made-up tale. Something to play inside your mind while you're

out here on your hands and knees, scraping lizard doo-
doo off some stranger's grave."

"Want to hear a *real* story?"

"Desperately," Willi says.

"It's heavy."

"Even better."

Wrecker takes out his flashlight and leads her to the
grave of Manuel Cabeza, where he halts, speechless. In
the middle of the plot stands a Mason jar filled with
new red, white, and pink roses. A fresh spot of candle wax, shaped like a teardrop, shines above the z in
CABEZA on the headstone.

The scene has put Willi on edge, too. Wrecker turns
off the flashlight and presses a finger to his lips. Under
the tan sliver of moon they stand together, listening,
but there's no sound of movement in the cemetery.

"Hello?" Wrecker finally calls out. "Anybody there?"

Nothing.

A police car comes hauling down Olivia Street with
blue lights flashing but no siren. Wrecker holds his
breath. The cop turns on Frances and keeps going.

"Whoever was here is long gone," Willi whispers.

"But how'd she get over the fence?"

"She?"

Wrecker tells her about the girl he watched singing
at Manuel Cabeza's grave, and then he describes what
happened on Christmas Eve in 1921.

"That's hideous." The words come out of Willi as a choked sigh.

"I bet that's who was here tonight. The same girl I saw."

"Anybody can bring flowers, Wreck. And they could have come this afternoon, before the cemetery closed." She reaches down to touch the roses. "What happened to Manuel's girlfriend after he was killed?"

Wrecker says he couldn't find much information about Angela. "The newspapers didn't say when she left Key West."

"How do you know she did?"

"Why would she stay after the Klan killed the man she loved?"

"To make a point," Willi says.

"Things were way different back then."

Wrecker doesn't mention it, but he knows that the pretty flowers on the Islander's grave will be gone tomorrow—breakfast for the iguanas.

"Let's bounce," Willi says restlessly.

"I've got one more stop."

"Is there another heavy story to go with it?"

"No story, just a job."

She follows him to the solo crypt of Silver Mustache's friend. Wrecker aims his flashlight at the front slab and sees that the name BENDITO VACHS is newly engraved in the plaque.

Below that are the words EVERYONE'S FAVORITE.

There are no rooster droppings or iguana turds to wash off, probably because the mason was working at the site. Lizards and chickens both prefer quiet over the noise of stone grinders.

"And this dude was who?" Willi asks.

"A friend of some guy who's paying me to keep the grave marker clean, same as I do for Sarah's."

"So this secret cemetery career of yours is catching fire."

"It's not a 'career,'" Wrecker says sharply. "The guy said his friend got the virus and died. He wants the tomb to look nice, and I said okay, since I'm out here every night anyway."

Willi pokes his arm. "Yo, I'm just givin' you grief."

"Why?"

"To avoid talking about what I promised to talk about when we were on the boat."

"Oh. You and Clay," Wrecker says.

"He dumped me for Juanita Mercer. You know her?"

"Not really."

"But you know she's hot, right? Of course you do," Willi says. "I could get away with telling people she stole Clay from me, but I'm pretty sure it was his idea. Anyway, I was definitely the dumpee, not the dumper. But I suppose I'll recover."

"You will. Big-time."

"That's the spirit. Thank you, Wreck."

"I'm serious."

"Yeah, but what do *you* know?"

In the cone of light he can see her wry smile.

"It's getting late, Willi."

"Take another look at that plaque and tell me what's wrong with it."

"You and your head games," Wrecker says.

Willi points at the dates. "Says the man died on April thirteenth."

"Yeah, so?"

"That's *tomorrow*, bro."

Wrecker hadn't noticed the mistake. Ever since the start of the pandemic, he sometimes loses count of the days on the calendar.

"I guess the stone carver messed up," he says.

"Slightly. You should call your buddy so he can get that fixed."

He's not my buddy, Wrecker thinks.

Later, back in his room, he dials the phone number that Silver Mustache scribbled on the fifty-dollar bill. A recording says the line is not in service.

Wrecker wonders if he should be worried, or just relieved.

Rain is beating on his window at half past eleven. Wrecker wakes up realizing his fake story about a storm system rolling in from the Gulf has turned out to be true.

His phone dings with a text, and he halfway hopes it's Willi. She'd said she doesn't sleep much.

But the message is from a number that Wrecker doesn't recognize:

Blue Bentley. End of yr street.

Who's this? Wrecker texts.

#1 Celia Cruz fan. And then a smiley-face emoji with a mustache.

Wrecker throws on some jeans and a sweatshirt, and peeks into the living room. Suzanne's asleep in her wheelchair next to the couch. The TV gives off enough light that he can see his way to the back door. He steps barefoot around the Deacon, also snoozing, and slips outside.

The rain has let up for now, the sidewalk is slick, and the humid night smells fresh from the squall. Wrecker spots the taillights of a blue sedan idling in a handicapped-only parking spot. The car's windows are down, and a sports talk show is on the radio.

"Hop in," says a husky voice from the driver's side.

"Why?"

"So we can solve the world's problems."

"I can hear you okay standing right here."

"Get in now." Silver Mustache reaches across and pushes open the passenger door.

The Bentley smells like stale cigars and heavy cologne. Its seats are plush; the doors and dashboard are paneled with dark polished wood. Wrecker has never seen anything like it.

Silver Mustache raises the windows and turns up the radio just loud enough to match the volume of his voice.

He says, "You called me earlier. What's up?"

"How'd you know I called? The number you gave me didn't work."

"Obviously it did."

Now Wrecker understands. Silver Mustache, not the phone company, put that out-of-service recording on his line.

"But how'd you know it was me on your caller ID?" Wrecker asks. "I never gave you my number."

"Wild guess, kid. Just tell me what this is about."

"The stone carver made a mistake on your friend's grave marker."

"Hmm."

"He put the date of death as tomorrow."

"Moron," says Silver Mustache. "He didn't come cheap, either."

"I knew you'd want to get that fixed before Mr. Vachs's family saw it."

"For sure. They've been through enough already. And poor Bendito."

"Anyway, that's the only reason I called," Wrecker says.

"The tomb looked all right otherwise?"

"Yup. Clean as a whistle."

"You're talking about the chicken crap," Silver Mustache says, "but I meant, did it look like anyone else had been messin' around there?"

"Like graffiti?"

"Yeah. Whatever."

"Why would anybody do that?" Wrecker says. "All I saw was the mason's mistake."

There's no music playing, only sports-jock chatter, but Silver Mustache's thick fingers are tapping some unheard beat on the steering wheel.

"And you were alone, right, Valdez?"

Wrecker's gut churns. *Did he just say my real name?*

"I always go alone."

"Good to hear that." Silver Mustache glances up at headlights approaching in the rearview mirror. A Jeep Wrangler packed with partying college kids races down the street.

"Trashed out of their skulls," Silver Mustache grumbles as the Jeep flies past. "Grow up to be smarter than that, would you?"

The rain starts slashing down again. Automatically the car's windshield wipers turn on. Wrecker says he'd better go.

"You're gonna get soaked," Silver Mustache says.

"I'll be okay. It's only a block."

"What's your sister gonna say, you walk into the house all sopping wet in the dead of night?"

Wrecker is jolted to hear him mention Suzanne, too.

"It was a car accident, right? Why she's in that wheelchair."

"Drunk driver," Wrecker rasps. "How'd you know?"

"Least they caught the dude." Silver Mustache offers a sympathetic nod.

What the hell's going on? Wrecker wonders.

He knows my name.

Where I live.

What happened to Suzanne.

Wrecker's hands feel like they're trembling, so he clenches them tightly on his lap.

"The guy who ran her down didn't even go to jail," he says.

"Sure, because he's an All-Star outfielder. What'd you expect?"

"She'll never walk again."

"I know, kid. But she's tough as nails, right?"

Silver Mustache pulls something from the pocket of his silky shirt, and Wrecker vigorously shakes his head no—maybe too quickly.

"We're good," he says.

"Yo, it's not money." Silver Mustache chuckles and holds out a small brass key. "This is for the cemetery gate. You won't need a ladder anymore."

Wrecker pockets the key. "Where'd you get it?"

"Friend of a friend."

Silver Mustache plucks a half-smoked cigar out of

the console. Raindrops thump like tom-toms on the hood of the Bentley.

"You're not wearing shoes, Valdez."

"I can run faster this way."

"A true island boy." Silver Mustache fires up the cigar. "Adios, now."

Wrecker is soaked to the skin by the time he reaches Suzanne's house. He drips a trail of water all the way to his bedroom, where he closes the door, peels off his clothes, and tries—with absolutely no success—to turn off his brain and fall asleep.

EIGHT

It's been more than a week since Willi met Wrecker at the cemetery, and she hasn't called or texted. The school started holding in-person classes again, but Wrecker hasn't seen her in the halls.

After getting sicker every day, Roger ended up in the hospital. Nobody was expecting that. Wrecker's mother isn't allowed to visit. She finally got tested for the virus—negative—and her cough turned out to be the harmless pollen allergy she said it was. Still, Roger's doctors advised her to self-quarantine, just in case.

Even though Wrecker's had both shots, he ventures no closer than the sidewalk when he stops by the house. Today his mother wrote a check for two hundred dollars to the Friends of Blue Waters and tried dropping it to him from the second-floor deck. A gust of wind sailed it into a neighbor's backyard Jacuzzi.

So she made out a new check, brought it downstairs, cracked the door, and hand-delivered it.

"Give this to Suzanne, please."

"Thanks, Mom. This'll help."

"How does my chin look? See how the swelling has gone down."

"You're as good as new."

"It's a Reese," she said proudly.

"Okay."

"As in Witherspoon? The adorable actress?"

"You two could be twins," Wrecker said. "How's Roger?"

"They say he's doing okay. Winking at the nurses, apparently."

"In Intensive Care?"

"By the way," she said before shutting the door, "your dad's back in town, and I don't wish to discuss it."

"Wait. What?"

So now Wrecker is pacing in front of The Boar, a new tavern on Greene Street, where "Austin Breakwater" is due to appear any minute. A one-man stage has been set up on the patio.

Wrecker hasn't decided what to say to his father, if he gets a chance. He doesn't even know what the Nashville edition of Valdez Jones VII looks like; the only photo on the official Austin Breakwater website is a twilight silhouette of a man in a cowboy hat. He's holding an acoustic guitar and sitting on a beach, and in the picture his face is turned away from the camera. The bio page says he's got "a country-fried soul and the steely nerve of a pirate." Whatever that means.

But here comes the man himself, ambling down the sidewalk carrying a scuffed guitar case. There's no doubt who he is—an older, wearier, slightly heavier version of the same person in the family photos that Wrecker keeps on his phone. He and his father have the same caramel skin, same strong jaw and wide brow, same angular shoulders. . . .

His hair looks different than in the pictures, though. Crazy different.

Either Valdez Seven is wearing a wig or he's spent a fortune straightening and coloring every strand on his head. The tips are beyond blond, like an electric banana.

He should stick with the cowboy hat, Wrecker thinks.

A sticker pasted on his father's guitar case says IM-MUNE DOUBLOON TOUR.

Stepping forward, Wrecker says, "Hey, Austin. Oops, I mean Dad."

His father rocks back on the heels of his snakeskin boots.

"Eight, is that you?"

"Wrecker. Everybody calls me Wrecker."

Valdez Seven sets down the guitar case and grasps him by the shoulders.

"Damn, son, you grew up!"

"One of us had to."

"I get that you're bitter. We'll talk after my first set, okay?"

Wrecker has no speech prepared. "What's the deal with your hair?" he asks.

"In my business, you either reinvent yourself or starve." Wrecker's father smiles extra wide to show off a mouthful of gleaming, perfect teeth. "Porcelain veneers, too!" he declares proudly. "I go to the same dentist as Tim McGraw."

Wrecker has already decided to stay for the show. He's not letting his father off the hook. Whether Valdez Seven wants to or not, he'll be explaining why he bailed out on his family all those years ago.

"Ladies and gentlemen," some guy with a heavy New York accent croons into the microphone, "let's give a warm island homecoming to Austin Breakwater!"

Wrecker's father strolls onto the mini-stage wearing a bright, baggy Hawaiian shirt that he must have packed with the guitar. He does six songs, ending with "Tequilaville Sunset," and his voice isn't terrible. But the three-chord melodies all sound alike, and the lines are totally predictable—broken hearts, smoky nights, lonely bus rides, whatever.

After each number the small crowd claps, more than politely. Most of them are tourists who are so thrilled to be in the Keys that they'd applaud for a sneezing parrot.

Still, Wrecker can't deny that it takes guts to stand up in public and do your own songs, songs that nobody's ever heard.

"What do you think, Eight?" his father asks him after the set, and doesn't wait for an answer. "This is how Jimmy Buffett started. James Taylor. Bonnie Raitt. All the greats!"

"You're braver than I am," Wrecker says, "at least when it comes to singing."

They're sitting at an outdoor table. Valdez Seven is drinking a beer that the manager brought him. Wrecker's got a can of Coke.

"Listen, I would've called you when I first booked this gig," his dad says, "but I don't have your number."

"Or Mom's? Or anybody in town's?"

"Truth is, son, it wasn't easy coming back to this place."

"Was it easier to leave?" Wrecker asks.

"Now, hold on."

"I just want to know why."

"I had a dream," Wrecker's father says, "one that your mother didn't share."

"And you couldn't call or write? All this time?" Wrecker had thought he'd gotten past caring about his father, yet now that the man's sitting right in front of him, he feels the old anger rise. "The way you disappeared like that was gutless. Pathetic."

Valdez Seven is jarred by his son's blunt words. He says, "You don't understand. Nothing was going right for me, until now."

" 'Tequilaville Sunset'?"

"My agent in Nashville says the buzz is incredible. I mean, except for the Eagles threatening to sue."

"*The* Eagles?" Wrecker says.

"Back in the day, they had a big hit called 'Tequila Sunrise.' Doesn't sound anything like mine."

I'm aware, Wrecker thinks. "What about 'Margaritaville'?"

"No way would Buffett ever take me to court! Again, my song's totally different. Way more soulful and country."

"How do you mean?"

"Sadder, you know," says Wrecker's dad. "My Tequilaville isn't Key West. It's every small town, every lonesome night."

"I gotta go."

"Why? Whatsa matter?"

"I'm late."

"For what?"

"My job," says Wrecker.

He can't take any more of Valdez Seven right now. Not the tinted hair. Not the cheesy python boots. Not his talking about himself in the same breath as legendary songwriters.

And especially not his flimsy excuse for skipping out on his family.

"I wish I could hang around for a few days so you and me could catch up," he's saying, "but tomorrow I've got a big show in Daytona."

A perfect place for that shirt of yours, Wrecker thinks.

"Thanks for the Coke," he says to his father. Then he stands up and walks away.

The cemetery gate is already unlocked and open. Parked in the driveway are Silver Mustache's blue Bentley and two black sedans. A burly dark-haired man in a brown suede jacket is leaning against one of the cars. He looks long and hard at Wrecker, standing there with a five-gallon bucket.

"You lost?" the man finally asks.

Wrecker knows he's seen him somewhere before—on the purple speedboat, with Silver Mustache and another man. Wrecker tilts the bucket to display the detergent bottle, scrub brush, and pile of rags.

"I'm taking care of some headstones," he explains.

"Not tonight, junior. There's a private ceremony."

"Okay, but—"

"We reserved the whole place."

Wrecker's never heard of someone booking an entire graveyard, day or night, but there's no point asking questions. Walking back to his bicycle, which he left under a streetlight, he's startled to hear somebody whisper his name from the shadows.

Running would be a reasonable option, but Wrecker is feeling curious tonight.

"Come out where I can see you," he says.

"Yo, it's just me."

"Me who?"

"*God*, really, Wreck?"

"Willi?"

"Duh."

She's hiding between a panel truck and a broken-down convertible in a short driveway that leads to a peeling old Conch house. The place is dark except for a one-bulb light mounted above the front door. Willi is wearing another hoodie, jeans, and black cross-trainers.

Wrecker kneels beside her and asks what's up.

"Those dudes in the cemetery saw me," she says.

"Doing what?"

"Just . . . you know . . . skateboarding along the road."

"So?"

"I think they got pissed," Willi says.

"Why? Lots of people walk their dogs or bike around these streets at night."

"All I know is . . . Never mind." Willi looks jumpy. She's biting a corner of her lower lip and twisting her braids with her fingers.

"Where's your board?" Wrecker asks.

"Somewhere in the bushes. I'll come back tomorrow and find it."

"Stay here." Wrecker gets his bicycle and rides it

back to the driveway where Willi is hiding. He hands her the grave-cleaning bucket and says, "Sit on the handlebars."

"But what if they see us?"

"Nothing's gonna happen, Willi. I know the main guy."

"How?"

Wrecker ignores the question. When they reach the stoplight at Southard and Simonton, Willi passes him the bucket, hops off the bike, and says she'll walk the rest of the way home.

"You all right?" Wrecker asks.

"Peachy. Thanks for the lift."

"Since I hadn't heard from you, I thought maybe you got back with Clay."

"No flippin' way," Willi says. "I've just had a crazy ton of stuff to do for my classes."

"I haven't seen you around school."

"No, I'm working remote. There was a spring soccer camp up in Miami."

Screwing up his courage, Wrecker says, "Maybe one night we could hang at the pier—"

But Willi's already waving goodbye, running down Simonton into the darkness.

Well, that *was weird*, Wrecker thinks.

He goes to the dock to check on his skiff. The tide's up, and a school of mangrove snappers is patrolling the water under the fish-cleaning table.

He steps on the boat and yanks the starter cord. The old Evinrude loyally growls to life, and he lets it idle while he leans back, looking up at the clouds. A spindle-legged blue heron, angling for a handout, settles a few feet away on the dock planks.

"No fish tonight," Wrecker says, and the bird immediately flies away, as if it understands English.

The waterfront is quiet, though the piers are packed with big boats. One go-fast in particular catches Wrecker's eye. He unties his skiff to motor closer. The grape-purple craft is dark and unoccupied, which is what Wrecker expects, since Silver Mustache and his crew are at the cemetery paying respects to their friend, the late Mr. Vachs. Afterward they'll probably return to one of the fancy guesthouses or hotels—anyone who drives a Bentley can afford something roomier than the cabin of a speedboat.

Wrecker ties the skiff to a piling and leaves the engine running as he steps up on the dock. Within seconds he's aboard the go-fast. The door leading below is locked—no surprise—so he creeps to the bow and tries lifting the front hatch. It won't budge.

The speedboat is rigged like a big-time offshore racer except the hull has no advertising logos or lettering on the glitter wrap. Flat on his belly, Wrecker stretches over the side and shines his flashlight through a plexiglass porthole. That's when he spots the gun on one of the salon seats inside.

Not a small gun, either. It's a military-style assault rifle, which is not something you'd normally need in a professional powerboat race.

Just then he hears men's voices and the clomping of footsteps on the wooden planks. Wrecker turns off the light and jumps from the speedboat to the finger pier. He hurries to his skiff, one-handedly unlooping the rope from the piling; his other hand is already on the tiller.

Quietly he steers toward a gray-blue slice of shadow between a pair of tall berthed yachts. There, sharing the water with a sleepy pelican, Wrecker watches Silver Mustache and the guy in the suede jacket amble down the long dock.

Moments after they board the purple speedboat, the running lights flick on and the big outboards rumble to life. As the go-fast backs out of the slip, Wrecker hears the men laughing boisterously.

And he wonders what could be so hilarious about a visit to a graveyard in the dead of night.

NINE

Suzanne says, "We're organizing a citizens' blockade!"

"What's that?"

"The day the first cruise ship shows up, hundreds of boats will be protesting in the harbor. You'd better be there, Valdez."

"Just say when," Wrecker says.

Like many people on the island, his stepsister is furious that the governor decided to ignore Key West voters and allow huge cruise liners to dock there again.

"The ship companies are spending millions of dollars trying to beat us down," she says, "but we're taking the battle to the sea."

Wrecker can't understand how the town's referendum got wiped out by politicians who don't even live there. The steal happened in Tallahassee, six hundred miles away. Suzanne had rented a bus for the Friends of Blue Waters and they were on the road for eleven hours. When they got there, the governor refused to meet with them.

"Our blockade will be peaceful," Suzanne is telling

Wrecker, "but we're not letting one single cruise ship get past us!"

They're at the bakery on Eaton Street, picking up apple Danishes and coffee. Suzanne wants to be near the waterfront, so they head down Grinnell, Wrecker walking at full stride to keep up with her wheelchair. She parks next to the anchor monument by the Half Shell Raw Bar. Wrecker sits down beside her.

It's a cool morning, a seam of low clouds blocking the sunrise. A breeze whips the flags on the ship masts in the marina. Wrecker can't stop thinking about the high-powered gun he saw inside the purple go-fast. Maybe it's legal, maybe it's not. The question is why Silver Mustache and his friends would bring one to sea.

Suzanne wipes a crumb from her lips and says, "Your mother told me who was in town last night."

"Yeah, I went to The Boar to see his show."

"Is he any good?"

"As a person?"

"His music, I mean."

"Oh, he's just chasing a dream," Wrecker says. "That was his excuse for walking out on us. Seriously."

"I'm sorry, Valdez. That sucks."

"What did I expect, right? Anyway, he's got an okay voice but the songs are lame."

"Your mom told me. 'Tequilaville' something?"

" 'Sunset.' "

Suzanne shakes her head. "Wow."

Wrecker doesn't tell her how the meeting with his father ended, how empty and disappointed he felt.

"Where's he staying?" she asks.

"He's not."

"I don't blame you for being mad."

"I gotta go to class now," Wrecker says.

"Don't forget to tell your friends about the blockade."

"The ones with boats, I will."

"Every human in Key West," says Suzanne, "either has a boat or knows someone who does. Get the word out, Valdez."

He stops by the house to pick up his book bag. On the bike ride to school, his phone starts ringing. It's Mr. Riley.

"I'm at Sarah's grave," he says to Wrecker.

"I can explain."

"Let's hope so. I'll be waiting."

The cemetery is out of Wrecker's way, but it's easy to make good time on the island when you know the side roads and alleys. In less than five minutes he's standing beside Mr. Riley, who is unhappily pointing his cane at a mound of iguana nuggets on Sarah Chillingwood's burial marker.

"That's disgusting," Mr. Riley says. "Horrific."

"I couldn't get in here to clean up. Some men were blocking the gate—they wouldn't let me by."

Wrecker doesn't want to complicate the conversation by revealing his connection to Silver Mustache, or his side hustle caring for the tomb of Bendito Vachs.

"What men?" Mr. Riley asks suspiciously. "That's ridiculous."

"They said they were holding a private ceremony."

"At night?"

"I know. It was weird," Wrecker says.

"Werewolves, perhaps—that's your story?"

"Sorry, Mr. Riley. You don't have to pay me anything this week."

The old man starts shuffling away. "I can't even look. Please take care of this now."

"Absolutely," Wrecker says.

He pedals as fast as he can to Suzanne's house to get his gravestone brush and cleanser, then races back to the cemetery. When he finishes scrubbing, every square inch of Sarah's stone is spotless. He snaps a picture and texts it to Mr. Riley, who probably checks his cell phone about once a year.

By the time Wrecker arrives at school, he's an hour late and smells like he just ran a marathon.

Boat ride?

That's his brilliant text to Willi, his big move, trying to break her silence.

It took him all morning to decide what to type. Famous poems have been written faster.

Pitiful, Wrecker thinks.

He's sitting by himself in the cafeteria at lunch hour. The alone part is fine, but the food isn't. Some sort of mystery meat, drowned in mud-colored gravy.

He spots a girl named Laura, a friend of Willi's. On the way out he stops to say hello.

"Hey, Wreck," she says, barely looking up from her tray.

"Can I ask you something? How does Willi spell her last name?"

"Are you serious?"

Wrecker nods uncomfortably. The truth is he doesn't remember Willi's full name, if he ever knew it.

"It's a tough one," says Laura sarcastically. "B-R-O-W-N."

"Oh. Okay."

"You need me to write that down for you?"

"Ha-ha-ha," Wrecker says.

"You want her number?"

"I've already got it."

"Yeah. Right," says Laura.

"Is she back with Clay?"

"*God*, Wreck. Just call the girl up and ask her."

"I will," Wrecker says.

"As if she actually gave you her number."

Hours drag by and Willi doesn't text him back. Standing in the parking lot after school, he takes a deep breath and dials her phone. It rings only once before switching to voicemail. He hasn't prepared a message, so rather than say something stupid, he hangs up.

Having Willi's last name isn't much of a help—an online cross-search turns up eighteen Browns with Key West addresses.

I'd have better luck knocking on random doors, Wrecker thinks.

When he returns to his stepsister's house, he sees a TV truck parked on the street. Suzanne is on the porch being interviewed about plotting the harbor protest. The reporter, who's dressed like she's going to party in Miami Beach, stoops beside Suzanne's wheelchair holding a microphone.

Wrecker avoids the scene by sneaking through the back gate. Minutes later he's gone again, riding off with his spinning rod and a small tackle box. The bait shop is out of live shrimp, so Wrecker buys a bag of frozens. They don't work as well on the larger snappers, but Wrecker doesn't care. Today it's not about catching fish, it's about calming his brain. He can't wait to get on the water.

Except there's a surprise at the dock: someone sitting in the bow of his skiff.

"I got your text," Willi says.

An olive hoodie is pulled over the Marlins cap on

her head. She's wearing wraparound sunglasses and a camo sun mask that covers the rest of her face and neck.

"Are you going duck hunting?" Wrecker says. He's happy to see her but too nervous to ask why she's there.

"Now you're giving fashion notes, Mr. Wharf-Rat Wardrobe?"

"It's good to see you, Willi."

"Yeah, yeah."

On the ride to the patch reef, she doesn't say a word until Wrecker points at a channel marker that's been sheared off above the waterline, leaving only a sharp stump.

"What happened there?" she asks.

"Looks like a big boat hit it going full speed."

"But how could anyone not see that thing?"

"Probably the middle of the night," Wrecker says. "There's no shortage of fools out here."

When they get to his fishing spot, he anchors the skiff up-current and baits the spinning rod for Willi. Finally she pulls back her hoodie and lowers her mask.

"You catch the first one," she says, "while I do some talking."

"No pressure."

"The reason I've been so hard to reach—there's major turmoil in Willi World right now."

"With you and Clay?" Wrecker says.

"No, bro, that's so over. This is something else. It wouldn't be cool to get you involved."

"Maybe I can help. Is it a guy problem?"

"He's nobody you need to worry about. But thanks, anyway."

Wrecker hasn't ever seen her so serious.

"Do I know him from school?" he asks.

She's almost smiling when she says no. "You two will never meet. That's a promise, Wreck. And he's not like a stalker or anything."

"Then how come you're hiding your whole face?"

"'Cause I'm freaked by what happened last night at the graveyard," she says. "I don't want those goons to recognize me. You said you knew 'em, right?"

"Just one. The boss."

"Who is he? What's his deal?"

"That's the guy who's paying me to take care of that new tomb," Wrecker says, "the one I showed you."

"Can you please find out if those thugs are after me?"

"That's crazy. Why would they be after you?"

"Next time you talk with the boss man," Willi goes on, "just ask if there was, like, an issue with a girl at the cemetery."

Wrecker reels in a small snapper, unhooks it, and drops it back in the water. He catches two more dinks on the next two casts. The big ones aren't biting.

"You're not telling me the whole story," he says to Willi.

Of course, he's not giving *her* the whole story, either.

She says, "Those dudes yelled at me and said to never come back."

"For skateboarding?"

"They said they knew how to find me."

"I don't get why they were so mad." Wrecker stops short of telling her that the men's threat was a bluff, because there's a chance it wasn't. Silver Mustache obviously had no trouble learning where he lived—and much more about him.

He reels in a puny striped grunt and says, "Let's try another spot."

Willi pulls the anchor while he starts the motor, tilting up the tiller so that he can stand while he steers. With the sun at their backs, they can see all the way to the bottom. Not even a pod of wild dolphins can lift Willi's mood.

As they go past the broken channel marker, Wrecker notices a heavy sheen on the surface of the water, something he missed on the ride out. He turns the skiff around to investigate.

"What *is* that?" Willi asks.

"Gas and oil."

"Where'd it come from?"

"Don't know." He steers a slow circle around the fuel slick, which shimmers like a rainbow-colored pond.

"There!" He points to a long bright shape on the bottom of the channel.

The instant that Willi stands up to look, she hears the engine cut off.

Then: two splashes behind the skiff.

The first is the anchor. The second is Wrecker, diving off the stern.

His head pops up like a cork. "I'll be right back!"

"Are you nuts?" Willi shouts.

And then, *bloop*, he's gone.

TEN

There's a dive mask and flippers in the skiff, but Wrecker forgot to grab them.

Another brilliant move, he thinks on his way down.

His eyes sting from the salt water and also from the rising plume of gasoline. Even so, the source of the fuel leak isn't hard to see.

The grape-purple speedboat rests upside down on the bottom, gleaming like a giant dead mackerel. There's a yawning hole in the bow, where it struck the channel marker. A jittery cloud of green minnows streams in and out through the broken portholes. With so much damage, the go-fast probably sank within minutes of impact. The propellers of its four drowned engines spin slowly in the current, like miniature chrome windmills.

Wrecker has always thought of himself as a good swimmer, but this is much different from snorkeling for lobsters. The speedboat went down in sixteen, maybe eighteen, feet of water—a routine free dive for an earlier, professional edition of Valdez Jones, but

Wrecker's lungs are already aching. The sweep of the tide is stronger than he expected.

Once he reaches the sunken craft, he has only enough time to swim the length of the broken hull before running short of breath. He shoots back to the surface, takes a gulp of air, wipes an arm across his eyes, and thinks:

This is not good.

The anchor didn't hold. His skiff is drifting away, down-current. Willi appears to be glaring at him from the bow. She throws up both hands as if to say, *Are you kidding me?*

Wrecker starts kicking hard, trying to chase down the boat. He's surprised to see Willi move to the stern and vigorously begin yanking the starter cord on the old Evinrude. Minutes later she pulls alongside and helps him aboard.

"Swim much?" she says.

He's embarrassed to be breathing so heavily. "Where'd you learn to run an outboard?"

"Sea camp for rich kids whose parents ditch 'em every summer."

"The boat that smashed into that post . . . it sank."

"What about the people?"

"Dunno. Take me back there," he says.

"If you're trying to impress me, this is a major fail."

"No, it's for real."

This time they stow the anchor and tie the skiff to

the stumped channel marker. The rainbow slick is dissolving, which means the speedboat's gas tank is nearly empty.

Now Willi, too, can see the shiny wreck on the bottom. "Oh God. We should call the Coast Guard!"

Wrecker puts on his mask and fins. "Keep a lookout," he says.

The second dive goes better because the current is slowing. The mask gives him a crystal view, and the flippers add power. He can't help thinking about his great-great-great-great-grandfather, who had no such advantages when exploring the pitch-black hold of the *Isaac Allerton*, in waters twice as deep.

The violent gash in the speedboat is wide enough for Wrecker to squeeze inside, fighting his fear of finding a dead body—Silver Mustache, or one of the others. Fortunately, the hull doesn't hold any bloated horrors.

Instead he ends up nose to nose with a five-foot nurse shark. It's a harmless, nearsighted creature, but Wrecker still blurts a bubble of surprise. Equally startled, the whiskered forager exits in search of another place to nap.

When Wrecker resurfaces, he's holding a package the size of a pizza box. It's wrapped in blue hurricane tarp and sealed with duct tape.

Willi snatches it from his hands and says, "What are you doing?"

"There's more down there."

"No, Wreck, let's get out of here."

"If you see anybody coming, throw that thing overboard."

"Is it drugs? It's gotta be."

"Maybe not."

Down he goes again.

Dozens of identical blue packages drift among the loose cushions and life jackets trapped inside the speedboat. Wrecker begins pulling boxes one at a time through the cabin door, releasing them to float toward the surface.

His lungs are burning, but he's wired. He's happy.

He's *wrecking.*

As he kicks upward for another breath of air, he hears metallic knocks coming through the water. It turns out to be Willi, banging Wrecker's pliers against the skiff's hull and trying to get his attention.

"Another boat!" she shouts when his head pops up.

He yanks off the dive mask and scans the water. What looks like a cabin cruiser is heading their direction, though it's still pretty far away. There is, however, nowhere to hide on a glass-calm sea.

Willi tugs up her sun mask. "Time to boogie, Wreck."

Four packages are stacked in the center of the skiff. Wrecker grabs a final loose floater and hands it up to her.

"What's wrong with you? Do you have, like, a brain bleed?" she says. "We need to dump whatever this is!"

"I got an idea."

"Stop! No more crazy ideas from you!"

"Untie us from the marker," Wrecker says, pulling himself aboard. He tugs off his flippers and starts the motor.

Willi presses close to his side as he points the skiff in the opposite direction of Key West, dead-on toward the Gulf of Mexico and the setting sun.

On any other night, the sixty-six-foot *Donna Rae* would be far out of sight, trawling for pink shrimp in the Gulf. But late on this afternoon there was engine trouble that the mechanic couldn't solve, so the captain was forced to turn around for the lurching, noisy ride back to port on Stock Island.

Now, out of nowhere, a small boat with a pair of teenagers has appeared under the starboard floodlights, cruising side by side with the shrimper. Both kids are wearing gaiters over their faces, and their skiff is matching the speed of the *Donna Rae*, staying directly beneath the wide net drooping from the long outrigger. When the captain of the shrimp boat hollers for the skiff to back off, the young driver replies with a smooth chill-out gesture.

"How come they're messin' with us?" the mechanic growls.

"I'm not sure they are," the captain says. It's clear

that the kid at the tiller of the small boat knows what he's doing. For miles he keeps his bow perfectly positioned on the smooth water ahead of the shrimper's steep wake.

Once the *Donna Rae* makes a turn up the ocean side of Key West, the kids drop back, fading into the darkness. By the time the shrimp boat limps into the Stock Island boatyard, the mystery skiff is tied to a dock at the end of Front Street in Old Town.

Wrecker's on the phone with his stepsister, apologizing for missing dinner. His fake story: he was fixing a hole in the boat's fuel line.

At the other end of the dock stands Willi, who's on the phone with her mom and likewise apologizing for being late. Her fake story: she lost track of time while researching an English paper at the library.

No longer is she wearing the hoodie. It's been converted into a sack concealing the five flat packages from the speedboat.

"Are you insane?" she'd asked Wrecker about seventeen times between the time they fled to the Gulf and the time they got back to Key West.

Finally he explained that shadowing the *Donna Rae* so closely had shielded the skiff from the view of all vessels on the shrimper's port side, including the cabin cruiser that appeared to have dropped anchor beside the sheared channel marker, at the wreck of the grape-purple speedboat. Wrecker had a good hunch that the occupants of the cabin cruiser were Silver Mustache and his goons, retrieving (and undoubtedly counting) their lost packages.

Wrecker chose not to share that theory with Willi, nor did he tell her that they were the same men who had chased her away from the cemetery.

From the waterfront, Wrecker beelines straight to Suzanne's house. Willi balances on the handlebars, clutching the bulky hoodie-sack with both arms.

"This is so stupid," she says in an agitated whisper. "Why didn't we just heave this stuff overboard, like I told you to?"

"Long story, Willi." He's thinking of the boxes as insurance, or maybe a bargaining chip.

"Are you going to clue me in before or after we get busted by the cops?"

"We will not be getting busted," Wrecker says.

At his stepsister's place he strips off his damp shirt, which reeks of gas, and tosses it in a garbage bin by the street. Then he opens Suzanne's garden shed and starts stashing the blue packages under plastic sacks of mulch.

Willi paces in a sulk. "So, we're seriously not going to open even *one?*"

"Suzanne's at a Blue Waters rally, but she'll be back any minute."

"Don't you want to see what we got? Come on, Wreck."

She tugs on his hand and pins him with a pleading gaze. He feels his cheeks redden, but he doesn't give in.

"I'll take you home," he says.

"Not necessary. It's a short walk from here."

"Whatever. Promise not to tell anyone about this, Willi."

"Only if you promise not to do anything deranged— like try to sell that stuff, whatever it is."

"That *would* be deranged. Also idiotic." He grabs the pail holding his headstone-cleaning items, shuts the shed door, and gets on his bike.

"Now where are you going?" Willi asks.

"Sarah's grave."

"This late? Let me come, too."

"Naw, I'm good."

"You can use my friend's ladder."

"Call you tomorrow." Wrecker pedals off without mentioning that he no longer needs a ladder to enter the graveyard.

Since the boss of the speedboat smugglers gave him a key.

His stepsister is dozing in front of the TV when Wrecker finally gets back. He picks up the remote and switches channels to Jimmy Kimmel, Suzanne's favorite. She blinks fuzzily and asks where he's been.

"My boat's fuel line had a leak, remember?" he says. "I didn't make it to the cemetery till after ten-thirty."

"Mmm."

"Honest."

"Do you have a girl in your life, Valdez?"

"No way!" Wrecker says, and that's how he feels. Willi's just a friend—he knows almost nothing about her, not even which street she lives on.

Except that she has some guy-related "turmoil" that she won't discuss.

"Sure there's no secret romance?" Suzanne says with a sly smile. "Hey, it wouldn't be the worst thing that could happen."

Wrecker refuses to take the bait. "How was the rally tonight?" he asks.

"Big crowd. I bet we'll have two hundred boats in the blockade. A bunch of us are flying to Tallahassee tomorrow to knock on the governor's door."

"Again?" he says.

Suzanne has a better chance of winning the lottery than getting an audience with the governor, but Wrecker admires her grit.

"Don't forget to feed the Deacon while I'm gone," she says. "I'm off to bed, Valdez. Do your homework, please."

"Night, sis."

Usually Suzanne falls asleep right away. Just to be

safe, Wrecker waits half an hour before sneaking out to the shed.

Cargo salvaged by an earlier Valdez Jones would have been stored with tons of other goods in a sprawling wooden warehouse along the old wharf, awaiting a judge's ruling on how much it's worth and who gets what.

Now, in the twenty-first century, Wrecker sits in a prefab metal hut holding a waterproof package that almost certainly doesn't contain cotton, tobacco, indigo dye, gold coins, or anything else that an earlier Valdez Jones would have risked his life to retrieve. Wrecker has no idea what he brought up from the sunken speedboat, but at least the packages are totally different in size and shape from the bales of dope that occasionally wash up on the shorelines of the Keys.

He slides the blade of his pocketknife through the duct tape and peels off the blue plastic, which reveals—to his puzzlement—an actual delivery box from a place called Peter Pan's Pan Pizza. He slips two fingers under the cardboard lid and lifts it by the corners. There's one more layer of clear plastic to be skinned away and then . . .

Okay, he thinks, studying the contents of the package. *Definitely not drugs.*

And when he realizes exactly what he's looking at, he begins rehearsing in his mind the dicey conversation he needs to have with Silver Mustache.

ELEVEN

Weeks pass, Wrecker clinging to his secret. School ends, and summer brings roasting heat to the island.

He hasn't seen or heard from Silver Mustache, which seems odd; the waiting keeps him on edge. Meanwhile, Willi's been ghosting him ever since he refused to tell her what's inside the salvaged pizza boxes.

The mud-churning cruise liners haven't yet returned to Key West Harbor, but the Friends of Blue Waters protesters are watchful and ready. Wrecker's mom and Suzanne are both in South Miami, staying in a hotel near the hospital where Roger was airlifted after his COVID symptoms got worse. The doctors first listed his condition as "critical but stable." It's been upgraded to "serious," though he's still in Intensive Care. Nobody is allowed to visit, but Suzanne and Wrecker's mother want to be nearby, just in case.

Wrecker isn't experienced at praying, but on one bright morning, alone in his skiff near Mule Key, he raised his eyes to a cloudless sky and said, "If you're up there and you're not too slammed, please help Roger get better."

It sounded less pushy than "Please *make* Roger get better."

He has a part-time day job stocking the shelves at Fausto's grocery, and at night he still faithfully brings a bucket and sponge to Sarah Chillingwood's grave marker. Even though Silver Mustache hasn't been around to pay him, he also tends to the tomb of Bendito Vachs, which has become a favorite poop zone for the roosters. Wrecker hasn't encountered the black-haired girl again, or found more telltale flowers on the grave of Manuel Cabeza.

Since no one is home waiting up for him, Wrecker has been staying out later. Sometimes, after leaving the cemetery, he rides his bike down Flagler Avenue and parks under a random light pole. If he shuts his eyes, he can practically hear the husky roars of the Klansmen at the hanging, and he's still blown away to think it happened only a hundred years ago, on an island he loves and thought he knew.

He finds himself wondering if any of his ancestors ever took a beating, or worse, from the Klan. Once in a while he'll even catch himself feeling guilty because his skin is lighter than the early, more Bahamian versions of Valdez Jones, and because he honestly can't remember anyone ever calling him the N-word to his face. That surely wasn't the situation for his forefathers in the year 1921, when El Isleño was being tormented for loving a woman of mixed race.

The next-to-last thing Wrecker does every night, upon returning to his stepsister's house, is make sure the blue packages from the speedboat are still secure in the garden shed. And then the very last thing he does, before going to bed, is scoop the Deacon's litter box, an act of true brotherly devotion that Suzanne greatly appreciates.

If Wrecker has trouble falling asleep, he sits up reading and listening to music. It's on one of those nights when the text he has long been anticipating finally pings on his phone:

I'm here. Let's talk

Wrecker walks out the door expecting to see the blue Bentley. Instead there's a gray Mercedes coupe parked in the driveway.

Silver Mustache leans out the driver's window and says, "Your sister's gone, right?"

Wrecker nods uneasily. It's so late that every house on the block is dark.

"What's up?" he asks the smuggler.

"Get in, kid. The bugs are savage."

"Where's your other car?"

"I said get in."

Wrecker does. Silver Mustache backs out crookedly

and starts driving toward Truman. He doesn't look great. There's a raw-looking crescent scar on his chin, and a bulky plaster cast on his right leg. He is twisted awkwardly in the seat, using the other leg to work the accelerator and brake.

"You gonna ask me what happened?" he grumbles. "Or maybe you already know."

Wrecker feels like his mouth is full of sawdust. He can't spit out a word.

"Some a-hole totaled the Bentley," Silver Mustache goes on, "with me inside."

"Unngh."

"Moron crossed the center line on Fleming and hit me head-on. Cops said he was wasted."

Wrecker clears his throat and says, "That sucks."

Thinking: *Fleming's a one-way street. There is no center line to cross.*

"My friend Leon, he got launched right through the windshield." Silver Mustache gives a grim shrug. "He always hated seat belts, so . . ."

"Wait—he died?" Wrecker wonders if Leon was the guy who wore the brown suede jacket.

"Paramedics said it happened so fast, he never felt a thing."

"When was this?"

"Few weeks ago. I can't believe you didn't hear about it."

Wrecker knows he's being tested, so he plays along.

"I remember one day when the road got closed because of a bad wreck."

"The other driver, he died, too. They airlifted me to Miami."

"Sounds like you're lucky to be alive," Wrecker says.

He's sure there was no fatal car crash on Fleming Street, because he *definitely* would have heard about it. Silver Mustache got injured when his speedboat plowed into a channel marker in the black of night.

"So, how's the fishing?" the smuggler asks, out of nowhere.

Wrecker says he hasn't been on the water much. "I took a summer job."

"I know. At the grocery."

"Are you spying on me?" Wrecker's blood is rising.

"Chill the bleep out." Silver Mustache grins. "It's a small town, junior. Speaking of which, did you hear anything about some packages—let's say, merchandise—washing up on the island?"

Merchandise? Wrecker thinks. *This guy talks like he wants to be the next Scarface.*

"You mean drugs?"

Silver Mustache shakes his head. "No, bro, these are boxes—not bales."

"Boxes of what?"

"Nothing of value to anyone but me and my associates."

"When'd you lose the load?"

"Around the same time as my car accident. And let's call it a shipment, not a load. My people got back most of the stuff, except for five boxes."

I was right, Wrecker thinks. *It was their cabin cruiser that anchored by the sunken go-fast.*

"I can ask around," he tells the smuggler, "but it would help to know what you're looking for."

"Don't ask anybody anything about *anything.* Just keep your ears open."

"Always." Wrecker is hoping his voice doesn't sound as shaky as he feels. The conversation isn't going as planned; he's lost his nerve to press for more details about what's in the pizza boxes.

Silver Mustache turns off Truman onto White Street, then hangs another left on Angela. Wrecker knows where they're going.

"Were you out here earlier?" Silver Mustache asks.

"You know I was. You've been following me."

"Not really. I just got back in town a few hours ago."

"Well, I'm here every night," Wrecker says flatly, "unless it storms."

On Passover Lane the smuggler whips the Mercedes into a space marked RESIDENTIAL PERMIT PARKING. He's got no such permit, of course. After grabbing a crutch from the back seat, he starts gimping toward the cemetery gate. Wrecker beats him there and unlocks it. A friendly moonglow lights the narrow roads between the burial sections, but the mosquitoes are vicious, newly hatched from the rain puddles beneath the cracked vaults.

"Ah, Bendito, mi compadre," Silver Mustache murmurs as they approach the site. Using the light on his phone, he carefully inspects the exterior stone from corner to corner.

Wrecker feels semi-insulted—anyone can see that the tomb of Mr. Vachs has been kept spotless and gleaming.

Flawless, in fact, except for the wrong date of death.

"I thought you were going to get that fixed," Wrecker says.

"Yeah, well, the engraver from Hialeah, he never showed up."

"Couldn't you find somebody else to do it?"

"Maybe I've had a few other things on my mind," Silver Mustache says, jabbing Wrecker with the tip of his crutch, "such as a major fracture of my right leg, four broken ribs, and my face split open like a tomato."

Wrecker drops the subject. Why should he care what dates are carved on Bendito Vachs's stone? He never met the man.

Time to cool the vibe and steer the talk in another direction: "Where was your friend Leon buried?"

"He was pure 3-0-5. We scattered his ashes up in Biscayne Bay."

"It must be rough to lose somebody close to you." No sooner has Wrecker spoken the words than he wishes he'd thought up something that sounded more sincere. "And hard for his family, too," he adds.

"Yeah. Super-hard." Silver Mustache pulls out four fifties, folded together. "Here's what I owe you for the last few weeks. Call it two hundred even."

"That's too much," Wrecker says.

"First rule of business: when you're being paid for professional services, there's no such thing as 'too much.'"

"Keep the money. Seriously."

Silver Mustache is wearing a peculiar smile. "Valdez, is this your way of ending our friendship?"

"No, it's not that—"

"Good, 'cause I'm depending on you for solid intel about those missing packages. Maybe a lobster fisherman found 'em floating somewhere."

"It's not lobster season yet," Wrecker says tightly.

"Then maybe it was a shrimper that picked up the stuff. Or one of the tarpon guides. I'm sure somebody's blabbin' their mouth off on the coconut telegraph." Again Silver Mustache pokes Wrecker with the crutch. "The boxes are square and wrapped in blue plastic. Should be five of 'em, like I said. Now be a smart young capitalist and take the damn cash."

Silver Mustache drops him at the end of the block. He jogs back to Suzanne's house and enters through the back door. After stashing the smuggler's payment in his dirty sneaker, he falls into bed and stares at the ceiling fan.

The room feels about eighty-nine degrees. Wrecker lies there sweating on the sheets, trying to design a plan that won't end with him in the cemetery, six feet under. After a while he shuts his eyes and dreams about Manuel Cabeza, covered with black tar and feathers, limping through the streets and firing a pistol at the houses of the Klansmen who'd tortured him. Next, men wearing pointy white hoods are tying El Isleño to the bumper of a Model T Ford, the most popular automobile in America in 1921. The lynching parade down the county road is bumpy and slow because the top speed of a Model T was only about twenty-five miles an hour. . . .

Wrecker awakens to the trill of doves, which is strange. Normally he can't hear noises outside because of the thick hurricane glass that Suzanne installed in the house. For some reason Wrecker's window is wide open, which explains the sound of the doves and also the fresh mosquito bites on his arms.

"Morning, sunshine," calls a voice, and at first Wrecker assumes his stepsister drove home from the mainland.

But the figure in his doorway isn't sitting in a wheelchair. She's standing.

And smells of lilac.

"Willi?"

"Gee, don't look so excited to see me."

She's wearing an extra-large Sloppy Joe's T-shirt, old jeans, rainbow flip-flops, and a white cap turned backward over her wild hair.

"I'm here to find out what's inside those packages we took off that boat," she says, casually leaning against the doorframe. "And I'm not leaving till you show me."

Wrecker's pulse is thumping, his palms are damp.

What if Silver Mustache or one of his thugs was watching the house when Willi broke in?

"Have you lost your mind?" he says.

"Don't be so dramatic. Your window wasn't even locked."

"*I'm* the one being dramatic? You vanish off the radar for weeks and then, boom, here you are, sneaking into my room like a burglar!"

"Maybe I was away at another soccer camp."

"Do they confiscate your phone at soccer camp? I don't think so," Wrecker says. "You were ghosting me."

"I kinda was," Willi admits. "You pissed me off, but I'll be over it as soon as you show me what's in those boxes."

"Don't get mixed up in this. The less you know, the safer you'll be."

"Snap! So it *is* drugs."

"It's not."

"Then, cash?" Willi presses on. "Stolen stocks? Government bonds?"

"No, no, and *no*."

The Deacon appears, fussing for breakfast. Willi feeds her in the kitchen while Wrecker rushes around the house lowering the shades.

When he's done, she says, "Chill out, bro. Frosted blueberry or mango?"

"What are you talking about?"

"Pop-Tarts." Willi is scouting the pantry shelves. "Those are the only two flavors you've got."

Wrecker, the opposite of chill, takes a seat at the kitchen table. Willi toasts two of the sugary shingles and presents them on a paper plate.

"The sunken speedboat," Wrecker begins, "belongs to the men who chased you from the graveyard."

"What? Those guys you said you know?"

"I said I've met the boss." He bites into one of the Pop-Tarts, instantly scalding his tongue.

Willi sits down across from him. "So your BFF is a smuggler. How fun is that?"

"He is *not* a friend. His boat ran aground one afternoon while I was fishing. A few days later he spotted me in the cemetery and asked me to watch over that crypt I showed you."

"The dude with the wrong date on his stone?"

"Bendito Vachs."

"Who supposedly died of the 'rona. Wink, wink."

Wrecker sighs. "I knew I shouldn't have told you about this. Swear to God."

"What did your BFF say about the night they yelled at me?"

"Not one single word—and I didn't ask. I'm pretty sure they've got bigger things to worry about than some crazy chick on a skateboard."

"Fine. Whatever," Willi says. "Enjoy your nutritious breakfast."

"Listen, the boss man knows almost everything about me. I can't figure out if he's spying on this place or what. He even knows about my job at Fausto's!"

"What's his name?"

"He won't tell me, and definitely doesn't want to be asked."

With something that almost sounds like pity, Willi says, "Oh, Wreck."

"Yeah. I'm an idiot."

"That's a bit harsh. Come on, let's go look in those boxes."

Fortunately, the door of Suzanne's garden shed isn't visible from the street. Wrecker hung a padlock on it, anyway. The combination is 2-0-0-3, the year that the Marlins beat the Yankees in the World Series, before Wrecker was even born.

Once inside the shed, Wrecker turns on the light and sits down next to Willi on the dusty slab floor. He reaches for the one pizza box that he unwrapped and places it on her lap.

"Spoiler alert," he says. "It ain't sausage and cheese."

She looks at the package and takes a slow, tense breath.

"This shed stinks like fertilizer," she says. "I don't suppose there's an air conditioner."

"Nope."

"Is there a fan we can turn on?"

"Nope."

"Then how about a window?"

"How about you quit stalling and open the box?"

"Fine." Willi does. Squints. Frowns.

Then: "What am I looking at, Wreck?"

"Blank vaccination cards," he says. "Uncut sheets of twenty, fifty sheets to a box. So there's five thousand of 'em here."

"Are these from the CDC?"

"The CDC doesn't deliver in speedboats, Willi."

She leans close, examining the top sheet. "But they look totally real."

"I'll bet you a brand-new skateboard they're either fake or stolen." Wrecker takes the box from her hands, closes the lid, and returns it to the stack.

"Who would pay for those things?" Willi asks.

"People who didn't get the shots but need a vax card for their jobs. Or to take a trip."

She pinches Wrecker's forearm. "We gotta call the FBI or somebody, like right this second."

"Not yet."

"Why not? What's wrong with you?"

"Well," Wrecker says, "to summarize my situation: I'm being followed around the island by a badass smuggler who might burn down my stepsister's house—or do something even worse—if I rat him out."

Willi rocks back slowly, folding her arms. "Okay, Wreck, fair enough. Let's hit the cosmic pause button and think hard. . . ."

"Thinking about this is all I do, day and night."

"Does that mean you've got, like, an actual plan?"

"It's more of a concept."

"Awesome," she says. "A masterwork in progress."

I wish, Wrecker thinks.

TWELVE

During his lunch break at Fausto's, Wrecker stands on the sidewalk eating a ham-and-olive sandwich and scouting the weather; he plans to take the skiff out later. He's also scanning the neighborhood for Silver Mustache lurking in his new car.

A commotion erupts when a shirtless dude carrying a stolen case of beer bursts from the grocery store and takes off running down Bahama Street. Wrecker crams the last of his sandwich into his cheeks while he chases down the fool, who isn't expecting to be tackled from behind, much less pinned to the pavement, by a teenage stock boy.

A policeman shows up right away. The thief claims that it's all a big misunderstanding, that he's a sophomore at Yale and why would he steal beer when his old man could write a check and buy the whole bleeping store. The cop, who is the stone-faced opposite of impressed, introduces the young man to the experience of handcuffs.

Wrecker carries the case of beer back to Fausto's

and spends the rest of the afternoon unpacking boxes of cereal and protein bars. By the time he gets on the water, an impressive summer thunderhead is forming over the Gulf, threatening to shorten his fishing trip. On the way out, Wrecker notices that the broken channel marker has been replaced. The go-fast is still resting on the bottom there, though somebody armed with heavy equipment has removed the four big engines.

Drifting across the reef, Wrecker lands a few keepers before lightning starts to crackle and the clouds turn from gray to violet. He barely beats the rain back to Key West. From a covered doorway on Front Street he calls his mother, who reports that Roger's condition is improving. He's out of ICU and family members are permitted to visit.

"He asked if you could come up here to see him," she says.

"I'm working almost every day, Mom."

"Oh, it would mean the world to him."

Wrecker isn't sure this is true. "Who would take care of the Deacon?"

"I'll buy your plane ticket, Valdez."

"All of us can FaceTime."

"You just can't stand to leave the island," his mother says. "That's very selfish."

After the squall ends, Wrecker wipes down the skiff and cleans the fish he caught. Back at the house, he checks the lock on the shed before sneaking around the corner to make sure his bedroom window hasn't been opened. The Deacon is waiting at the door.

Wrecker grills four snapper fillets and donates one to the nagging cat. After a quick shower he rolls into bed and texts Willi. He falls asleep waiting for a reply.

An hour later, his phone dings: Meet me at Catholic corner of g-yard

Wrecker sits up groggily. Right now? he texts back.

Don't look for me. I'll find u

The roads are slick from the rain, the trees still dripping. Wrecker dodges deep puddles all the way to the cemetery, where he chains his bike to the Angela Street side of the fence. Not wanting to draw attention, he shoves both hands in his pockets and starts walking at a casual-looking pace. Within moments, Willi materializes and whisks him into the shadow of an old strangler fig.

"I saw grave robbers!" she whispers.

"Where?"

"They're gone now. I think."

"What were you doing here all alone?" Wrecker asks.

"Skateboarding. The usual."

"After what happened last time?"

"I couldn't sleep," Willi says.

She leads him to a dead-end alley between two old houses that are being remodeled. Hidden in the shrubs is the same six-foot ladder she was carrying the night he met her at the little dog park. That's what they use to climb over the fence; Wrecker doesn't want Willi to know that the smuggler gave him a key to the gate.

Once inside the cemetery, they run to the mini-mausoleum of Bendito Vachs. "Look what they did," she says excitedly. "Sledgehammers!"

A pumpkin-sized hole has been smashed in the heavy wooden door. Visible through the opening is the lower end of a casket, resting on a stone platform inside the crypt chamber. Above the battered doorway, the memorial plaque has a crack down the middle.

Willi levels her phone light at Bendito's epitaph: EVERYONE'S FAVORITE.

"Apparently not true," she says.

A car with its headlights off slows to a crawl in front of the cemetery gate.

"Get down," Wrecker says, pulling Willi next to him behind a random headstone.

The car speeds off. Wrecker tells her not to stand up yet.

"Am I allowed to breathe?" she asks.

"Quietly."

"There were two robbers, Wreck. They got scared off by a siren. It turned out to be a fire truck, but the dudes were already gone. . . ."

"Did you see their car?"

"Red Hummer," Willi says.

Wrecker is thinking ahead to the call he'll be making

to Silver Mustache, who'd warned him that intruders might "disrespect" the grave of Bendito Vachs.

My friend had some enemies, he'd said.

Possibly an understatement.

Wrecker takes a picture of the damaged tomb.

"Let's split," Willi says.

Back on the other side of the fence, she stashes the ladder in the same shrubs in the same dead-end alley. Wrecker says they should return it to her friend's house.

"Not tonight, Wreck. I'm fried."

"What about your skateboard?"

"Just take me home."

They fly down Southard Street, Wrecker pedaling as if he's in the Tour de France. Like before, Willi hops off the handlebars as they reach Simonton—only this time she twists an ankle landing on the pavement.

Her vocabulary of cuss words is vast and colorful.

"What's your actual address?" Wrecker asks as she bounces like a pogo stick on the sidewalk.

"I'm good," she replies through gritted teeth.

But she's not good. She's in semi-serious pain. Wrecker helps reseat her on the handlebars.

"I live on Whitehead Street," she says.

It's a classic old Key West estate, not far from the Hemingway compound. Some people would call it a mansion. Floodlights bathe towering banyans and lush fern gardens, and a metal plate on the brick gate says the site is officially "historic." Clearly, Willi didn't want Wrecker to know her family was rich. That would explain why she never wanted him to take her home, and why she'd claimed her mom and dad both work late, like they're waiting tables at some all-night diner. Wrecker decides not to comment on the size of the Brown family manor.

Willi types in the code and opens the gate. The first floor of the house is dark, but the lights are on upstairs.

"It appears the parental units are still awake," Willi says.

As Wrecker helps her hobble up the front steps, he's surprised to see an electric skateboard propped against one of the pillars.

"I thought you rode it to the cemetery," he says.

"Oh, this one's my backup." She takes out her house key.

"Get some ice on your ankle," Wrecker tells her.

Unexpectedly she pecks him on the cheek. "Don't be a dork and go back to the graveyard tonight."

"I won't," he lies.

He taps in the phone number, connects to the same fake recording. While waiting for a callback, he unlocks the cemetery gate. A sense of duty leads him first to Sarah Chillingwood's grave, where there's nothing to clean up; the rainstorm did its job.

Next stop: Mr. Bendito Vachs.

Wrecker examines the damage to the mahogany door. The hole doesn't look large enough for a person to climb through, and the brass handle is still locked.

His phone vibrates.

"Are you, like, a night stalker?" Silver Mustache says on the other end. "Don't you ever sleep, bro?"

"I'm with Mr. Vachs. You need to come see something."

"And this can't wait till morning?"

"I'm texting you a picture," Wrecker says.

Ten seconds later: "Don't go anywhere, kid. I'm on my way."

Wrecker spends the time walking among the undisturbed dead. Most normal people avoid cemeteries at night, but for whatever reason, he's never been creeped out by the place. It helps to not believe in ghosts, spirit forces, or flesh-eating zombies.

One grave of interest belongs to a young Black sheriff's deputy. Wrecker ran across some old newspaper clippings about him at the library. His name was Frank E. Adams, and in 1901 he was shot dead while trying to make an arrest near the Key West courthouse. He was buried in an unmarked plot and basically lost for almost a century before the local Catholic church and cemetery workers located his remains and put up a headstone.

Wrecker knows that a white deputy killed in the line

of duty would have been laid to rest with fanfare and a fine marble marker—and nobody would have ever forgotten where he was buried. Frank Adams left a wife and six children who didn't even have a tombstone to visit. Now one of his sons and one of his daughters are buried beside him, which was a nice thing for the Catholics to arrange. Wrecker hunts around for a smooth rock to place on the deputy's marker; it's more of a Jewish tradition, but the only flowers in sight belong to other graves.

He returns to Bendito Vachs and slaps mosquitoes while he waits. Soon the sleek Mercedes comes flying down Angela and screeches to a halt outside the cemetery gate.

Brilliant, Wrecker thinks sourly. *Honk the horn while you're at it.*

Silver Mustache is panting like a plow horse as he crutches through the dark. Wrecker waves to him with his phone.

"I see you, dude. I see you," the smuggler wheezes as he approaches.

Wrecker shines his light on the punctured door of the vault. "At least they didn't get the body," he says.

Spitting curses, Silver Mustache hurls his crutch into the gravestones and begins hopping in circles. It's the second angry, one-legged performance that Wrecker has witnessed tonight, although Willi's was not nearly as loud.

"YOU'RE ALL DEAD!" the smuggler thunders into the darkness.

Wrecker doesn't ask who, because he wouldn't get a true answer.

He tells Silver Mustache that a friend of his in the neighborhood said the grave robbers were two men in a red Hummer. "They were already gone when I got here," he adds.

"Who's this eagle-eyed 'friend' of yours?" Silver Mustache asks.

"Dwight."

"That's a worse fake name than Charles!"

"Whatever. Leave him out of it, please." Wrecker has no problem lying to protect Willi.

"Did 'Dwight' see anything else?"

"The robbers took off when they heard a siren. You know any bad guys that drive a Hummer?"

"Do *you*?" Silver Mustache asks acidly.

The smuggler turns around and makes a short phone call. Then he turns back to Wrecker: "Okay, smartass, go find my crutch. We're gonna take a ride."

The coupe's air conditioning is so awesome that Wrecker doesn't mind listening to Silver Mustache rant and ramble as they wait for his "associates" to arrive: two skinny white dudes lugging power drills and plywood. It takes only minutes for the pair to board up the crypt, but then Silver Mustache orders them to remain on-site until dawn. From what Wrecker can see of their reaction, they would rather be almost anywhere else on the planet.

Once he gets back in the car, Silver Mustache starts driving back and forth across the island—not too fast, not too slow. His temper is winding down, but he still doesn't offer any hints about the identity of the would-be grave robbers, or why anyone would want to steal the corpse of Bendito Vachs, everyone's favorite.

"You earned your pay tonight, Valdez," he's saying. "What happened to my friend is a sin, a crime, and an outrage."

Wrecker manufactures a sympathetic-looking nod. "Who would try something like that?"

"Bendito wasn't easy. Sometimes he rubbed people the wrong way, but the men who did this are sick in the head. Call me if you hear anything—even crazy rumors."

It's the opening that Wrecker's been waiting for. "Speaking of rumors," he says, "that 'merchandise' you asked me about?"

"Yeah?"

"I know this guy who buses tables at the A&B. He heard a shrimper from Texas talking about some packages he found floating in the Northwest Channel. He said it wasn't drugs. This was a few weeks back."

Wrecker's on a roll now. One big fat lie after another.

Silver Mustache stiffens behind the wheel. "What's the name of this shrimper's boat?"

"He didn't say." Wrecker has rehearsed this story so often that he'd believe it himself if he heard someone telling it.

"Here's the weird part," he goes on. "What the shrimper said was inside the packages?"

"Tell me," Silver Mustache says.

"Blank vaccination cards!"

"Hmm."

"Insane, right? My friend at the lobster house said the guy was half-drunk, so it might be a load of bull. But I wanted to pass it along, just in case."

"Glad you did," the smuggler says tightly.

"The shrimper's long gone."

"Where to?"

"Galveston," Wrecker says, and why not? That's where lots of the commercial boats come from.

"Galveston. Okay." Silver Mustache looks like he's gripping the steering wheel hard enough to snap it in half. He doesn't say anything more until they're back at the cemetery gate. Before Wrecker can slide out of the car, the smuggler presses the button that keeps the doors locked.

"Don't ever 'Dwight' me again," he snarls. "I ask for a name, you better give it to me. This ain't a game, you little creep."

Wrecker can't squeak out a response. It feels like there's a boot on his chest.

"Listen up," Silver Mustache says. "There's lots of

people who don't want COVID shots. Maybe they're scared of needles, maybe it's a political thing, or maybe they're just dumb as dog turds. Who cares? But there's also lots of places won't let you in the door—or past the border—if you don't have proof that you got the vaccine. And my customers? They like to travel big. Eat at five-star restaurants. Go to the theater. Maybe even take a tropical cruise. So guess what, Valdez? If some rich weasel wants a fake CDC card, he's happy to pay a sharp businessman like myself to make it happen. Don't sit there all innocent, pretending you don't understand how this stuff works."

Wrecker manages to push out the words: "I get it."

"Excellent. Muy bueno." Silver Mustache unlocks the doors. "It ain't pills we're sellin', and it ain't powder. It's just pieces of paper, kid."

"Sure."

"Now go home and grab some sleep." Silver Mustache places four fifties in Wrecker's palm.

"No, seriously, that's not—"

"Take the money!" the smuggler snaps.

Wrecker is too stressed to argue. As soon as the gray coupe rolls away, he slips through the gate and fades into the darkest part of the cemetery. For the moment, he feels safer there.

The Plywood Twins are undoubtedly standing watch at the crypt of Bendito Vachs, far out of earshot.

And they're undoubtedly not happy to be spending the night in a graveyard.

Leaning against an old chipped vault, Wrecker wonders how deep and dangerous is the mess that he's stumbled into. A screech owl whinnies from the top of a tamarind tree. Somewhere down Olivia Street, a tomcat yowls. Blessedly the sky is silent; the airport doesn't open for a few hours.

After a while, feeling calmer, Wrecker makes his way toward the modest resting place of Manuel Cabeza. The mosquitoes pursue him, but he stops swiping at them the moment he reaches El Isleño's grave.

In front of the headstone sits an empty Mason jar. Beside the jar is a round white candle that hasn't been lit.

And, cast into the branches of a nearby ixora bush: a dozen red, white, and pink roses, bound at the stems by a florist's twine.

The black-haired girl was here tonight, Wrecker thinks. *The tomb bandits must have scared her away.*

Dejectedly he retrieves the roses and places them in the jar. There are no matches to light the candle, so he leaves it untouched.

The tomcat on Olivia is wailing again as Wrecker locks the cemetery gate behind him and trudges down the sidewalk to his bicycle.

THIRTEEN

Silver Mustache could have cross-checked Wrecker's cell number to find his name and address. It's easy. Costs about twenty-nine bucks online. Then, for free, he could have entered the address on the property-records website, which would reveal Wrecker's step-sister as the homeowner.

After that, the smuggler only had to google Suzanne's name to learn about the car accident that put her in a wheelchair, and the famous baseball player who was speeding drunk when he hit her. . . .

Wrecker is alone at the top of the lookout tower at the shipwreck museum. His back is turned to the waterfront as he watches the planes landing and taking off at the airport. He's waiting for an afternoon sea breeze, and still trying to figure out how Silver Mustache knows so much about him.

It wouldn't take James Bond to notice that Suzanne was out of town. If the smuggler drove past the house more than one night in a row, he would have spotted that only the lights in the back bedroom were on.

The source of his intel on Wrecker's job at Fausto's isn't as obvious. Maybe he tailed Wrecker to work, or maybe one of his men happened to walk into the store. Practically everybody in Old Town shops there.

Willi's ex-boyfriend, for instance.

Earlier, during his morning shift, Wrecker had spotted Clay in the aisles. He had a can of black beans, a bag of white rice, and a handful of KitKats. He saw Wrecker at the same moment, though he pretended he didn't.

Wrecker walked up to him anyway. He wasn't trying to spook the guy. They exchanged wassups, then Wrecker said:

"You still with Juanita?"

"Basically. You still with Willi?"

"No way. We're just friends."

"Whatever." Clay always seemed nervous around Wrecker, as did some of the other older guys in school. Wrecker found that interesting. He'd never started a fight in his life, though he'd been obliged to finish a few.

"How's your uncle?" he asked Clay.

"Which one?"

"The Frances Street uncle."

Clay was caught off guard; he knew exactly what Wrecker was aiming at.

Lowering his voice: "Wreck, he didn't tell anybody else besides me about you crashin' the graveyard."

"Yeah, Clay, but who did *you* tell?"

"Only Willi. Swear to God."

"Then how come there's a guy from Miami," Wrecker said, "who knows all about it? Older dude with a thick gray mustache."

Clay's ears turned red. "Yo, I did *not* rat you out! I don't know anybody from up there, anyway."

Wrecker decided to believe him. "Okay if I go see your uncle?" he asked.

"He's movin' to Homestead tomorrow. The landlord kicked him out."

"Why?"

"The city was gonna cut off his water at the house," Clay said. "Last month he got a humongous bill for, like, two hundred fifty bucks. He told 'em it's gotta be a mistake, but they said to pay up or we'll shut your water line. He doesn't have the money, so he's bailin'."

"That's not right," Wrecker said, feeling like a jerk. He was the one who had left the uncle's garden hose running all night long, racking up that astronomical bill. It was the same night he'd fled the cemetery instead of introducing himself to the black-haired girl at Manuel Cabeza's grave.

"He boozes like a maniac, my uncle," Clay was saying. "Probably good for him to get off the island."

"Still sucks," said Wrecker.

After his shift at the grocery ended, he hurried to Suzanne's place and removed four fifty-dollar bills from his disgustingly stinky sneaker—the same four fifties that Silver Mustache had given him for reporting the attempted grave robbing. To the two-hundred-dollar wad Wrecker added another fifty from his wallet, the most recent payment from Mr. Riley.

When he arrived at the lavender house on Frances Street, he found Clay's uncle packing—clothes, picture frames, pots and pans, liquor bottles. Cardboard boxes filled the front yard. Wrecker introduced himself and apologized for borrowing the ladder and hose without asking permission. He told the man about leaving the water running one night, and then handed him the cash to cover the bill.

"Sweet," Clay's uncle said, counting out the fifties. He wasn't mad at all. "I didn't even know you were using the hose," he added. "I can't see that side of the yard from my window."

He had droopy gray bags under his eyes, and he was missing a few key teeth. "I used to play in a band with your daddy. How's he doin' these days?"

"Still making music," Wrecker replied, trying to sound proud. "He did a solo gig at The Boar a while back."

"Awesome. I heard he got hisself a new name."

"Yup. Austin Breakwater."

Clay's uncle cackled. "Well, that's showbiz!"

"Question," Wrecker said. "Did you tell anyone about my visits to the graveyard? Besides Clay, I mean."

"Some cop came by not long ago. Guess he saw you take my ladder one night. He asks, do I want to press charges for trespassing. 'Trespassing?' I says. 'Does this look like bleeping Buckingham Palace?'" Again Clay's uncle laughed. "I told him I don't know what you're doing with the ladder, but you always bring it back, like a good neighbor."

Wrecker asked if the policeman was wearing a uniform. Clay's uncle said he was in plain clothes, maybe a detective, stocky and mustached.

"Dude had a proper-lookin' badge," he added.

"I'm sure he did."

"And he wore enough French cologne to gag a maggot."

Clay's uncle lifted one of the boxes and began carrying it back toward the house. Wrecker offered to help, but Clay's uncle said no.

"I got this," he called over his shoulder. "Just be sure and tell your old man that Ricky Leek says hey. Rickenbacker Ricky. He'll remember."

A line of chatty tourists is clomping up the steps of the lookout tower, so Wrecker packs up his thoughts and leaves. On the way to the dock he stops to buy a cup of coffee. It's the only thing he brings on the boat besides a cap and sunglasses; no fishing gear, because he's not in the mood. He can't get his mind off Silver Mustache, a police impersonator on top of everything else. That's probably how he conned a gate key out of the cemetery manager.

Fortunately, the smuggler doesn't seem aware of Willi's presence in Wrecker's life. There'd be no reason for him to hold back that juicy tidbit, either; he makes a point of mentioning Suzanne whenever he wants to put Wrecker on edge.

Also, Silver Mustache never mentioned hollering at a girl on a skateboard by the graveyard, an incident that definitely would have sparked a phone call if he'd suspected that she and Wrecker were friends.

Keeping Willi safe—and anonymous—is a crucial part of the brilliant plan that Wrecker should have laid out by now, the plan to free himself from the smuggler's web.

Except there's still no plan, brilliant or otherwise. Every scheme that Wrecker tries to formulate has flaws. . . .

The skiff is riding as smooth as a glider. Wrecker takes off his hat and pushes the throttle to wide open, creating his own personal breeze. The Gulf is pale green and glassy. From hundreds of yards away he can see the chrome flashes of a big tarpon free-jumping in Pearl Basin.

Weaving through the parasail boats with their hooting airborne customers, Wrecker makes his way toward Calda Bank. There he finds the channel blocked by law-enforcement vessels, blue lights flashing—Coast Guard boats, the state marine patrol, and an outboard catamaran from the National Park Service.

Wrecker motors slowly toward the scene until he's intercepted by one of the marine patrol boats. He recognizes the officer, who frequently shops at Fausto's.

"What's going on?" Wrecker shouts.

"Recovery operation," the officer calls back.

"Somebody's boat sink?"

The officer motions for Wrecker to raft up beside him.

"It's not a boat. It's a dead body," he says soberly. "No idea what happened. He's been out here a long time, and so have the bull sharks."

Wrecker turns off his motor. "It's a man?"

"Was," the officer says. "All that's left of him fits in his jacket."

"He had a life jacket?"

"No, a *jacket* jacket. Fancy brown suede."

"Suede?" Wrecker says.

"There was ID in the pocket."

"What's the guy's name?"

"Leon Davila, according to his vaccination card."

"The vax card was his ID?" Wrecker asks.

"Good thing he got it laminated to be waterproof. Otherwise, his remains wouldn't be identified until who knows when. Maybe never."

Wrecker says, "I don't know anybody named Leon."

Thinking: *But I know someone who does.*

"We'll be done here soon," the marine patrol officer tells him.

"I need to get back anyway. See you around."

Wrecker isn't even halfway to Key West when a neon-green speedboat with quad Mercs blows past going the other direction. Wrecker automatically draws back on the throttle to deal with the wake. The bright go-fast circles back and approaches the skiff from the starboard side.

Seated on the front passenger side is Silver Mustache, another cigar wagging in his mouth. The new scar on his chin shines with zinc sunblock, and his right leg—still cased in plaster—is propped up on the dash panel.

Wrecker tosses him a rope and pulls the two boats close.

"Hello, Valdez." Silver Mustache waves a hairy tan arm toward the police commotion at Calda Bank. "What's the deal with all the grouper troopers?"

"They found a dead man named Leon in Jack Channel."

"Uh. Just now?" Silver Mustache looks down and wipes the spray off his shades. The driver of the go-fast doesn't say a word.

"Wasn't that your friend's name?" Wrecker says. "The one that got killed in the car wreck?"

"So what. The world's crawling with Leons."

Wrecker nods. Best to let it go. "New boat?"

"Pretty much," says the smuggler. "I traded the other one."

The one that Leon died in, Wrecker thinks. *The one that's now a sunken condo for stone crabs and lobsters.*

"How fast does it go?" he asks, as if he really cares.

"It's a bullet, kid." Silver Mustache turns and whispers something to the driver.

Wrecker asks when Mr. Vachs's tomb will be repaired. Silver Mustache says the family is arranging it.

"Meantime, they hired private security for Bendito," he adds. "Nothing personal—you did everything you were supposed to. But after what happened last night, we need to take it to another level."

"That makes sense." Wrecker is secretly delighted to be off the smuggler's payroll. The would-be grave robbers did him a favor.

Then Silver Mustache says, "Don't worry, bro, I got another job for you. The pay's even better."

"Huh?"

The smuggler throws Wrecker's rope back into the skiff. "I'll tell you about it later."

"No, tell me now," Wrecker says.

"Gotta run." Silver Mustache adjusts his sunglasses, braces his single flip-flop against the dash panel, and nods to the driver. The neon-green bullet blasts off, angling far away from Calda Bank.

Downcast, Wrecker drifts alone, waiting for the froth to calm.

Later, after dinner, he goes to Willi's house. The gate stands open, so he walks up the driveway and raps on the tall front door. There must be cameras somewhere, because her voice crackles from an intercom speaker: "I'll be down in five, Wreck."

Sixteen minutes later she comes out. They sit on the steps, and he says, "We shouldn't hang together till this is over."

"For sure."

"Don't worry. Nobody followed me here."

"God, look at us," Willi says dejectedly. "Eighty-two degrees out, and we've got hoodies on our heads like it's freaking Detroit in December. We might as well be fugitives."

"These are not the guys to piss off. They're the guys to avoid."

"Gee, ya think? Smugglers and grave robbers."

"Are your folks home?" Wrecker asks.

Willi throws one of her sideways smiles. "Why? You wanna make out?"

"That's not why I asked."

"I'm just messin' with you, Wreck."

"You told me your mom and dad work late."

"Did I?"

No more games, Wrecker thinks wearily. *I don't have time.*

"What Mother and Father do is called 'managing their wealth,'" Willi says. "Does that count as work? They also travel a lot. This week it's either St. Barts or St. Croix, I forget which."

"So you're here all by yourself? That's the only reason I brought this up."

"Believe it or not, I've got an actual live-in nanny. She's about as old as that banyan tree." Willi turns and raises her voice to the intercom: "BUT I LOVE YOU, MISS BASCOMB, IF YOU'RE EVEN STILL AWAKE."

"Just be super-careful," Wrecker says quietly, taking her hand. "Keep the doors locked, windows shut, all that stuff."

She laughs. "Do you not see this place? Does it look like the parental units skimped on security?"

"I'll call you soon, Willi."

"Can't you stay for a while? We're totally safe here. I'll shut the gate."

"Graveyard duty," he says. "Also a hungry cat at home."

"Okay, Wreck. You did good for a rookie, though."

"What?"

"This innocent hand-holding ploy of yours." Willi winks. "Pretty solid."

Once again she's got him rattled. Instantly he lets go of her hand.

She stands up looking highly entertained. "Yo, how's that master plan of yours coming along?"

"DOA," Wrecker says. "Gotta start over."

"You're the one that needs to be careful."

"Naw, I'm like a ninja."

"Definitely," says Willi. "A fearsome bicycle ninja."

On his way to the cemetery Wrecker swings by the house on Pearl Street to pick up his money. It's been a couple of weeks since he's been there, and now a real-estate sign is planted in the yard.

Except for the light above the steps, Mr. Riley's place is dark. The doormat under which he hides the money envelope is gone, so Wrecker checks the mailbox: nothing but random travel magazines and a flyer promoting the Friends of Blue Waters flotilla.

He doesn't want to wake Mr. Riley by knocking, so he lights up his phone and peeks through the windows to make sure the old man hasn't fallen down again.

The house is completely bare—no furniture, no rugs, no family photos on the pine walls.

And no Mr. Riley.

Maybe he didn't pay his water bill, Wrecker thinks, *like Rickenbacker Ricky.*

But then the lawn sprinklers come on, so obviously the water company hasn't cut Mr. Riley off.

Wrecker tries the doorknob, which is, predictably,

locked. So is the door to the Florida porch, where a rust-pocked barbecue grill is the only evidence that the place was recently occupied. Returning to the front yard, Wrecker darts through the sprinklers to take a picture of the real-estate sign.

He rides away wondering why the old man didn't tell him he was moving.

FOURTEEN

On his day off, Wrecker flies to Miami. His mother got him the ticket and a bag of N95 medical masks. It's a short plane ride from Key West, but long enough for Wrecker to get a stomachache worrying about his new unknown assignment for Silver Mustache.

Suzanne picks him up at the airport, which is a madhouse, and drops him off at the hospital. Although Roger has been moved out of Intensive Care, he remains connected to an oxygen machine. It's startling to see him so weak and worn, but nobody looks great with tubes in their nose.

Wrecker's mom isn't there—she had an appointment to audition a new plastic surgeon—but Roger is allowed only one visitor at a time, anyway. He seems truly glad to see Wrecker, who has been outfitted with a clear plastic face shield by one of the nurses.

Out of nowhere, Roger says, "You should move back in the house with Carole and me. What do you think, Valdez?"

"Let's talk about it when you're all better."

"First thing on my to-do list is getting the vaccine!"

"Excellent idea," Wrecker says.

"I don't care if the CIA injects microchips into my blood. I just don't ever want to get this sick again."

"There are no microchips in the shots," Wrecker patiently tells his stepfather, "just medicine."

"I should've listened to you and Suzanne." Roger's weary eyelids close. "It's like I failed the world's easiest IQ test."

"You'll be golfing again soon. Get some rest."

Outside the hospital, Suzanne is waiting in the car with Wrecker's mom. Wrecker gets in the back seat. His mother says he looks good, but she wishes he'd worn a collared shirt instead of a faded T.

"I've got some personal news," she clucks on.

"You're trading in your chin?"

"That's so mean, Valdez. I love my Reese."

His stepsister says, "Carole got her first COVID shot yesterday."

"I'm proud of you, Mom." Wrecker's not being sarcastic. He doesn't want her to go through the agony that Roger did.

"Nobody forced me to vax, either. My body, my decision."

"And it was a smart one." Wrecker happens to know that a woman in his mother's spin class caught the virus and was gone four days later. She was a Key West city firefighter, only forty-two years old, and her death scared all the fool stubbornness out of Carole Dungler. That, on top of seeing Roger so sick.

"There's one more headline in our lives, Valdez," she says, "but I'll save it for lunch."

"Why?"

"Entertainment, of course."

They go to her favorite Italian restaurant in Coconut Grove and sit outdoors, Wrecker rearranging the chairs to make room for Suzanne's wheelchair. While skimming the menu, they discuss when Roger might be able to return to Key West. Wrecker doesn't mention his stepfather's invitation to move back into the house; it's possible Roger was too medicated to realize what he was saying. Besides, Wrecker likes his current living situation. Suzanne seems cool with it, too.

Wrecker's mother orders the salmon, Suzanne selects the vegan lasagna, and Wrecker goes for good old-fashioned spaghetti. He's starving.

"Okay, Mom, what's the other big news?" he asks.

She bites a breadstick in half and says, "It's about your father, the musician. Apparently he's got himself a hit record."

"Where? On Mars?"

"The *Billboard* Top One Hundred."

"Not possible," Wrecker says.

His mother shrugs and attacks the other half of the breadstick like a heron pecking a minnow. Suzanne confirms the story, adding, "I read it in *Rolling Stone*."

It seemed Valdez Jones VII was finally squeezing some good luck from one of his bad ideas. Unexpectedly, the Eagles are following through on their threat to sue—not because the title of "Tequilaville Sunset" was a rip-off of "Tequila Sunrise" but because Valdez Seven had blatantly lifted three and a half lines from the original song for his own. News of the lawsuit had spread among Eagles fans on the internet, resulting in thousands of curious downloads of the new Austin Breakwater single, whoever Austin Breakwater might be.

The following week, "Tequilaville Sunset" reached number 98 on the *Billboard* Hot 100 music chart, college kids started playing the lame cut for laughs at frat parties, and a Memphis record company signed Wrecker's father to an actual contract. In his interview with *Rolling Stone* magazine, Austin Breakwater was quoted as saying he hoped Jimmy Buffett would sue him, too.

"The steely nerve of a pirate," Wrecker thinks sourly, spearing a meatball.

Suzanne says Valdez Seven is booking a long road tour. "Twenty-eight cities, including Key West."

Wrecker's mom declares she will *not* be attending.

"I'm sure he'll be crushed," Wrecker says.

"Valdez, where did this snide streak come from?"

"He doesn't care about us," Wrecker answers. "All he cares about is himself."

"The music business is brutal," Suzanne chips in. "Eventually he'll have to write a good song to survive."

A pulse from Wrecker's phone saves him from prolonging the conversation. It's the real-estate agent who put up the for-sale sign at Mr. Riley's place; Wrecker had left a voice message for her. He steps away from the table to take the call.

"So, Mr. Jones, you're interested in the house on Pearl Street?" the real-estate agent begins. "Please call me Lucinda, by the way."

"Actually, I'm a friend of the man who used to live there."

"Mr. Riley?"

"Do you know where he moved?" Wrecker asks.

Lucinda doesn't answer right away. Then: "I'm very sorry, Mr. Jones. Your friend passed away a week ago."

"What?" Wrecker tries to swallow. "I, uh, didn't know."

"They said it was a stroke."

"At home?"

"Yes, in his sleep. The house cleaner found him."

"When's the funeral?" Wrecker's voice cracks.

"I believe the service will be held in Ireland," says Lucinda. "That was Mr. Riley's wish—to go home."

"I remember. What about his sister?"

"I wasn't aware he had one. Did they live together?"

"Not exactly." Wrecker doesn't feel like sharing the tragic tale of Sarah Chillingwood with a stranger.

"It's a shame you didn't get to say goodbye to him, Mr. Jones."

"He was a nice man."

"I understand he also had quite a way with words. Have you read any of his stories?"

"No. What did he write?" Wrecker thinks about the antique typewriter he saw when he visited the old man.

"Travel features," the real-estate agent says. "He was published in all the top magazines. I'm surprised he didn't tell you."

"I wish he had," Wrecker says.

"Well, if you happen to know anyone who's looking for a house, Mr. Riley's place is a cozy little gem—central air, new kitchen appliances. And, of course, all that glorious Dade County pine."

"Definitely a gem," Wrecker says, biting back a few choice words.

"Call me if you have any friends who might be in the market. You've got my private cell number, Mr. Jones."

"I sure do, Lucinda."

He deletes it two seconds after hanging up.

That night, on the plane returning from Miami, Wrecker watches for the lights of Key West, the brightest star in Florida's southernmost constellation of islands. He tries to imagine how the town looked from the air a hundred years ago. The flight is smooth, though the airport's short runway requires commercial pilots to brake firmly and fast. A Danish tour group in the front of the plane applauds the landing.

Wrecker's glad to be back. His bicycle is right where he left it, double-chained to a bus bench on South Roosevelt. He's tempted to stop by the White Street Pier to see if Willi is among the skateboarders, but there's no time. The Deacon will be waiting for supper.

Before Wrecker makes the turn onto Elizabeth, he gets passed by a light-colored Mercedes coupe. It's moving too fast for him to see if Silver Mustache is the driver, but the possibility makes him pedal faster. Once inside Suzanne's house, Wrecker turns on all the lights, feeds the cat, and prepares the scrub bucket for his graveyard run. Before leaving, he sneaks out to the shed to check on the stash of fake vaccine cards. The combination padlock reads 3-4-4-3, exactly as he'd set it. He always leaves the same numbers showing so that he'll know if anybody messes with the lock. After thumbing the dials to 2-0-0-3, he cracks the door and peeks inside the shed. Nothing has been moved.

He takes a roundabout route to the cemetery, cutting through alleys and side streets in a way that no car could follow. After opening the gate he pedals straight to Sarah Chillingwood's grave, where it hits him hard that the only relative who ever visited her won't be coming back. Even though Wrecker didn't know Mr. Riley well, the thought of the old man dying alone makes him sad. There's no question in Wrecker's mind that he'll continue tending to Sarah's marker, even though he won't be getting paid for it.

After scrubbing off the day's iguana insults, he starts rinsing the poop brush and rags under a weak faucet he found near the battleship *Maine* monument. Two men approach him wearing black coats that are loose enough to be covering guns.

"What're you doin' here?" the taller man demands.

"Cleaning the tombstone of my friend's sister."

"How sweet is that," scoffs the shorter one, who's wearing a plastic neck brace.

Wrecker has seen him before. He was driving the grape go-fast with Silver Mustache and Leon when it ran aground that first afternoon—which means he was probably aboard the night it crashed into the channel marker.

"Call your boss," Wrecker says to the men. "He knows me."

The shorter one steps closer. "Aren't you the punk in that little boat that tried to drag us off the flats?"

"That's right."

"And you're hangin' around this boneyard after dark because . . . ?"

"I already told you. My friend's sister is buried here. And up till yesterday, your boss was paying me to take care of Mr. Vachs, too."

The men in black coats glance skeptically at each

160

other. The taller one whips out a cell phone and walks away. When he returns, he whispers something to Neck Brace, who turns stiffly to Wrecker and says, "So you're here every single night?"

"Unless it storms."

"And you're the only one that comes?"

"I work alone." Wrecker wonders if they've seen the mystery girl at the grave of Manuel Cabeza.

The taller man says, "Someone wants to talk with you."

"What about my bucket?"

"We'll keep an eye on it."

Silver Mustache is waiting in the gray Mercedes, double-parked on Passover Lane. The windows are down, so the cigar stench smacks Wrecker even before he opens the door.

"Hop in," says the smuggler. He turns down the stereo and waves off the Black Coats. Wrecker asks if both of them were hired to guard the tomb of Bendito Vachs.

Silver Mustache says, "The family decided two sets of eyes are better than one."

"They got guns?"

"Come on, bro. What would be the point of me answering that question?"

Wrecker notices that a lightweight Aircast has replaced the heavy plaster one on Silver Mustache's right leg.

"Valdez, were you off the island today?"

Wrecker is pleased to hear that Silver Mustache doesn't know his exact whereabouts every single minute.

"I went up to the mainland to see a friend. He just got out of ICU."

"The corona?"

"What else," says Wrecker.

"That blows."

"Did Mr. Vachs end up in a hospital, too?"

Silver Mustache seems thrown by the question. "Uh, no. Bendito passed away at home." Then, tapping the ashes off his cigar: "He didn't trust doctors."

"Did you find out who tried to break into his tomb?"

The smuggler shrugs. "The cops found a red Hummer is what I heard. Torched in the woods on No Name Key. Dude that owns it—some dirtbag from North Miami—he's missing, along with his cousin. They probably skipped out of the country."

Wrecker is certain that the would-be grave robbers didn't skip off anywhere, and that Silver Mustache knows exactly what happened to them. More likely than not, they now have unmarked graves of their own.

"Let's talk about something else, Valdez. Like Galveston."

"'Kay." Wrecker's right foot begins to tap, which happens sometimes when he's nervous.

"The shrimp fleet over there—we asked around," Silver Mustache says. "None of those boats have been to Key West in months. So whoever found those missing packages of ours . . . See, what I'm sayin' is, your intel about the loudmouth shrimper was no damn good."

"I was only telling you what I heard around town."

"Bar talk, I guess." The smuggler hitches an eyebrow.

For one reckless moment Wrecker wonders what the smuggler would do if he got out of the car and walked away—or ran. Then he thinks about Suzanne, and how Silver Mustache could make her disappear, like the men in the red Hummer.

"Let's discuss your new gig, Valdez. You're stoked, right?"

"How much does it pay?"

"That's the homeboy spirit! Remember, you saw me out cruisin' the Gulf in my mean green machine the other day?"

"Yeah, it's a sweet ride," Wrecker says.

"Well, congratulations. You're my new driver."

"Can't I be an astronaut instead?"

"I'm dead serious, kid."

"Then you're seriously crazy."

"Careful." Silver Mustache wags a finger.

"But I can't run that thing!" Wrecker protests. "It's got, what, twelve hundred horsepower? My skiff only has a forty."

"You'll learn quick. And the money's good, to semi-answer your question."

Wrecker is thunderstruck. "You already have a driver," he says.

"Not anymore. He has to leave Florida for a bit. Family emergency," says Silver Mustache. "Besides, I need somebody who grew up on these waters."

"Look, man, I definitely can't get involved in . . . you know . . . this business."

The smuggler smiles. "Son, you are *so* involved."

"But I don't want to be!"

"Your mother doesn't have to know. Suzanne, either. You want to keep them out of it, right?"

Wrecker gets the point, the unspoken threat.

"So I've got to quit Fausto's?"

"Why would you do that?"

"'Cause now I'll be too busy."

"No, you won't," the smuggler says. "The only time you'll be working for me is at night."

"Wait—what?"

"Except for your first captain's lesson, of course. Ten a.m. tomorrow."

Wrecker's skiff is only a sixteen-footer. The smuggler's new go-fast is almost three times longer, ten times heavier, and thirty times more powerful. Driving it will be like switching from a golf cart to a Ferrari.

This nerve-racking turn of events weighs on Wrecker as he pedals away from the cemetery. *Why would a sane person put a teenager at the helm of a half-million-dollar speedboat?*

One thing is clear—he's in even deeper trouble than before.

He could go to the police, except that he's the one holding five thousand counterfeit vaccination cards. Since the salvaged pizza boxes are the only evidence of a crime, the case would boil down to Wrecker's word against Silver Mustache's. The grape-purple smuggling boat, sunken and stripped, would be useless to the prosecutors.

And once Silver Mustache learned he was talking to the authorities, nobody in Wrecker's family would be safe. . . .

Leaving Key West is another option—Wrecker could go camp out on one of a dozen little mangrove islands on the Gulf side. But as soon as he disappeared, Silver Mustache and his gorillas would show up at Suzanne's door.

By the time he gets home, Wrecker feels hopelessly trapped. The feeling gets worse when he goes to the shed.

The padlock lies unlatched on the ground, the dials turned to 2-0-0-3. Somebody either guessed the combination—almost impossible—or used a professional tool to line up the tumblers. Wrecker knees the door open and turns on the light.

The pizza boxes are gone, of course. Silver Mustache sent someone to snatch the fake vax cards.

Which means he must have figured out that Wrecker's been lying to him all along.

Yet earlier, at the graveyard, the smuggler acted so friendly and chill. In a way, that's even scarier. Suddenly his proposal for Wrecker to drive the hot new speedboat makes sense—it's meant to be a one-time, one-way trip.

Wrecker sits down heavily on a sack of garden mulch.

I'm a moron, he thinks, *and I'm going to die for it.*

He wouldn't be surprised if the gray coupe was parked down the street right now, Silver Mustache having a good laugh.

Wrecker knows he's down to one move: go to the cops and hope they believe his story. Maybe they'll assign a patrol officer to watch Suzanne's house, so at least she'll be safe.

The police station is only minutes away. It's his best—and maybe only—chance to shake free of this mess. He stands up and reaches to switch off the light in the shed, and that's when he sees it.

A crisp white envelope propped on a shelf next to a carton of snail bait.

The envelope is addressed to "The Honorable Valdez Jones VIII." Inside is a one-sentence note, written by hand.

Revealing that, once again, Wrecker was dead wrong about what's happening.

FIFTEEN

The corner of Southard and Margaret rings with the sound of dueling roosters. Wrecker stands under the Iguana Tree, where the crusty old-timer that Willi named Ichabod is climbing slo-mo up the trunk, positioning himself for some morning rays.

Wrecker was up early. He'd hardly slept, and kept the house lights on all night. He took a sneaky zigzag route to the intersection so nobody could track him. Tucked in a pocket is the envelope that was placed inside Suzanne's garden shed.

"Yo, Wreck!"

He whirls and there's Willi, holding two cups of coffee from 5 Brothers. She hands him one and says, "You look like crap, bro."

"Wonder why."

"Try meditating before bed. I use an app called Dream Chants."

"I'd rather sit on a sea urchin," Wrecker says.

"That kind of snark is not attractive. *God.*"

Willi's fashion choice for their meeting is camo-themed, from the backward cap on her curly head to her yoga pants to the straps on her flip-flops. Having been assured that the Black Coats aren't hunting for her, she is no longer hiding her face like a bank robber. She brightens at the sight of Ichabod in the tree.

Wrecker says they should go somewhere quiet to talk, Southard being one of the busiest streets in town. In his imagination, every gray car that drives by turns into a Mercedes.

"I don't want that guy to see us together," he says to Willi.

"Well, I intend to finish my coffee."

They end up sitting side by side on the tombstone of Dr. Frederick Weedon. It's located at the opposite end of the cemetery from Bendito Vachs, though Silver Mustache can't station his goons at the crypt during daylight hours. The graveyard is teeming with tourists.

The late Dr. Weedon, 1784–1857, was a prison physician assigned to treat Chief Osceola, the legendary leader of the Seminoles. In his diary, Weedon wrote that he became friendly with the captured warrior, who was often ill with fevers and other ailments. After Osceola died in 1838, the doctor cut off the chief's embalmed head, took it to St. Augustine, and displayed it at his drugstore. Family accounts say he also liked to place the gruesome relic above his children's beds when they misbehaved. Eventually, the head of Osceola ended up at a New York medical college, where it was supposedly destroyed in a fire.

Willi didn't know the bizarre story. After hearing it from Wrecker, she says, "Maybe this is why you don't have a girlfriend."

"History isn't pretty."

"FYI—severed heads? Don't bring up that subject on a first date. Maybe not even the second."

"This isn't a date," Wrecker says tightly. "Not even close."

"Really? Thanks for clearing that up." Willi stands to address the long-dead Frederick Weedon: "Doc, you were one seriously twisted dude."

Wrecker takes out the envelope. "Here's the reason I asked you to come."

"Okay." Willi shrugs.

He reads the short note aloud. "'Don't worry, partner, I've got our pizzas.' Explain, please," he says.

"Which do you want first—the how or the why?"

"The how." Wrecker's starting to lose it. "Did you pick the padlock?"

Willi smiles at the question. "Seriously? That night we went into the shed, I was standing right behind you when you dialed the combination. Two-zero-zero-three!"

"So you were spying, stealing personal information. Because that's what friends do to each other."

"I'm not nosy by nature, Wreck. Just observant."

"Why'd you take the pizza boxes?" he snaps. "And what did you do with them?"

"Wait, I wasn't finished with the how. My nanny has a car, she goes to bed insanely early—and I've got a learner's permit."

Wrecker's anger at Willi is slightly shaded by relief, knowing it wasn't Silver Mustache who snatched the bogus vaccine cards.

"I'm gonna ask again," he says. "Where are they, Willi?"

"The smugglers would have found 'em at your place. It was only a matter of time. You even said they might be following you."

"WHERE ARE THE BLEEPING BOXES?"

"Super-safe, I promise."

"Give them back to me. *Today.*"

"Here's a freaky fact," she says. "Nobody named Bendito Vachs died in the Keys this whole year."

"What? How do you know that?"

Willi explains that she went online pretending to be a niece of Bendito Vachs. When she tried to order a copy of his official death certificate, she was informed that no such document existed. Next, she ran a search of all obituary notices posted since January by funeral homes in Monroe County, and found not one dearly departed person named Vachs.

Wrecker admires her detective work but he's in no mood to admit it.

"So, the first mystery is who's really buried in that grave," Willi goes on. "The second mystery is why anyone would want to steal the body. Theories, please?"

Wrecker gets up to shoo a pair of curly-tailed lizards basking on the cracked marker of a child who died in 1904. He keeps on walking, Willi trailing behind him.

"I thought I could trust you," he says over his shoulder.

"We're in this together."

"You stole the vax cards to keep it that way, right?"

Willi catches up, whispering: "Wreck, I did *not* steal them. I just moved them."

"You're unbelievable."

"Anyhow, they're mine, too. I was there when you found 'em."

"Only one of us went diving on that wrecked speedboat," Wrecker says sharply. "The crazy part is, from the start I've been trying to keep *you* out of this mess. I told you these people are hardcore. And what do you do? Sneak over to my sister's house and take what the bad guys are hunting for, just so you can stay in the mix."

"That's mean, Wreck. I may require an apology."

"Yo, the red Hummer you saw at the cemetery? Somebody burned it to a crisp. And the guys who tried to rob Bendito's grave? Disappeared. Permanently is my guess."

Willi stays silent for a full minute. Then: "Stop

worrying. They'll never find where I hid those pack-ages, not in a jillion trillion years."

By now they're standing on Angela Street, away from the cemetery and the safe flow of tourists.

"Bring me those pizza boxes," Wrecker says.

"Text me later."

"I will."

"You better," Willi says.

"I *will*. Now please get outta here."

"Rude."

"Fast," Wrecker says. "I'm not kidding."

Down the block, a sleek gray car is easing up to a stop sign at Passover Lane. The windows are open, and Wrecker can hear Celia Cruz singing, pure as an angel. By the time he turns back around, Willi's gone.

He takes a deep breath and runs the other way.

Like the purple speedboat, the neon-green one doesn't have a name. It's a secondhand Cigarette Rough Rider, forty-six feet long, that looks brand-new. Silver Mus-tache got it repainted. To create more cargo space under the aft deck, he replaced the factory inboard engines with quad Mercs. The console panel features high-def GPS map screens, a steering wheel that belongs in an Italian sports car, a stiff full-handed throttle, and too many rocker switches to learn on one test drive.

But Wrecker is doing okay—pretty good, actually—

until a Coast Guard inflatable Zodiac appears with its chase lights flashing. Silver Mustache tells Wrecker to throttle down and keep his mouth shut. The Coast Guard crew is a man and a woman, self-introduced as Petty Officers Webster and Coltrane.

"This is my nephew," Silver Mustache tells them. "We're taking it easy today. Thirty, thirty-five max."

"He's pretty young to be driving a beast like this, isn't he?"

"Even though he's only fifteen, he's got more time on the water than a lot of the so-called captains out here."

Wrecker tries to act like he appreciates the compliment. He isn't surprised that Silver Mustache knows his age, but he wonders if the Coasties believe it. Because of his size, most people think he's older. Under Florida's boating law it doesn't really matter, because you've only got to be fourteen to operate a private vessel of any size. No driving test, either, and the marine safety course is online. Ridiculous.

"What's your name?" Petty Officer Webster asks Wrecker.

"Valdez Jones. I go to Key West High."

"Do you have a boat of your own?"

"Yes, sir," Wrecker says, "but not like this one."

"I bet."

Because gaudy go-fasts are so popular with smugglers, they're magnets for the Coast Guard patrols.

Wrecker's not surprised when Petty Officer Coltrane steps aboard and asks to see the registration.

"Uncle Mo-Mo's got it," says Wrecker, and Silver Mustache shoots him a poisonous look.

After examining the paperwork, Coltrane goes through the boat counting life preservers and checking the gauges on the fire extinguishers. Wrecker is hoping Silver Mustache isn't reckless enough to be hauling anything illegal in broad daylight.

Coltrane eyes the smuggler's cast and asks what happened to his leg.

"Bad car accident," Silver Mustache says. "This is my first day off crutches."

"Another reason to take it easy out here. Okay, you guys are good to go."

As soon as the Zodiac pulls away, Silver Mustache turns on Wrecker. "Uncle *Mo-Mo*? Is that your idea of funny, Valdez?"

"What was I supposed to say? I don't know your real name—we've never officially met, remember? And we never will, you said."

"Yeah, yeah."

The two of them had met up at the Half Shell Raw Bar, where Silver Mustache had parked the gray coupe in a handicapped spot. He was finishing a plate of jumbo fried shrimp when Wrecker walked in, his shirt still damp after his unplanned jog from Passover Lane.

The Cigarette boat sat gassed up and ready to go at one of the finger piers behind the restaurant.

The smuggler's mood was unusually friendly and positive, which naturally had made Wrecker fear the worst. He was so nervous that he barely spoke a word as they were leaving the harbor. He suspected that it could very well be his last day on earth, and that his body would never be found. Briefly he'd considered jumping off the speedboat, but he figured that Silver Mustache would just turn it around and run him over—or shoot him dead—in the water. . . .

Yet here he is, nearly two hours later, still very much alive. The smuggler hasn't said anything to indicate he knows that Wrecker's been lying about the missing packages of forged CDC cards. Until the Coast Guard showed up, Wrecker's driving lesson had been the only topic of conversation. Now the go-fast is drifting with a light breeze on the Atlantic side of Key West, where Silver Mustache has been letting Wrecker buzz up and down the shipping channel.

The smuggler had lied to the Coasties about how fast they'd been going. At one point Wrecker had pushed the Cigarette to fifty-two miles an hour and it felt practically airborne, as if only the propellers were touching the water. The sensation had both thrilled and terrified him, while Silver Mustache stayed totally chill behind his wraparound sunglasses. Clearly the man was comfortable at high speeds; he'd bragged to Wrecker that he once raced from Key Largo to South Bimini in seventy-two minutes—insane, though not impossible.

"I'd better get back soon," Wrecker says. "For work."

"Switch places with me, kid. I'll take 'er in."

The boat blasts off, and Wrecker's hat flies away. Holding on to his seat with both hands, he stops peeking at the digital speedometer when the number hits seventy. Silver Mustache delivers him to the dock with plenty of time to spare, and Wrecker's delighted not to have been killed on the ride, either accidentally or on purpose.

A surprise is waiting at his stepsister's house: her van in the driveway.

"Man, your nose got fried," Suzanne says when Wrecker walks through the door. "You forget your sunblock again? And where's your hat, Captain Bulletproof?"

"When are Mom and Roger coming back?"

"Next week, hopefully, when he's off the O-2. Check this out, brother."

She thrusts a copy of the *Key West Citizen* into Wrecker's hands. The front-page headline says a cruise ship named the *Princess Pandora* will be docking at Key West within days—the first mega-liner to return since the beginning of the pandemic, and a punch in the gut to all the locals who'd voted to limit the size of passenger vessels entering the harbor.

"Blockade time, baby," says Suzanne. "There's a major meeting tonight."

The newspaper story says the *Princess* is eleven hundred feet long and nine stories high and carries seven thousand people. The tourist tanker has a rock-climbing wall, an ice-hockey rink, a wave pool for surfing, and a driving range where golfers whack "biodegradable baked tofu balls" off the fantail into the ocean.

"A floating fun-fest," Wrecker says acidly.

"Yeah, and also . . . a zip line for handicapped passengers? NO THANK YOU!" Suzanne is fired up. "I wish that reporter would've called *me* for a quote."

Wrecker takes a shower to wash off the salt rime from the bouncy speedboat ride. The water pressure in the bathroom is so weak that he can hear Suzanne through the walls, ranting about the cruise ship to somebody on the phone. Still, she has a Cuban sandwich ready and wrapped before he leaves. He devours it on the bike ride to Fausto's. Before walking into the store, he shoots a text to Willi:

Pizza tonight?

By the end of his shift, six hours later, there's still no answer.

Lightning above a graveyard makes the tombstones flicker in electric blue. The scene is strangely beautiful to Wrecker.

I never claimed to be normal, he thinks.

After work he'd gone home, eaten two hamburgers, and watched *Jeopardy!* with Suzanne. The cannon booms of thunder began when he got to Sarah Chillingwood's grave, and now the whole tropical sky is pulsing. No rain yet, though it's rolling in fast from the Gulf; Wrecker can taste it. He could probably make it back to the house before the squall unloads, leaving Mother Nature to rinse the lizard crud from Sarah's stone.

Still, he keeps on scrubbing, even after the first fat raindrops splat in his hair. Silver Mustache's two Black Coats have already taken cover in a plain black car parked outside the cemetery gate; Wrecker heard them griping as they hustled to beat the incoming weather. He knows they don't have the patience to wait it out and will be gone shortly.

Leaving unguarded the tomb that holds the mystery of Bendito Vachs.

Soaked to the skin, Wrecker slinks low between the vaults and tombstones until he reaches the Toppino family mausoleum, the largest structure in the Catholic part of the cemetery and an excellent shelter from storms. More important, it's got a clear view of the sedan on the street.

Sure enough, barely ten minutes into the downpour, the car carrying the Black Coats speeds away. Wrecker's glad he remembered his pocket flashlight because, unlike his phone, it's waterproof. He runs through the rain to the Bendito Vachs memorial and finds that the smashed door has been replaced, the name marker has been fixed, and the stonemason has finally changed the date of death—from April 13 to April 1.

Either it's an ironic coincidence or Silver Mustache has a twisted sense of humor. One thing for sure: whoever's inside that coffin is long past caring whether or not he actually died on April Fools' Day.

The roof of the tomb is splattered with chicken poop—the lazy Black Coats obviously haven't been cleaning it, and even heavy rain can't dissolve some of the hard-as-plaster plops. The new door of the vault is locked, of course. Wrecker runs a hand across the thick wood, imagining how hard he can swing a sledge-hammer.

Again he tries to reach Willi. Still no reply, which is odd since she'd practically ordered him to text her. Wrecker decides to go see her. He wants her to take him to wherever she hid the smuggler's packages.

From the road, the Brown family mansion looks dark—and it's only nine-fifteen. Willi had said her parents were away traveling, so Wrecker figures it's safe to press the speaker button on the security box mounted at the foot of the driveway.

"Hey, Willi, it's me. I'm outside your gate."

Nothing.

"Getting my butt soaked," he adds.

A fuzzy click comes from the speaker box.

"Willi? You there?" He pushes the button again.

From the other end comes a sound not like breathing, more like someone trying to hold their breath.

"Yo, what's wrong?" Wrecker says. "You told me to text, and I did."

Still no answer.

"Willi? We need to talk."

Another click, then the box goes silent again.

Riding off through the puddles on Whitehead Street, Wrecker feels like his nerves are strung tight as a piano wire.

SIXTEEN

"What's the issue with the ravioli?"

"It's fine, Mom. I'm not super-hungry, that's all."

Ah, the Dungler family dinner. A cherished tradition.

I wish I was fishing, Wrecker thinks.

It's been five days of frustrating silence from Willi, but still he constantly checks his phone for a text. She knows he intends to take back the pizza boxes, and clearly she's dodging him.

"Dad, could you pass the rolls?" Suzanne asks.

"You betcha," says Roger.

He lost twenty-one pounds in the hospital, but he looks pretty good for somebody who almost died on a ventilator. The Key West sunshine helps.

"Have you thought any more about moving back with us?" he asks Wrecker, who hadn't really thought about it at all.

"I, uh, I don't know, Roger—"

"Oh, Valdez comes and goes at all hours," Suzanne cuts in, with a fake tone of sisterly disapproval. "Dad, you need your rest at night. Isn't that right, Carole?"

"We're always in bed by nine sharp," says Wrecker's mother. "I struggle with sleep issues, too, Valdez."

"I remember, Mom."

"But it's been good having him stay at my place," Suzanne says. "He's a huge help with the chores."

Right now Wrecker wants to hug her.

"Well, just know that you can have your old bedroom back anytime you want. It's the same as when you left," Roger says.

"Except we repainted it," his mother adds. "Periwinkle blue."

Bold choice, Wrecker thinks.

The talk turns to another delicate subject—his father, the song poacher. Wrecker's mom reports that "Tequilaville Sunset" tumbled off the *Billboard* chart after one measly week. The Eagles shrugged and dropped their lawsuit, and now tickets for Austin Breakwater's big concert tour are selling online for the humiliating sum of eleven dollars and fifty cents, including the service fee.

"Isn't he playing here tomorrow night?" Suzanne asks.

"I'll be busy," Wrecker says, "washing my socks."

"You don't own any socks."

If Roger is bothered by the conversation about his wife's ex-husband, he doesn't let on—even when Carole reveals that Valdez Seven phoned and personally invited her to the show.

"With you, honey, of course," she says to Roger. "He's saving us front-row seats."

At The Boar? Wrecker thinks. *What front row?*

Roger pipes up randomly: "They're reseeding the seventh fairway at the golf course. Grass weevils, they said. It's like a plague!"

"Oh Lord," sighs Wrecker's mom.

This is a good moment for Wrecker to stage his exit. He says he's too full for dessert, and—as casually as possible—excuses himself from the table.

It's time for his first nighttime practice run. When he arrives at the empty cruise-ship pier, Silver Mustache beckons from the neon-green speedboat. As they motor out of the harbor, toward open water, the smuggler warns him to watch out for the channel-marker posts.

"Only a jackass would hit one of those things," Wrecker says with a straight face.

Silver Mustache grunts testily. "You heard any more chatter about my missing merchandise?"

The man is obviously not giving up on those five packages.

"Matter of fact," Wrecker says, "I think I got the name of that shrimp boat."

"Talk to me, Valdez."

"It's called the *Last Laugh*."

"I'll pass that along to my people."

"I left you a voice message."

"That was my old number," Silver Mustache says. "I got a new one."

They run the Cigarette up and down the shipping channel. The seas are choppy and the current is heavy, so Wrecker is more than glad to hold the speed down. Even so, the long hull of the go-fast slaps hard on every wave crest. To spare their teeth, Wrecker and Silver Mustache remain standing for the ride, the smuggler balanced on his one good leg. Of course he spotlights every channel marker on the way in.

When they get to the dock, he hands some cash to Wrecker, saying: "You did all right for a rookie. That wasn't exactly smooth water out there."

"I can't take this money."

"Since when?"

"This isn't like soaping a gravestone."

"You're right, dude. This is a real job. My vax cards? They've tripled in price this summer. I'm not even jokin'. We can't print enough of 'em." Silver Mustache smooths his windblown hair. "That means—"

"I know what it means," Wrecker says.

"Then you shouldn't be surprised that I can afford to pay my new boat captain a lot more than he was making on lizard-crap patrol in a boneyard."

"That's not the point."

"In my world, it is," Silver Mustache says. "I'll be in touch soon, Valdez."

Wrecker heads home to get the cleaning bucket for

his graveyard run. Riding past Willi's house, he spots a light in an upstairs window. A friend of hers told him she's vacationing with her parents on Cape Cod, which might or might not be the truth. Cell phones work fine in Massachusetts, so she's got no excuse for ignoring Wrecker's messages.

He waits until the road is quiet, scales the entry gate, and follows the shadow line to a twisting old ficus tree next to the house. He doesn't have to climb very high to see inside the lit room.

Willi is sitting cross-legged on the bed, swiping through Instagram posts. She looks fine. Wrecker dials her number and watches her expression change when his name pops up on her phone. He doesn't want to scare her by rapping on the window, so he shoots her another text (I thought u were out of town). Immediately she hops to her feet, turns off the lights, and disappears through the door.

This is more than a ghosting, Wrecker thinks glumly. *It's an arctic freeze.*

Scrambling down the tree, he wonders what's going on in Willi World to make her act this way. It might have something to do with the pizza boxes—did her parents find them? Or somebody else? Maybe she threw them in a dumpster and doesn't want to tell him.

Wrecker rings the front doorbell and leans close to the speaker: "Willi, I know you're home. Please open the door."

A click of static comes from the intercom box, followed by a stranger's voice: "This is Miss Bascomb. Whom am I speaking with?"

"Uh . . . my name's Valdez. Valdez Jones." Wrecker is sure that he sounds totally flustered. "I really need to talk with Willi."

"I'm sorry. She's on vacation with her mother and father."

The words sound mechanical and distorted, like a robot talking in a tunnel. Willi's parents need to invest in a new speaker.

"Look, I know she's home," Wrecker says. "I just saw her."

"Please leave the property, young man."

Wrecker can see where this conversation is headed. He sprints down the driveway and hops the gate. As soon as his feet touch the sidewalk, somebody tackles him from behind.

"Don't move," a man's voice snarls in his ear.

"I think I'm bleeding."

"Shut up and do what you're told, boy!"

"Excuse me?" Wrecker says.

His attitude could have been better, for sure.

After all, he'd been caught red-handed fleeing a gated private estate. On the plus side, he was carrying no stolen items or even burglary tools. The only crime they could charge him with was trespassing.

And getting slammed to the ground? Not that huge a deal.

It was when the policeman called him "boy" that Wrecker lost interest in being polite. He was keenly aware what that word was intended to mean.

The officer is a white dude, early thirties, narrow-eyed, and built like a linebacker who traded a football career for the buffet line at Cracker Barrel. He must be new on the force because Wrecker's never seen him before.

"This'll teach your dumb ass to stay in Bahama Village," he says, referring to a historic Key West neighborhood where many Black families live.

Wrecker sits rigid in the back seat of the police SUV. His wrists are cuffed in front of him, and his bloodied T-shirt smells like the rum bottle that shattered when he fell on it. He doesn't say much during the short ride to the station, and he winds up alone at the same bare table in the same bright interrogation room where they brought him on the one night he got busted at the cemetery.

A bored-looking nurse comes in and says, "Lift your shirt, young man."

She tweezes several brown glass shards out of his chest, wipes him down with an antibiotic ointment, and tapes gauze over the cuts, which aren't deep. Wrecker doesn't tell her what happened, and she doesn't ask.

Later the arresting officer enters the room carrying a printout. In the light, Wrecker can finally see the nameplate on his uniform: NUGENT.

"I wasn't breaking into that house," Wrecker says. "A friend of mine from school lives there."

"Sure, he does. What's his name?"

"Willi Brown—and she's a girl."

The cop looks irritated. He's rereading the information on the printout.

"Good thing nobody was home," he mutters. "You could've got your dumb burglar butt shot off."

Obviously Willi wouldn't come to the front door, even for the police. Same with Miss Bascomb. Officer Nugent just happened to be driving past when Wrecker was coming over the fence.

"Stay where you are," Nugent says curtly, and walks out of the room again.

Wrecker's aim is to talk his way out of this fiasco so that the police won't call his stepsister. When Nugent returns, he says, "It's your lucky night, boy. The homeowner doesn't want to press charges."

"That would be Mr. Brown, right?"

"They're away on a trip, which I'm sure you already knew. We got hold of him on his phone."

"What did he say?"

"That you're trying to hook up with his daughter."

Wrecker shakes his head. "Not true. We're just friends."

The cop gives a creepy grin and waves the printout. "You're not foolin' anybody, 'Mr. Jones.' We found your name in the system."

"The system?"

"I get it. You're tryin' to pass for white."

"You mean because I don't live in Bahama Village?" Wrecker is glaring daggers at the man.

"What kind of first name is 'Val-deez,' anyway?"

"What kind of last name is 'Nugent'?"

The cop clearly wants to lunge across the table and slug him. Wrecker's heart is racing—not from fear, but anger.

A second officer enters the room. His nameplate says VAN ZORN. He's built thin, with graying sideburns and a deep tan. Wrecker has seen him out boating with his kids on weekends. He's got a twenty-one-foot Grady-White, teal blue, with a T-top and an old two-stroke Evinrude.

He and Wrecker haven't spoken before, but they make eye contact.

"There's a fight at Mallory Square," Van Zorn informs Nugent. "Let's wrap it up here, Ned."

"Can I please have my money back?" Wrecker asks.

Van Zorn looks narrowly at Nugent, who says, "This punk had two hundred bucks in his pants! I'm sure he stole it from somewhere."

Wrecker didn't know it was that much money; he hadn't gotten around to counting the wad that Silver Mustache handed him.

"I work at Fausto's," he says. "They let me cash my paycheck there."

Van Zorn nods. "No law against that. We gotta roll, Ned."

Wrecker holds out his wrists. Sulking like a brat, Nugent uncuffs him.

"How's fishing?" Wrecker asks the other officer.

"It's been good. I sure don't miss the mud from those cruise ships."

"Me neither." Wrecker shakes his arms to get the circulation going. "Are you coming to the harbor blockade?"

"If I can get off work," says Van Zorn.

Nugent can't stand it anymore. He slaps Wrecker's speedboat cash on the table before stalking out.

On the way home—because, really, that's what his stepsister's house has become for him—Wrecker hears the sirens of police cars racing toward Mallory Square, where the famous laid-back vibe is being spoiled by drunken fools punching each other.

"What on earth happened to you?" Suzanne asks when he tries to sneak in the back door.

"Fell off my bike."

"No, you didn't. You stink like booze."

Wrecker removes his ruined shirt, Suzanne raising her eyebrows at the sight of the tape and gauze.

"Tell me the truth, Valdez."

"Okay. Some cop body-slammed me on Whitehead

and I landed on a bottle of rum that obviously wasn't empty. That's what happened."

"So, just another night in paradise."

"Basically," Wrecker says.

Suzanne looks concerned but also suspicious. Wrecker can't blame her.

"It's all good, sis. No stitches necessary, and the police let me go."

"Really? Who posted your bail?"

"Not funny." Wrecker ducks into his bedroom to hide the cash he got from the smuggler.

His phone dings. Finally, Willi texting:

sorry u got busted, dude. my fault

Yup, he replies.

She sends a remorseful-looking emoji, then:

I shoulda opened the door for you. I was being super surly

Yup, Wrecker types.

Dad's got cameras all over. I saw that whacked cop take you down

how's Cape Cod, Willi?

I don't blame u for being mad. Call me tmw!

Doubtful, Wrecker texts, and turns off his phone.

He's got a theory that being tall and muscular for his age has spared him from being bullied, or getting called racist names. One of his friends who moved away during the pandemic was a Black kid who weighed about eighty-five pounds. The kid was a stone genius at math and piano, but he was also shy and quiet. He shrewdly never left Wrecker's side whenever they were in the gym or cafeteria.

Still, one afternoon the kid came out of PE and found that a crude hangman's noose had been drawn with a yellow Sharpie on his backpack. Nobody would tell on who did it, which, looking back, was a good thing for Wrecker. Otherwise he probably would have ended up in another police car.

Now, after a long and confusing night, he's riding his bike up and down Flagler Avenue amped to the max. The dark side of his imagination is once again transforming the modern utility poles into old wooden telegraph posts, just tall enough for a hanging rope. Some people would say El Isleño shouldn't have taken the law into his own hands and shot that Klansman who'd tortured him the day before. Clearly Manuel Cabeza had been overcome by rage, humiliation, and the bitter certainty that nothing would happen to his abductors if he told the sheriff about what they'd done to him—all because he was in love with someone who wasn't white.

Wrecker is not fully raging but he's still boiling mad, and shaken up. He believes his run-in with Officer Nugent was something that was bound to happen. It was an infuriating but useful reminder that, even on a tourist island fabled for its tolerance, hateful people are still out there; they just know better than to put on white robes and march down Duval Street.

It was after midnight when—still hot about Nugent—Wrecker had left Suzanne's and gone to the cemetery. The visit began and ended with jolting distractions. He went first to check on Sarah Chillingwood's gravestone, only to discover that the gravestone was gone.

The soil on the site looked newly turned, then raked. Wrecker had snapped a low branch from a gumbo-limbo and plunged it into the ground as deep as it would go; nothing as solid as a casket was there.

Which meant Sarah was gone, too.

Then the singing began, and this time it wasn't Celia Cruz. Wrecker ran to Manuel Cabeza's grave, and of course the mourning girl was there. He couldn't tell if she was crying; she wore a veil over her face and a simple dress that matched her coal-black hair. Her head was bowed as she sang:

Los corazones llorosos deben preguntarse por qué
Y espero que los arcoíris iluminen el cielo

The Islander's headstone stood illuminated by a single white candle, set beside a jar filled with fresh long-stemmed roses. Wrecker watched the scene, hiding in the muggy summer shadows, his back snug against the wall of some nameless tomb. He touched the recording app on his phone and waited for the singing girl to finish so he could step forward and speak to her.

But before that could happen, the two Black Coats appeared out of the darkness.

"What the bleep are you doin' here?" one of them barked at the girl, who turned and ran away.

Their job of scaring off a harmless trespasser accomplished, the Black Coats didn't bother to give chase. The heavier man kicked over the candle on Manuel Cabeza's grave, and the other grabbed the roses. Together they ambled away in the direction of the nonexistent Bendito Vachs.

As soon as they were out of sight, Wrecker dashed from his hiding place to find the girl in black. On Angela Street he heard a person running ahead of him, but he was too far behind to catch up. By the time he reached the crossroad at Frances, the footsteps had faded and he didn't know which way to go.

That's when he'd spotted something that belonged to the young graveyard singer snagged on the top of a chain-link fence. Wrecker hurriedly untangled it and ran back to get his bike.

The object he found is still clutched in one fist as he rides up and down Flagler.

It's more than a clue. It's a thunderbolt.

SEVENTEEN

Wrecker hears the wheelchair rolling around the kitchen, and he smells bacon frying. He's glad to have the day off from work.

"I'm goin' fishing," he tells Suzanne.

"Shocker."

"Want me to bring back some snapper?"

"Valdez, I texted you six times last night."

"My bad. Low battery."

"You mean that battery between your ears?" Suzanne says.

"I was at the cemetery, sis."

"No more unpleasant interactions with the police, I hope."

"Gimme a break," Wrecker says.

"Let's put some clean bandages on those cuts."

"I'm good. Doesn't hurt."

The island sky is pearly and the morning air smells sweet. On the way to the dock, Wrecker stops by the cemetery office to find out what happened to Sarah

Chillingwood's coffin. The sexton asks if he's a relative.

"No, but I knew her brother," Wrecker says.

"Well, now they're at eternal peace together. She's back home in Ireland."

"That would make Mr. Riley happy."

"Oh, he's the one who arranged it," the sexton says. "He put it in his will. There was a life insurance policy that paid for all the shipping expenses—and also a new memorial marker. It was waiting when she got to Belfast."

So she'll be Sarah Riley from now on, Wrecker thinks. *The old man thought of everything.*

"They're buried side by side in the family plot," the sexton adds. "The best possible ending to a terribly sad story."

Wrecker is relieved to learn that no crime was involved in the removal of Sarah's remains. He's also glad that Mr. Riley arranged for a new gravestone; otherwise, visitors to the Irish cemetery would be left wondering: What rumor was true?

It's a Key West story that should stay in Key West, buried under Johnny Chillingwood's anonymous tombstone, wherever that might be.

Wrecker goes to the tackle shop and scoops four dozen live shrimp into his bait bucket. At the dock he tops off the skiff's gas tank using a jerry can that he strapped to his handlebars. While kneeling to lock his bicycle to the fish-cleaning table, he finds himself staring at a pair of ridiculous old snakeskin boots.

He straightens up and says, "It's Mr. Breakwater himself."

"What happened to plain old 'Dad'?"

"Funny, that's the same question I asked Mom all those years: 'What happened to Dad?'"

"Are you coming to the show tonight?"

"Can't. I've got sort of a date." Although it's far from being a date, he and Willi are meeting up later.

"Can we go somewhere private and talk?" his father asks.

"Not right now. I've gotta catch dinner."

"I'll tag along. There's plenty of time till my rehearsal."

"Wait—you rehearse?"

"Lighten up, Eight."

"I told you to call me Wrecker," he says. "Hop in the boat."

His dad's cowboy hat blows off three times on the ride to the patch reef. Now the man is clutching the wet hat on his lap, letting it drip all over his jeans. He isn't much of an angler, but he can outtalk a car salesman. While Wrecker reels in one snapper after another, Valdez Seven prattles on about a new song he just finished that's guaranteed to be a smash hit, even bigger than "Tequilaville Sunset."

The title: "Here Comes the Moon."

"Sounds a lot like 'Here Comes the Sun,'" Wrecker says.

"No, no, no! The lyrics I wrote are way different."

"So now you're ripping off the Beatles, the most famous band in the history of bands. That's really smart."

"I play my song in the key of G. Theirs is A major," Valdez Seven declares. "Hey, let 'em sue! Trust me, that kind of publicity sells tons of downloads."

"Unbelievable."

"If there's a moon tonight, I'm opening the show with that new number."

Another reason to be elsewhere, Wrecker thinks.

"Listen, *Dad*," he says. "The Beatles aren't going to sue you, just like the Eagles didn't sue you."

"We'll see about that, *Wrecker.*" His father gives a cocky nod. "You don't know the music business like I do."

"Are you gonna fish, or not?"

The song pirate runs both hands through his pressed, tinted hair. "I need to get some sun on these highlights," he says. "They weren't cheap."

"I wouldn't know." Wrecker can't imagine what the hardcore seafaring generations of Valdez Joneses would have thought of Number Seven.

"Next weekend I'm booked to play a yacht party up in Destin. I hear that place is in-*sane*," he says.

"You'll kill, Dad."

Wrecker stows the rods and cranks the motor. Heading back to Key West, he spots an old loggerhead trailing twenty feet of loose rope from a lobster trap. He stops the boat, whips off his sunglasses, grabs the fillet knife, and dives overboard.

Bewildered, Valdez Seven stands up to see what's going on. He watches his son snatch the free end of the trap rope just as the frightened turtle zooms to the bottom. Dragging Wrecker, it hunkers in a lush bed of seagrass. Hand over hand, he pulls himself close enough to grasp the crusty front rim of the reptile's shell. Swiftly he yanks the knife from his belt and cuts off the tangled rope, liberating the ancient traveler.

"You're bleeding!" Valdez Seven exclaims when his son climbs back into the boat. "Did you stab yourself?"

"Turtles have barnacles," Wrecker says, catching his breath. The scrapes sting his arms, but it's no big deal.

"That was amazing, son! Who taught you how to swim like that?"

"What're you doin', Dad?"

"Taking a video for my Facebook."

"Put your phone down," Wrecker snaps.

"Aw, come on."

"You better hope that thing floats."

"Okay, okay," says Valdez Seven. "I'll turn it off."

Suzanne fries the fish fillets in a coating of pancake mix and eggs. Wrecker fixes a salad with fresh greens, tomatoes, and black olives.

Halfway through the meal, Suzanne says, "I'm a little tired today," which means her arms and back are sore from covering a lot of territory in the wheelchair. She had staged another fundraising event for the Friends of Blue Waters, but it brought in less money than she'd hoped.

"People on this island need to dig deeper," she complains. "We're up against some mega-powerful companies."

She'd shown the audience some drone footage of a mammoth cruise ship turning around in the harbor, churning vast plumes of milky gray mud off the bottom. The disturbing scene was recorded before the pandemic hit, when monster ocean liners were still docking in Key West every morning.

"Some guy from Jersey dropped a twenty in the jar," she says, "but that's the biggest donation we got."

"Don't let up, sis."

She's feeding morsels of fried snapper to the Deacon, poised like royalty on her lap. Later, when she empties her BLOCKADE FOR BLUE WATERS! collection jar, she'll find two hundred more dollars than she counted the first time.

"Guess who went on a boat ride with me today," Wrecker says. "International recording artist Austin Breakwater."

"How'd *that* happen?"

"He just showed up at the dock."

"Really?" Suzanne says curiously. "So, did you two enjoy some quality time?"

"We didn't exactly bond, if that's what you mean. He's got a new rip-off song coming out."

"I'm afraid to ask."

"This time he's trying to get himself sued by the Beatles." As Wrecker describes his father's ambitions for "Here Comes the Moon," Suzanne starts laughing.

"Are you going to see him play tonight?" she asks.

"Negative. Is Mom dragging Roger to the show?"

"He says he's still avoiding crowds, but I think he just doesn't want to have to clap for your dad. Your mom's taking him to dinner at Louie's, out on the deck."

"A rare victory for sanity," Wrecker says.

"And Roger's self-respect," Suzanne adds. "You off to the graveyard?"

"I am."

"How're things with Ms. Chillingwood?"

"Peaceful," says Wrecker.

He hasn't told his stepsister that Sarah is gone, because Sarah will continue to be his excuse for leaving the house after dinner. Tonight his only stop is the White Street Pier, one of his favorite places on the whole island. It's a sentimental coincidence that Mr. Riley's most treasured picture of his sister was taken here.

Wrecker rides his bike to the square plaza at the end of the pier. Baby tarpon are gulping shrimp under the lights by the pilings. Lots of people are fishing. The locals are easy to spot; they're more patient than the tourists, and their lines don't turn into bird nests when they cast. Nobody is bothering the little tarpon because they're hard to fool and no good to eat.

Offshore is a passenger ship the size of a shopping mall, probably heading to Kingston or Cozumel. It could be the dreaded *Princess Pandora*, or one of the other jumbo liners that use Miami or Fort Lauderdale as a home port. Snapper boats and shrimp trawlers are natural features on the water at night, but a cruise ship this large looms sharp-edged and out of place. Wrecker is happy to observe that it's bypassing Key West, at least for now.

The soundtrack drifting from Old Town is a collision of songs being performed at various outdoor bars. Wrecker listens for his father's voice, though it's unlikely that an acoustic performance of "Here Comes the Moon" stands any chance of being heard over an Allman Brothers cover band.

Willi rolls up on her skateboard wearing her usual outfit. She says, "I guess we oughta talk."

"Yup."

"Again—super-sorry I didn't let you in the house last night. I still can't believe that cop flattened you right on the street."

"And I can't believe you wouldn't answer your door. This whole ghosting thing you do is such a head game. It's not cool, Willi. Actually it sucks."

"The pizza boxes are in a safe place. That's no lie."

"I'm talking about all of it," Wrecker says.

They stand in uneasy silence looking out at the Atlantic, smooth as indigo tile. The hulking outline of the cruise ship is dwindling to a smudge of orange light.

Finally Willi says, "It wasn't a hard ghost. Sometimes I just don't feel like communicating with anyone."

"Sometimes your friends need to hear from you. Sometimes it's important."

She sighs out another half-hearted apology. Then: "Tell me your big plan for the vax cards."

"Thing is," he says, "I need a partner I can trust."

"That's harsh, Wreck."

"You speak any Spanish?"

"Sí, mi amigo."

"I thought so." From his backpack he takes out a piece of paper. "Tell me what this says in English."

Willi's face clouds as she stands beside one of the pier lights reading the words that Wrecker had transcribed from the recording he made at the grave.

"Uh, well," she begins, "it starts off like, 'Sorrow was never meant to stay, but a pain so deep goes on for years.'"

"That's heavy. Could you do it in Spanish?"

"I guess. 'El dolor nunca tuvo la intención de quedarse, pero un dolor tan profundo dura años.'"

"Sing it for me, Willi."

"What? No!"

"It goes like this." Wrecker presses the Voice Memos app on his phone.

At the sound of her own singing, Willi goes stiff, arms clenched.

"You're the one playing head games," she says hoarsely. "I'm so outta here."

"Not yet," Wrecker says. "There's something else you need to see. I found it last night down the street from the cemetery."

Willi bites her lower lip as she watches him reach once more into his backpack.

When he holds up the silky black wig, she says, "I hate you right now."

"Don't cry. That's not fair."

"I've got allergies, jackass!"

"All you had to do was tell me the truth."

"How'd you know that stupid thing was mine?"

"The lilac smell," Wrecker says, half-embarrassed. "It's what you always wear."

"Oh God."

"You're Manuel Cabeza's great-great-granddaughter, aren't you?"

"No, I'm not," she sobs, stepping off her skateboard. "But I wish I was."

From secret family papers, Willi had learned of the events that took place in Key West on Christmas Eve in 1921:

That afternoon, a ship carpenter heard frantic knocking on his door. It was a friend coming to tell him that El Isleño had shot Bill Decker and was now holed up in the Solano building. Like everyone in town, the carpenter knew what had provoked the shooting. El Isleño's real name was Manuel Cabeza, a tavern owner also known as "Head." The night before, he'd been hauled from his shop, severely whipped, and covered with tar and feathers.

That vicious crime was carried out by the ship carpenter and half a dozen fellow Ku Klux Klansmen, including Bill Decker. The reason for their attack on Cabeza was simple: he'd been living openly with a brown-skinned woman named Angela, and spoke of her as his wife. The Klan had decided to teach him a lesson.

The fiery Cabeza had taken revenge, Decker was dead,

and the ship carpenter once again donned his white robe and pointed hood. He would join the mob that mauled El Isleño in the jailhouse, cheer in the morbid parade as the man was dragged through the streets, and even help tie the noose in the hanging rope.

Willi's voice is scraped with emotion by the time she finishes the story.

"The carpenter was my great-great-grandfather," she says. "On my mother's side . . . like it matters."

Wrecker, stunned, never saw that coming. It's more than sadness over the Islander's death that weighs so darkly on Willi; it's also shame and anger over the lethal role of her own blood kin.

"What was his name?" Wrecker asks.

"I will never speak it. *Ever.*"

"But he's the one you were talking about, right? The turmoil in your world."

"I can't let it go, Wreck, no matter how hard I try. And I *am* trying."

During the pandemic lockdown, she had accidentally discovered—hidden in a storage space under the stairs—a box of old correspondence between relatives discussing Willi's great-great-grandfather's part in the lynching.

"He never got arrested for it. Nobody did," she adds. "And he never quit the Klan. They found his white robe hanging in the closet after he died. Age eighty-one, by the way. Never had a change of heart."

After reading the letters, Willi had, like Wrecker, looked up everything she could find about Manuel Cabeza. And like Wrecker, she'd turned up no clues about what happened to Angela, the dead man's true love.

"I go stand at his grave because there's no one else left to do it," Willi says. "And yeah, because a person in my own family was one of the monsters that put him there."

In her voice Wrecker hears the unearned guilt, and the helplessness.

He says, "That ladder you loaned me at the cemetery doesn't belong to a friend. It's yours, right? Because that's how *you* get over the fence. And you weren't just randomly skateboarding along the street on the night those goons chased you off. You were there, on the inside, visiting the Islander."

"Duh."

"And you only go after dark because you don't want anyone to see you."

"But I put on that damn wig in case someone does," she says. "It's a small town, Wreck. Lots of people know me, and I've got no desire to broadcast my family connection to the freakin' KKK. It would crush my mother and father."

"Willi, you don't have a connection to the Klan, and neither do they. It happened a hundred years ago."

Now her eyes are dry, her tone flat. "So, what are you planning to do with my dirty little secret?"

"Pretend I never heard it."

Wrecker tosses her the wig. With a rueful smile, she places it crookedly on her head.

"That song you sing at the grave," he says, "what's it called?"

"You won't find it on Shazam, Sherlock. I wrote the words myself."

"This isn't a move or anything, but your voice sounds beautiful. Really."

"Oh, just shut up."

She doesn't pull away when he puts his arms around her. A seagull blinks from its perch on a light post. Farther down the pier, two girls are dancing to Taylor Swift while their boyfriends cast shiny barracuda lures on spinning rods.

Willi presses her cheek against Wrecker's shoulder. He breathes in lilac and hears her say, "Last night I ran past Sarah's grave. What happened?"

"They took her back to Ireland."

"So I guess I won't be seeing you at the cemetery anymore."

"Why not?"

"Well, because she's gone."

"Yeah, but El Isleño is still there," Wrecker says,

"and I've got a perfectly good key to the gate. You and I can go together."

"Now *that's* a move, Wreck."

"Possibly."

"But what about the Black Coats? I hate those goons."

"We'll start with them," Wrecker says. "Then we'll take care of their boss."

EIGHTEEN

For days Wrecker and Willi didn't reenter the graveyard. Instead, they hid behind trees or shrubs along the
boundary streets, observing the Black Coats from a distance.

Usually the men showed up around sunset and departed early in the morning, before the cemetery opened
to the public. Passover Lane was the henchmen's favored
place to park. The shorter one would be driving, sipping
from a coffee mug. After exiting the black sedan, they'd
open the trunk to collect their guns and long coats. Even
at night they must have been sweating like swamp hogs.
It was, after all, Key West in the summer.

Surveillance also confirmed that the Black Coats
liked to skip out early when the weather turned bad.
So the mission would depend on a heavy rain.

"Special tools, too," Willi said during one of their
nighttime strategy meetings on the pier. "I say we try to
crack the lock."

"We don't need to break inside," Wrecker reminded

her for about the tenth time, "just do enough damage to make 'em *think* we did."

"Guess what? We get that vault open, this girl is for sure goin' in."

"Where do we find a lockpick?"

"Burglar Depot?" said Willi.

"I'm serious."

"Yes, and borderline cute." She tweaked Wrecker's chin.

From then on he started checking the weather app regularly and, for the first time in his life, hoping for a long hard downpour.

One afternoon, while mopping up a milk spill at Fausto's, he gets a call from Silver Mustache's new number. He's too busy to answer the phone, and there's no voice message or follow-up text. Later, after his shift ends, he walks out of the store and spots the smuggler sitting on the fender of the gray Mercedes, which is double-parked. Silver Mustache is wearing reflector sunglasses and a glossy black jogging suit. The cast is gone from his right leg.

"Time for a dry run," he says to Wrecker.

"Right now?"

"Right freaking now."

"Can't I go home and change?"

"It's not Holy Communion, kid. It's a boat ride."

The truth is that part of Wrecker enjoys driving the

sleek Cigarette. Who wouldn't? Roaring at highway speeds across an open sea could take anybody's mind off their problems—if the problem wasn't sitting next to them in the cockpit.

While the engines are warming, Silver Mustache activates the GPS screens to illustrate the route—basically a straight shot down West Channel to Boca Grande Key. The far side of the island has a white strip of beach that's popular with day-trippers but usually deserted at night.

"There's a decent lee there," the smuggler says. "That's where my associate from down south will be waiting."

This alarming detail is delivered as they're pushing away from the dock.

"Wait—what's going on?" Wrecker demands.

"First you need to stop at Ballast Key and drop me off." Silver Mustache taps on a blue waypoint displayed on the screen. "Right here."

"But you said this was a dry run!"

" 'Dry' in the sense that I don't plan on getting wet."

"Are you serious?" Wrecker says. "I'll be the one that gets locked up if the Coast Guard shows up at Boca Grande."

Silver Mustache grins so broadly that, in the orange glow of the control panel, his face looks like a Hallow-een pumpkin. "They can't throw you in prison, bro.

You're a minor! Why do you think I picked you to be my wheelman?"

Steering out of the harbor, Wrecker anxiously thrashes through his options. There aren't many. He'd hoped it would be weeks before the real smuggling run was scheduled, and that by then he and Willi would have gamed their way out of this fix.

"My associate's name is Rodrigo," Silver Mustache is saying, "and he speaks perfect English. He'll be with a couple other dudes in a fifty-two-foot Hatteras called the *Zoolander*. Brand-new ride, he said. You give him that big Yeti cooler, which you will *not* open, and then they'll transfer the pizza boxes to my boat."

"Pizza boxes? Here we go."

"Deep-dish, bro." The smuggler cackles.

"Will the guys on the other boat have guns?" Wrecker asks.

"Now what would be the point of me answering that question?"

"I don't want to get shot would be the point."

"Rodrigo would never hurt a kid," Silver Mustache says, "even a pain in the butt like you. After the pickup, drive straight back to Ballast. It's already plotted on the GPS."

"I won't need the GPS."

"Well, excuse me, Señor Columbus."

Soon the boat is going so fast that the flying fish

barely have time to clear out of the way, skimming on silvery fin-wings across the wave tops. The chop is brisk enough for Wrecker to keep a grim grip on the throttle. Silver Mustache reaches for the handheld spotlight as they begin slowing into a wide turn toward Ballast Key. Wrecker weaves smoothly through the winding, slender channel. Slowly he noses the bow up to the long wooden dock, where Silver Mustache steps off gingerly, favoring his healing leg.

"Careful on the way out of here," he growls at Wrecker. "Don't screw this up."

From there it's a short hop to the larger, uninhabited island of Boca Grande. The *Zoolander* is waiting exactly where Silver Mustache said it would be, the tall twin outriggers swaying like mutant insect antennae. A person high on the flybridge signals with a red laser pen as the Cigarette draws closer.

Wrecker can't understand why he feels so suddenly, weirdly calm; maybe he inherited a stay-cool gene from his great-great-grandfather, the brazen rum smuggler. He kills the running lights and steps on the foot switch that lowers the anchor. Before long he hears the *putt-putt* of a small motor—a rubber dinghy is approaching with three figures aboard. They're wearing ball caps and, to conceal their faces, sun masks. The thinnest one introduces himself as Rodrigo.

"I'm Charles," says Wrecker.

"You got the cooler?"

"Right here."

The men take it back to the Hatteras. Wrecker waits nervously.

What if they keep the boxes and drive off with the money? he thinks. Silver Mustache gave him no instructions for that particular scenario.

Five minutes later, though, the dinghy returns. After tying up snug to the Cigarette's transom, the men climb aboard with the first load. They seem more amused than surprised that Wrecker has come alone.

"How old are you?" asks one of Rodrigo's companions.

"High school," Wrecker says.

The guy snorts and makes a snide-sounding remark in Spanish. Wrecker is tempted to make a joke about the lame butterfly pattern on the guy's gaiter, but he holds back.

Several trips in the dinghy are needed for Rodrigo's crew to finish ferrying the counterfeit vax cards from the *Zoolander* to the speedboat. Wrecker doesn't offer to help with the loading, and the men don't ask him to. It doesn't look like they're carrying guns, but who knows what's on the Hatteras. The man with the laser pointer in the tuna tower is also equipped with binoculars. He is obviously the lookout.

Wrecker knows it's possible that only a fear of Silver Mustache is stopping Rodrigo and his crew from jacking the cash, keeping the blank cards, stealing the valuable speedboat, and heaving him overboard. He opens a lukewarm can of Coke, thinking it's not a long way to shore, if worse comes to worst. He could swim most of the distance underwater, which would make him a hard target to shoot.

But after the last of the pizza boxes are loaded, the only thing Rodrigo says is: "See you next time, junior." Then he unties the dinghy and shoves off.

Wrecker doesn't wait around to watch which direction the Hatteras goes. He raises the Cigarette's anchor and starts the engines, all the while scanning for other vessels. His heartbeat ticks up slightly on the return ride to Ballast Key, where Silver Mustache is pacing the dock like a panther with a limp.

The smuggler nearly does a face-plant when he jumps aboard. Once steadied, he hurries down into the cabin, where the boxes are stacked, and shuts the door behind him. Wrecker patiently motors to deeper water before gunning the engines. The rush of salty air stings his eyes, so he gropes in the console for a pair of racing goggles that he saw there. The strap breaks while he's putting them on, confirming his mother's observation that his head is larger than average.

The boat is riding lower now, the hull catching more drag from the weight of the load. Silver Mustache comes out and shouts at Wrecker to slow down while he fires up the nub of a cigar. He also wants to have a conversation, which is impossible while the powerful outboards are at full howl.

Wrecker throttles back to a crawl. Once Silver Mustache can hear himself speak, he says, "Good job with Rodrigo, kid. You're a natural."

"Why'd you make me go alone?"

"So if there was a bust, I could testify I wasn't there and never saw the dude. But he was super-chill with you, right?"

"Oh yeah. We're besties now," Wrecker says.

"How'd that new Hatteras look?"

"Sweet," Wrecker says. "I like the name, too."

"*Zoolander* is Rodrigo's all-time favorite movie."

"I figured."

"Speaking of boat names," Silver Mustache says, "fun fact: there are twenty-seven commercial fishing vessels in this country called the *Last Laugh*, and not one of 'em is a Gulf shrimp boat. My people searched all up and down the Texas coast. Louisiana, too."

Wrecker is secretly pleased that Silver Mustache went to so much trouble. He'd made up the nonexistent boat name as another false lead to distract the smugglers, and it seems to have bought him some time.

He says, "Maybe the shrimper who found your stuff freaked out and painted over the letters on his boat. Or maybe he sold it and the new owner renamed it."

Silver Mustache reports that his "people" located

a shrimping vessel registered as the *Last Call*, which is pretty close to *Last Laugh*. "It's in Port Arthur," he adds, "but the captain says he hasn't fished Key West in years."

"Then I guess I got more bad intel."

"Would that be coming from your old pal 'Dwight'?"

"Nope. Dwight's in Saskatchewan, visiting his sick grandmother." Wrecker turns his face to hide a smile, and also to avoid the cloud of cigar smoke. "I need to get home soon," he tells Silver Mustache.

"Don't you want to know how much this load is worth?"

"Now what would be the point of me asking that question?"

Silver Mustache isn't a huge fan of sarcasm. He says, "You're lucky I'm in a good mood."

"Can we go now?"

"Pedal to the metal, smartass." The smuggler tosses what's left of his cigar into the water, where it dies with a hiss. "Welcome to the business," he says.

The words hit Wrecker later, while he's riding his bike home through the muggy darkness.

It's true, he thinks. *I drove the boat, so I'm one of them.*

Which explains why the new wad of cash in his pocket feels like a plug of hot iron.

Another night of dream-cursed sleep:

A mob of white robes laughing and twirling on a

long, empty beach. A man's body hanging from a cell-phone tower.

In the center of the gathering, a cross burns, the sparks riding a breeze to the sea. The light cast by the fire reveals a frightened dark-skinned man wearing a cowboy hat and carrying a guitar. He begins to sing:

Here comes the moon, here comes the moon
I say it's okay
Little sweetheart, shining so bright, feels like days
*   since you've been here*

The lynch mob stops dancing and begins to jeer.

"You suck, boy!"

"Rip-off!"

"Thief!"

The singer drops his guitar and tries to escape, but his snakeskin boots get stuck in the mud.

"Here comes the moon! Here comes the moon!" the Klansmen chant gravely as they advance.

"What are you people doing?" the singer cries. "The key is G, not A major . . . !"

Wrecker wakes up and tries to shake off the nightmare. Lying on the floor is the old sneaker where he stashed the latest payoff from Silver Mustache. It looks like there's a tennis ball crammed inside the toe.

Wrecker doesn't want to be anywhere near this particular money. Fortunately, he knows of a place to hide the cash where it could never be traced to him, in the unlikely event that someone finds it.

Twenty fifty-dollar bills. Unbelievable.

He stays in his room pretending to be asleep until Suzanne leaves the house. Then he takes the money to the garden shed and tediously rolls each fifty into its own little tube. One by one he slides them into the hollow shaft of a long-handled gaff made for landing strong offshore species such as mahi and tuna. Once the cash is secured, Wrecker reattaches the steel head of the gaff—basically an oversized fishhook—by screwing it tightly onto the aluminum handle.

Now who's ghosting who? Willi texts, with a scowling-face emoji.

Evidently she's been trying to reach Wrecker for a while, but he'd turned off the volume on his phone during the night. If he hadn't, Willi might have spared him from that depressing dream.

Call u in 1 hr, he types, knowing it will probably take longer.

Only in the Keys would nobody glance twice at a kid carrying a deep-sea gaff on his bicycle. Once he reaches the dock, he hops on the skiff and positions the hook end of the device a safe distance from his bare legs.

There's no time to top off the gas tank, so he holds to a medium speed, conserving fuel. The handheld GPS guides him straight to the destination—the unmarked remains of a small barge that went down in a tropical storm long before he was born. A coral-encrusted ruin, unrecognizable as anything created by humans, the barge now rests in seventeen feet of water near Cottrell Key. Small gray snappers swarm over the flat deck, while thick solitary groupers lurk in rusted-out holes in the sides.

Wrecker drops anchor and strips to his underwear, stacking his clothes on top of the phone to shield it from the heat of the sun. He puts on his dive mask, picks up the gaff, and slips over the side of the skiff.

This is wrecking in reverse, he thinks on the way down, *sinking something valuable instead of raising it.*

Below, the cloud of snappers dissolves in a panic. Wrecker swims toward a narrow gap at one rotted corner of the barge; the gaff should fit inside easily.

It does—but the moray eel living in the dark hidey-hole isn't pleased.

The eel that Wrecker didn't know was there until it buried its fang-like teeth in his left hand, which he is now unable to extract from the hull.

Blood darkens the water, and jolts of pain sizzle up his arm. The infuriated moray has knotted itself like a ball python around Wrecker's wrist, and he's running out of breath.

Let me go! he rages silently, pulling and yanking and jerking. . . .

Then, unexpectedly, he wrenches free of the barge. He kicks upward with a burn in his lungs, the writhing eel still attached to the meat of his hand. Only when he bursts to the surface does the speckled fighter unfasten its jaws and slither-dive back to its lair.

Gasping and light-headed, Wrecker boosts himself into the boat. He wraps his dry T-shirt tightly around his bleeding hand and struggles into his pants. For a while he sits motionless and hunched over. He probably needs stitches, but it's not life or death. The sunlight feels good on his back. He can't figure out why the Gulf looks so hazy until he realizes he's still wearing the dive mask, which has fogged in the humid air. He sheepishly tugs it off and one-handedly hauls up the anchor.

The foul-tempered eel wouldn't have been an issue if Wrecker had first cleared the hidey-hole of toothy occupants by probing it with the gaff, like any diver with half a brain would have done.

I deserved to get chomped, he thinks.

The phone dings from Willi World.

Where u at? she texts.

Boat

Must be nice

wassup? Wrecker says.

check the weather?

I'm sitting in it. Sunny and nice

No, dummy, Willi shoots back. The 4cast!

Wrecker taps on his radar app. A bright swath of

rain is rolling south from the Everglades toward the Keys.

Stormy night, he texts.

Willi responds with an umbrella emoji.

Ichabod's crib, Wrecker types. @ 10 pm

Yo, guess who got a lockpick?

Wrecker isn't even slightly surprised.

I'll bring a hammer, he texts back, just in case

NINETEEN

The sky unloads.

Wrecker zips the rainsuit up to his neck and takes shelter under a restaurant awning across from the Iguana Tree. Gnarly Ichabod is nowhere in sight.

Willi rolls up in a white car and tells Wrecker to get in. She's wearing a plastic garbage bag as a poncho.

"What happened to your hand, Wreck?"

"Eel bite."

Willi laughs. "Stop trying so hard. I know you're a tough guy."

"It's the truth! There was a moray on a wreck."

"Or . . . you burned your fingers on a waffle iron. Nothing to be ashamed of. They say most accidents happen at home."

"Just drive," Wrecker says.

The wind moans and thunder shakes the island like a bombing raid—a perfect night to hang out at a grave-yard, if you happen to be a bat or a werewolf.

True to form, the fair-weather Black Coats are already gone. They hadn't even paused to shut the gate behind them. By the time Wrecker and Willi reach the mini-mausoleum, the rain is slashing hard. He aims the flashlight over her shoulder as she struggles to spring the lock on the door.

"Forgive me, Bendito," she says, "or whoever you are."

She'd purchased the picking device at a hardware store. It resembles a pocketknife, but instead of folding blades there's a row of thin wire prongs that fit various types of lock cylinders. Wrecker brought a crowbar, not a hammer, though he has no intention of prying open the coffin of a dead gangster, whatever his real name might be. The plan is to mess up the vault enough to make the Black Coats freak out and call Silver Mustache, who'll freak out even worse. Wrecker wants to rattle the boss smuggler, but he does *not* want Willi and him to end up like the careless tomb invaders in the red Hummer.

Between crashes of thunder, he prods Willi to hurry.

"Lightning never strikes in a graveyard," she says. "Don't you know that?"

"That's the dumbest thing I ever heard."

"Look it up, Wreck."

At that very moment, at the opposite end of the cemetery, a blue-white bolt zaps the copper soldier on the U.S.S. *Maine* monument. Wrecker flinches and covers his ears. Willi bobbles the lockpick and cusses.

After the thunderclap fades, Wrecker steps in front of her and says, "My turn."

With a single overhead swing of the crowbar, he whacks the brass handle off the door of the crypt. The lock doesn't last long after that.

"Show-off," Willi says, smoothing the wrinkles in her garbage-bag poncho.

The thick bandage on Wrecker's injured hand is soaked. He wedges the pry end of the crowbar into the gap where the lock cylinder had been.

"Ready?" he says.

"Oh, just do it."

He does. The door to the tomb surrenders.

Willi whistles. "Whoa," she says. "That's a proper coffin."

"Red cedar, I think."

"It's annoying you would even know that. What next, Wreck?"

"We roll."

"Oh no. Not just yet."

"Don't even think about it," Wrecker says.

In his mind he's adding up the crimes they've already committed—trespassing, vandalism, breaking and entering, destruction of private property. Disturbing a dead body would be a much creepier charge in court.

"I've got a theory," Willi says. "Hand me the crowbar."

"Not happening."

"Fine, I'll do it myself."

The gusts are blowing rain into the funeral vault.

"It's probably sealed," Wrecker says.

"But is it?"

"First tell me your theory." Wrecker's trying to stall. He doesn't want a close-up peek at a human corpse.

Willi snaps her fingers and says, "Give me the flashlight."

There's nothing he can do to stop her. The casket isn't sealed. When she lifts the lid, her eyes widen.

"Well, hello," she says. "So this is the afterlife? Not bad."

There's no dead body. The coffin of Bendito Vachs is packed with cash.

Wrapped bricks of twenties, fifties, and hundreds.

Everyone's favorite, thinks Wrecker. Silver Mustache, being clever.

"Obviously, Vachs isn't pronounced 'vox.' It's 'vax,'" Willi says, "as in 'vaccine' cards. At least your smuggler friend's got a sense of humor."

"Stop calling him my friend."

Wrecker can't wait to get out of the graveyard. Willi can't stop staring at the money.

"How much do you think is here?" she asks.

"Enough to get us killed."

"Let's count it."

"Shut the lid," Wrecker says impatiently.

"We should get a picture first. Where's your phone?"

"No selfies, Willi. Just take a shot of the money."

She snaps a couple of photos and closes the coffin. Wrecker motions for her to step back.

"Why? What're you gonna do?" she asks.

"This." He brings the crowbar down so hard that it splinters the polished wood.

"*Now* I'm impressed," Willi whispers.

"That wasn't for you," Wrecker says. "That was for the bad guys."

The inside of Miss Bascomb's car smells like bacon and stale peppermint. It's an old white Honda that attracts zero attention, which is good because Willi's not supposed to be driving without an adult beside her. She assures Wrecker that Miss Bascomb sleeps like a grizzly and never notices when Willi borrows the car. He's not sure why Willi has a nanny, but she says that keeping Miss Bascomb at the house makes her mother and father feel like responsible parents, since they travel so much.

Wrecker himself doesn't have a learner's permit. He doesn't know how to drive a car, and has no interest in getting his license; a bike and a boat are all he needs in Key West. His mother told him to go to the DMV and take the test so he could drive Suzanne around on the days she didn't feel great, but Suzanne got irritated when he offered to do that. She's glad to be independent.

Willi doesn't drive too fast, and she's careful to

mind the road signs. It would suck to get pulled over by the police when you're not street-legal.

"You think anyone saw us back there?" she asks, steering around a puddle.

"Not in the middle of that monsoon."

The thunderstorm has rolled offshore, and the rain has slacked to a drizzle.

"Now we know what those grave robbers in the Hummer were after," Willi says.

"And the real reason those two goons are guarding the tomb."

"They're in deep doo-doo now, those stupid Black Coats."

I would not *want to be them,* Wrecker thinks, *when Silver Mustache finds out.*

"Here," Willi says, braking at a stop sign, "grab the wheel for a second."

"What? No!"

"I'm gettin' outta this wet garbage bag." She starts tearing it off in pieces.

Wrecker clamps his bandaged and still-throbbing hand on the steering wheel. They're on Amelia Street, which is narrow but luckily has little traffic. When a convertible full of drenched tourists pulls up behind the Honda, Wrecker says to Willi, "Just to be clear, I don't know how to drive."

"You can steer, bro. *Anybody* can steer. Didn't you see that monkey steal the golf cart on TikTok?"

"Then next time bring a damn monkey."

The driver of the convertible beeps the horn. Willi sticks her arm out the window and waves the tourists past. Once freed from her homemade poncho, she retakes control of the Honda and turns right on Simonton Street.

"There's something I've gotta tell you, Wreck. But you've gotta promise not to get pissed."

Wrecker's nerves are almost shot. "What now?"

"Those pizza boxes I took? They're in the trunk of the car."

"*This* car?"

"Correct."

"Right now?"

"Get a grip, Wreck. I peeled off the blue wrapping, so they don't look like packages of dope."

"Seriously? Your super-safe, super-secret hiding place for five thousand fake vaccination cards is your nanny's Honda?"

"She'll never find 'em," Willi insists. "Her key fob hasn't worked for years, and I've got the only spare that opens the trunk."

"Uh-huh."

"See, you're mad. *God!*"

"Maybe ease off the accelerator," Wrecker says stiffly, "since we're behind a police car."

"Yes, I'm aware."

"Are your mom and dad home?"

"Portugal," Willi says. "Tomorrow they're off to some coast of Spain."

"Good, then here's what happens now. We go straight to your house and figure out a halfway intelligent place to hide the boxes. You sure Miss Bascomb's asleep?"

"Comatose. A marching band couldn't wake her up."

"You better be right."

"Honestly, Wreck, I'm not loving your attitude."

But, of course, as the gate to the Brown estate swings open, a figure that can only be Miss Bascomb looms in the driveway. She squints at the car's headlights like a confused old opossum.

Wrecker sighs. "Please go get her a robe."

"Yeah," says Willi, "that's not a good look."

Two-thirty in the morning. Wrecker's laptop is open on the bed. He's wide awake, searching online for information about Swanson Paul, a ship's carpenter who took part in the hanging of Manuel Cabeza.

Paul was Willi's great-great-grandfather. Tearfully she'd shown Wrecker one of the family letters that confirmed Paul's lifetime membership in the Ku Klux Klan.

This was after the nanny had been calmed and led

back to bed. Wearing sketchy pajamas, odd Miss Bascomb had been roaming the property in pursuit of a rooster that, for reasons unknown, started crowing in the dark of night.

Miss Bascomb had announced her intention to wring its neck. Wrecker told Willi to bet on the rooster.

The internet turns up only one mention of a Swanson Paul in Key West. It's a newspaper article from June 1922 about a passenger steamship damaged by a galley fire while moored at the waterfront. Paul was one of those hired to do the repairs. He was quoted as saying the job could take weeks.

Wrecker is scrolling through the story when a text dings on his phone:

Wake up and meet me out front

The accompanying photo shows a coffin impaled by a crowbar.

Wrecker is trying not to shake when he gets in the gray Mercedes. "What happened? Did they take the body?" he asks. "Where were your security guys?"

"Drinking beer and chowing down on conch fritters. It was a meal they won't soon forget." Silver Mustache starts driving, eyes straight ahead. His voice is granite. "Were you at the graveyard tonight, Valdez?"

"You mean with my snorkel and fins?"

"Know what happens to smartasses in my business? *Our* business."

"You didn't see how bad it was raining?"

Silver Mustache says, "I asked a clear question. Answer it."

"That's crazy!" Wrecker is struggling to sound insulted. "Who goes to a cemetery in the middle of a lightning storm?"

"Grave robbers do, obviously. Strange part is they didn't take anything."

"Did they mess with the body?"

"Nope. Busted a hole in the casket and ran."

"Maybe they got scared off, like the Hummer guys," Wrecker says.

"So you definitely weren't there. That's your official answer."

"Why would I go? I don't even have my cemetery job anymore—the person's grave I was getting paid to watch, she's gone. The family moved her back to Ireland."

The smuggler parks the coupe along the walkway at Smathers Beach. Nobody else is around. The waves are still rough, the sky still cloudy and starless.

"What'd you do to your hand, kid?"

"I got bit by an eel."

"Let me see."

"For real?" Wrecker asks.

Silver Mustache nods. "If I see one teeny, tiny wooden splinter in your skin, I'll know you're lying about tonight. Bendito's coffin is made of cedar."

Wrecker unpeels the Ace bandage and strips off

the underlying gauze. The smuggler turns on the car's dome light to study the wounds—bloodied V-shaped imprints of the moray's upper and lower jaws.

"Count the holes if you want," Wrecker says.

"You should be more careful where you stick your fingers, kid." Silver Mustache turns off the light and rolls down his window. "Those eels, they're basically pit bulls with fins. Go see a doctor before it gets infected."

"Naw, I'm good."

"I hope so. You'll need both hands to drive my boat," the smuggler says.

"Don't worry."

"Aren't you curious to know why people keep breaking into Bendito's tomb?"

"You told me he had enemies," Wrecker says.

"There is no Bendito Vachs, dead or alive. The coffin's full of money."

"Yeah, right." Wrecker, acting as if he doesn't already know.

"One million four hundred thousand seven hundred and sixty dollars."

"No. Way." This time Wrecker isn't pretending to be surprised. He had no idea there was so much in the casket.

"Me and my associates don't do Venmo, dude. It's purely a cash business at both ends," Silver Mustache says. "But the people who were at the cemetery tonight, they didn't steal even a twenty. I know this because I watched my guys count all of it—twice—after they washed the conch juice off their mitts, of course."

Wrecker rolls down his window, too. He inhales the tangy salt air, a relief from the reek of the smuggler's cologne.

"Why do you think they didn't take the money?" he asks.

"I don't know. It's extremely freaking weird, and I'm not a fan of weird."

"Especially in a graveyard," Wrecker says.

"Yesterday they busted some kids from your high school selling fake vax cards—not my brand, by the way. Forty bucks a pop those clowns were charging." Silver Mustache chuckles coldly. "Point is, the market for our product is growing so fast, I don't need to risk my butt doing these offshore pickups. No disrespect to Rodrigo, but my profits will go way up if I simplify the supply chain. One more ocean run, I'm done. After that, me and my group will be making our own CDC cards—I just bought a printing press and a trucking company up in North Miami."

"Does that mean you won't need me anymore?" Wrecker asks.

"Are you bummed out, Valdez?"

Crushed, Wrecker thinks sardonically.

"This virus, it's the gift that keeps on giving," the smuggler goes on. "Whenever there's a new variant, my phone blows up. Seems like everybody wants a phony card—ballplayers, movie stars, airline pilots, Silicon Valley millionaires. Dude, some college frat house in Tallahassee just ordered two hundred blanks for Pledge Week!"

"So when's our last job?" Wrecker asks.

"Soon enough." Silver Mustache plucks a cigar from his jacket.

If he lights that thing, I'll puke, Wrecker thinks, *all over his leather seats.*

"Question, Valdez."

"Okay."

"Why do you think I'm trusting you with the truth about Bendito?"

"Tell me."

"You're a bright young man," Silver Mustache says. "You'll figure it out."

Wrecker already has. Bendito's grave will be empty soon, and the truth about the million-plus dollars won't matter. No one would believe such a story.

Unless there was something more.

Two hours earlier, a plain white Honda had wheeled into the parking lot of the Key West Police Department on North Roosevelt. What appeared to be a young man got out of the passenger side of the car. He was wearing a rainsuit, a baseball cap, and a fishing gaiter for a COVID mask.

The night-shift desk officer buzzed him in, and why not? The guy was delivering a tall stack of pizza boxes.

"These are for Officer Nugent," he said.

The desk officer was surprised, because Nedrick Nugent was possibly the cheapest human on the planet. He never paid for anything.

"How many did he order?"

"Five," said the delivery guy.

"I'll go get him. He's in the back, interviewing an inmate."

"We're good. He already paid with the app." The guy placed the pizza boxes on the counter and started for the door.

"Hold on." The desk officer took out his wallet.

The young deliveryman said, "Don't worry, the tip's included." Then he walked out and got back in the Honda, which sped away. Later, when the desk officer replayed the security video, he would discover that the car's license plate had been crisscrossed with black tape, hiding the numbers and letters.

But before that, Officer Van Zorn stopped by the front desk. He eyed the boxes and said, "What's Peter Pan's Pan Pizza? Never heard of it."

"Must be a new joint on the island," the desk officer said. "These are from Nugent, believe it or not."

"Did hell freeze over? That guy wouldn't buy his own mother a cup of coffee."

Van Zorn texted Nugent and told him to come out front. When he showed up, folding somebody's rap sheet into a paper airplane, Van Zorn asked, "Did you order all these pizzas?"

"Why? For who?"

"I don't know. The night shift?"

"Uh, no way. Definitely wasn't me," Nugent answered with a dry chuckle. He grabbed the top box off the stack. "But God bless the sucker who did."

With a hungry grin he flipped open the lid.

"What the hell?" The expression on his face was half disappointment, half confusion.

Van Zorn smiled. "I was wondering why they didn't smell like pepperoni."

The desk officer reached for the phone. "Don't go anywhere," he told Nugent. "I'm calling the lieutenant."

TWENTY

"How's Sarah?" Suzanne asks.

"Same."

Wrecker hasn't set foot in the cemetery since the crowbar incident. Most nights after dinner he leaves the house carrying his grave-cleaning kit, but it's an act. He's actually going to the White Street Pier to hang with Willi. If Suzanne found out, she'd drill him with endless questions about his new best friend, girlfriend, whatever.

"Princess High Maintenance had her eyes done," she says. "So maybe say something nice about the way she looks."

"What does that mean, getting your 'eyes done'?"

"A surgeon snips out the wrinkles and tightens the skin."

Wrecker grimaces. "Who's Mom trying to look like this time?"

"Nicole Kidman," Suzanne says, "which is aiming high."

"Slightly."

"But the eyes are all she wanted."

"And that makes it *not* insane?"

"Don't be mean when you see her, Valdez."

They're on their way to Roger and Carole's place. It turns out that Roger is what doctors call a long-hauler, meaning he no longer carries the virus but some of its exhausting symptoms still haven't gone away. He tries to play golf but seldom makes it more than six or seven holes. His joints ache so much that it hurts to walk, and on some days brutal headaches keep him in bed. Wrecker feels bad for him.

Yet there he is, happily waving from the porch as Wrecker and Suzanne pull up in her van. The man doesn't look well, but he's wearing a big smile and a new haircut. Wrecker and Suzanne mask up before unloading the wheelchair.

"Is it too early for a drink?" Roger asks, holding the front door open.

Wrecker says a Coke is fine. Suzanne says she'd love a beer. Roger's already holding a small glass of whiskey. They settle in the living room to await Carole Dungler's grand entrance.

Suzanne asks Roger if he heard about the scandal at the police department.

"Sure, it's been all over the front page of the *Citizen*," he says. "Fake vaccine cards in shoeboxes!"

"No, Dad, pizza boxes. First they thought one of their cops was involved. That hammerhead they just hired from Arizona—Nedrick Nugent? But now the chief's saying it was locals pulling a prank, not a smuggling operation. I know Nugent, and trust me, he's not smart enough to smuggle fungus under his toenails! That's the same jerk who tried to shut down one of our Blue Waters rallies at the cruise-ship dock. . . ."

Wrecker listens to his stepsister go off, and he doesn't say a word about the curious delivery to the police station. The newspaper reported that the pizza boxes were dropped off by a tall, broad-shouldered male wearing a gaiter-style sun mask. According to the desk officer on duty, the deliveryman appeared to be in his late teens or early twenties, a wrong guess that once again made Wrecker grateful he was big for his age. The story said the man came to the police station in a white Honda sporting a Conch Republic bumper sticker, which had since—Wrecker happened to know—been removed, crumpled up, and dropped in a garbage can outside Willi's house.

The illegal vaccine cards—a total of five thousand—were turned over to an FBI squad that's investigating counterfeit operations during the pandemic. No charges would be filed against Officer Nugent, which was okay with Wrecker. All he'd wanted to do was mess with the guy, a minor sting of payback.

". . . and this Nugent kept waving his arms and yelling that we needed a permit to assemble on the public waterfront, and I said, 'Yo, Constable, assemble *this*—'"

Suzanne halts midsentence as Wrecker's mother appears on the stairs.

Roger, beaming, sets down his drink. "Why, there she is!"

Wrecker can only gape. He hasn't seen many Nicole Kidman movies, but he's pretty sure that both her eyes are located in the same zip code. The doctor who worked on his mother stretched her face like he was shrink-wrapping a Christmas ham.

"You look amazing, Mom," Wrecker says anyway.

"So elegant," Suzanne chips in.

"Isn't she?" Roger motions for Carole to join him on the sofa. "Sit down, honey bear."

She's wearing more makeup than a street mime, probably to hide the new surgery scars. Wrecker wonders how long before the swelling goes down and she doesn't look so—what's the word?—ripe.

Part of him is bummed, and part of him is angry at Roger for not talking her out of the serial remodel— neck, nose, chin, and now this. Then again, she probably would have steamrolled the poor guy if he'd tried to stop her.

The fact is that Wrecker thought she was pretty the way she looked before. Roger did, too.

Her lips could be next, Wrecker thinks gloomily. *It's Kardashian World.*

"What I heard," his mom is saying from her sofa

throne, "is that students at the high school are selling those faux vaccine cards for a hundred dollars each! Obviously they're getting them from somewhere—maybe not that cop, but it's got to be somebody connected to the island's criminal element."

"Which criminal element?" Suzanne teases. "There are dozens to choose from."

Wrecker says not many kids are walking around with a hundred bucks to spare. He chooses not to pass along what Silver Mustache had told him—the price for blank vax cards in the local high-school market is only forty dollars.

"You don't get it. The students are buying them for their parents!" his mother continues excitedly. "Bridget Albertson's father told me."

"Did he get one for himself?" Suzanne asks. "That fool."

"He always wears his mask like a chin strap," Wrecker remarks. "Plus, Bridget said he never got the shots."

"His body, his choice," says Carole, stiffening.

Roger, bless his heart, interrupts with an update on the grass-weevil crisis at the golf course. The group moves to the dining room, where the subject pivots to lunch—fried grouper fingers and shrimp, a menu upon which the whole family can hungrily agree. Roger doesn't have much of an appetite but he hangs in there, battling another long-hauler headache, until dessert arrives—mango sorbet with a blueberry on top. Roger nudges his bowl toward Wrecker, quietly excuses himself from the table, and walks slowly up the stairs.

Wrecker's mother says, "Don't worry. He'll be fine after a nap."

"He's not fine." Suzanne puts down her spoon with a deliberate *clunk*. "What if he catches it again, Carole? What if there are no ICU beds next time? You guys really should get out of Key West for a while. Rent a place in the mountains, away from the crowds and the germs."

"I do love North Carolina this time of year," Carole Dungler says wistfully.

"High-altitude yoga for you. World-class golf for Dad."

"That's not a bad idea, Suzanne. The summers here are so sticky and stifling. I'll go on Vrbo tonight."

Wrecker flashes his stepsister a fingers-crossed sign. The latest variant of the virus recently landed in Key West. In Roger's weak condition, he might not survive another wave; the farther he can get from Duval Street, the better.

After lunch, Suzanne and Wrecker head off in different directions. She has a meeting with an environmental lawyer that she's hoping will turn into a date. Wrecker is going fishing near Man Key; the sea is flat, the tides are right.

His phone rings while he's gassing up the skiff. He peeks at the caller ID and frowns at the number.

It's the criminal element calling.

Wrecker turns off the phone, thinking:

Why spoil a perfectly nice afternoon?

Did the ship carpenter go fishing on his days off? Did he drift the same patch reefs as Wrecker does?

Swanson Paul was more than just another face in the mob that hanged Manuel Cabeza. He was all in; he helped make the noose. Plainly there wasn't a shred of remorse—he kept his cherished Klansman robe until the day he croaked, a doddering old bigot.

Willi still refuses to talk about her great-great-grandfather, which is understandable. Wrecker can't stop thinking about the man, trying to understand how a person so warped by hate lives a long, ordinary life.

That Christmas morning in 1921, after the Islander was killed—did Swanson Paul hand out brightly wrapped presents to his children by the family tree? Maybe he even dressed up like Santa Claus, a jolly figure slightly hung over from the murderous festivities near the trolley station. Pass the eggnog and sugar cookies!

Something yanks hard on Wrecker's line and he sets the hook. After a sturdy fight he leads a grouper to the boat. A ripe orange would fit in its bucket mouth, but the fish measures one inch shorter than the legal limit. Wrecker puts it back in the water.

He wishes there was something he could say to make Willi feel better, to help free her from being haunted by the awful deed of a relative she never knew. Swanson Paul's descendants long ago exiled his memory to a closet, yet generations after his crime, it's Willi who carries guilt to the graveyard and sings.

Some pain can't be packed away, Wrecker thinks.

He catches several decent snappers before losing his rig on a coral head. It's a good time to quit. He turns on his phone, which immediately starts ringing. He puts it back in his pocket and lets the call go to voicemail. Probably Silver Mustache again. The smuggler has been silent and invisible since the pizza boxes showed up at the police station, but apparently he's back in action now.

A minute later, another call comes. Then another, and another. Wrecker gets aggravated and pulls out the phone. It's not Silver Mustache on the other end; it's his stepsister.

"Where are you, Valdez?" she asks.

"Out fishing. What's wrong?" He throttles down in order to hear her better.

"But *where* are you fishing? Gulf or ocean?"

"Ocean side. I'm heading in."

"And you don't see it?" Suzanne asks. "How can you not see it?"

"See what? Which way?"

"In Hawk Channel, straight off the airport."

Wrecker looks to the northeast and quickly stops the skiff.

"No way," he says, mostly to himself.

"See it now?"

"Yeah, but I don't understand."

"Simple. They lied." Suzanne's voice falters. "It's a week earlier than they told everyone."

"Maybe it's going to Jamaica or Mexico."

"Valdez, they already made the turn. They're doing this to beat the flotilla!"

"I'll call you back, sis."

Wrecker guns the motor wide open. Minutes later, he's inhaling diesel fumes, steadying the skiff in a roiling current behind the *Princess Pandora*. As the cruise liner rumbles toward Key West, a volcanic cloud of milk-chocolate-colored mud spews from beneath its mammoth propellers. Wrecker sorrowfully watches a pair of bottlenose dolphins leaping through the turbid mess, frantically searching for clean water.

The *Pandora* is almost a hundred feet high and as wide as a soccer field; to passengers on the upper decks, Wrecker's puny skiff must look like a speck of debris in the wake. He's aiming his phone, taking video while he steers. The sight is beyond sickening. By the time the ship docks, the swirling brown grit will be settling on the reefs and channel bottoms—killing the seagrass, gagging the sponges, driving away the fish, crabs, and lobsters.

Twice the *Pandora* sounds its horn to alert the harbormaster. The blasts are so deep that Wrecker can feel the vibrations through the tiller as he steers.

You could hear that thing halfway to Havana, he thinks, stowing the phone.

Something makes a splash in the waves near the skiff's starboard side. To Wrecker it didn't sound like a baitfish. There's a second splash on the other side, causing him to look upward to see if a flock of seagulls is taking random dumps.

The next time it's not a splash, but a sharp bang in the front of the boat. Wrecker covers his head and peeks around the cooler. A small round object is rolling down the deck toward him.

"Pitiful," he says, grabbing the dimpled white sphere: a ball stamped PRINCESS PANDORA DRIVING RANGE.

And in very small script: BIODEGRADABLE TOFU PRODUCT.

Wrecker looks up just in time to see another one coming. Tourists are blindly hitting golf balls off the fantail of the cruise ship.

Splash, splash, splash into the murky turbulence.

"Ahoy, Captain, please back off!" calls a British-sounding voice from a bullhorn. Some clean-cut young dude in a pressed white uniform is hailing him from one of the *Pandora*'s lower decks.

Wrecker is amused to be addressed as "Captain."

He replies with a friendly wave and motors closer—probably too close, if he's being honest. His skiff isn't much bigger than the dot over the *i* in the word "Princess" on the ship's stern.

"Captain, back off now!"

No "please" this time. Meanwhile it appears that the golfers have been instructed to hold their fire.

"Captain, if you do not comply immediately, we will alert the Coast Guard!"

"I don't blame you!" Wrecker shouts up at Bullhorn Boy. "You're just doing your job!"

The churning wash behind the liner's giant engines is causing the skiff to skate and skitter like a leaf on a windswept lake. To hold course, Wrecker pins the end of the tiller under one leg.

Bullhorn Boy watches with alarm as the sleek little outboard draws ever closer to the moving ship—all two hundred thousand tons of it—until suddenly the young renegade captain rears up and, with a wild shout, hurls what is clearly a tofu golf ball straight at the *Princess Pandora*.

It pings off the towering hull and plops harmlessly into the water.

Oh well, Wrecker thinks, speeding away. *It felt good, anyway.*

TWENTY-ONE

Willi isn't singing. And no candle this time, only flowers. She's wearing a loose black dress, lacy veil, and dark running shoes with tape covering the fluorescent stripes.

And that ironed-looking wig, shiny as black chrome.

"Early Katy Perry," she tells Wrecker.

"I'll take your word for it."

They're holding hands at the grave of the man her great-great-grandfather helped to kill. The night is gummy and hot, a honey-colored slice of moon peeking through the wispy clouds.

The two Black Coats are gone—fired, no doubt, or worse. They've been replaced at the Bendito Vachs tomb by four even larger, more disagreeable-looking individuals. Their nearby presence rules out the possibility of any songs, or the scent of candles. Willi has dubbed them the "No-Neck Quartet" due to their weightlifter body types. They wouldn't be here unless the cash was still stashed inside the coffin; Wrecker wonders if the new goons even know what they're guarding.

He's been waiting for the right time to reveal the astounding sum to Willi. Her eyes are closed as if she's praying, though the closest thing to a religious conversation they've ever had was her hopeful fantasy about Jesus on a water bike.

Wrecker's thoughts keep drifting back to his stepsister—tonight was the first time he'd seen her cry. She broke down while watching the video he'd taken in the silt contrail behind the *Princess Pandora*. He was standing beside her wheelchair when she started sobbing. There wasn't much to be said. The cruise-line company had foiled the citizens' blockade of Key West by sending the *Pandora* a week earlier than scheduled. Now it was comfortably docked at the harbor, spitting out thousands of tourists.

"Those ships aren't even allowed here at night," Suzanne fumed. "They're supposed to be in and out by sunset!"

"I know, sis."

"First the state throws out our referendum, and now this sleazy trick. It's a sewer of greed!"

"What do we do? Is there a plan B?" Wrecker asked.

Suzanne dried her eyes and gathered her emotions. Her phone kept dinging like a railroad gate—the Friends of Blue Waters were planning an emergency meeting at the library on Fleming.

"You should come, Valdez. Everyone who cares about this island needs to see your video!"

"I can't be there tonight, but I'll text it to you."

"And would you please go on the dreaded social media and post it? Instagram, TikTok, whatever you can handle. Just this once!"

"I've got a friend who's into that," Wrecker said. "She'll help me put it out there."

Willi was the reason he couldn't attend the meeting. He'd promised to accompany her to the grave of Manuel Cabeza; it was too dangerous for her to be there alone. Wrecker assumed that Silver Mustache had beefed up the force in the cemetery, and he knew what kind of men the smuggler liked to hire.

In case he was being watched, Wrecker had left his bicycle in front of the house, snuck out the back door, and hopped a neighbor's fence. He and Willi had met up at St. Mary's Convent and walked a pinball route to the cemetery, mostly dark alleys and overgrown lanes. Before entering, they'd scouted the grounds from outside the fence to locate Silver Mustache's thugs. As expected, the men were posted by the false Bendito tomb. From that spot they couldn't see Wrecker and Willi open the main gate.

Standing in front of the Islander's tombstone, Willi squeezes Wrecker's hand and says she's glad he came.

"I bet those dudes have serious guns," she whispers.

"The odds they do are about one million four hundred thousand seven hundred and sixty to one."

She turns and grabs his shoulders. "*That's* how much money is in the coffin?"

Wrecker nods. "The boss man told me he made the Black Coats count every dollar on crowbar night."

Willi sighs heavily. "This is bat-bleep crazy, Wreck."

Across the gray ramble of crypts and headstones, the glow of four cigarettes confirms that the No-Neck Quartet is staying close to the fake funeral vault.

"Look at those baboons," Willi says.

"Baboons with firearms."

"Some night, I'm going to sing here again."

"When it's safe," Wrecker says.

"It won't ever be safe, not totally. If I didn't wear this stupid black mop and hide my face, somebody would recognize me and start with the questions: 'Why are you here?' 'What do you care about some dude who died a hundred years ago?' And if they ever put the true story together—about what my great-great-grandfather did—my family'd have to pack up and leave Key West."

"It was a mob that night at the lynching," says Wrecker. "You're not the only one on the island carrying this secret from one generation to the next."

"So maybe I should start, like, a KKK descendants' support group?"

"They could fill a big room in this town."

"Wreck, you *do* understand that I'm not telling

another human soul about that particular carpenter in my past? Have I not made that clear?"

Crystal, he thinks.

"I'm not saying you should tell anybody. And I'm not saying you shouldn't feel sick about what happened. But you weren't even born then, so maybe cut yourself some slack."

"Easy for you to say."

"And I'm right, Willi."

"Every now and then you are."

Wrecker sees that Silver Mustache's thugs are on the move, cigarettes bobbing as they stride four abreast down one of the cemetery's narrow avenues.

Willi pinches her nose. "God, I can smell those nasty cigs that the No-Necks are smoking."

"The wind shifted."

"Gross."

"Also, they're coming this way."

"Let's bounce, Wreck."

"Fast," he says.

Heads low, they steal toward the gate.

Silver Mustache had wanted to pick up Wrecker at the house, but Wrecker said no. They'd agreed to meet in front of the public aquarium on Whitehead Street. The neighborhood was guaranteed to be busy with wandering passengers from the *Princess Pandora.*

Midnight comes and goes—and no sign of Silver Mustache in his Mercedes coupe. Wrecker decides to wait another hour, a smuggler's schedule being hectic and unpredictable. The phone rings, though it's not the caller that Wrecker is expecting.

"Yo, Eight!"

"How'd you get my number?"

"Your mother was decent enough to give it to me. You sound mad."

"I'm busy, Dad."

"Doing what? It's the middle of the night! Don't be like this, Eight."

"It's not a great time to talk."

"I wouldn't be callin' so late," says Valdez Jones VII, "if it wasn't super-important."

He's probably short on money, Wrecker thinks.

"I'm coming home for good, son. Back to the island!"

"Who's chasing you, Dad?"

"That's not very nice. I thought you'd be happy."

It turns out that Austin Breakwater's surprising streak of good luck is over. His brazen Beatles rip-off, "Here Comes the Moon," was the final blow to an already shaky career. The surviving Beatles didn't sue him over the song; it was worse than that. Their fans flew into a mass cyber-rage.

"I got slaughtered all over the internet. I mean, it was a *massacre,*" Wrecker's father is saying. "I'm sure you saw some of the memes. The vicious parodies. Even Weird Al called me out!"

"I missed all that. I don't do social media."

"Not even Insta?"

"Gives me a rash," Wrecker says.

"Do you know how ridiculously popular they are? Those Beatles?"

"I'm aware, Dad. Everyone in the solar system is aware."

"I got death threats! Some troll posted my Destin gig and memed a ferret's face on mine, or maybe it was a woodchuck. Doesn't matter—haters are haters. Then my record company, some psycho mailed a box full of poo to their office!"

"Maybe don't play that song in your show anymore," Wrecker says.

"It was cow poop, by the way. They did the forensics."

"Here's a crazy idea: try writing something original."

"I'm done, Eight. You can stick the proverbial fork in me—another innocent victim of the cancel culture. I'm afraid the Breakwater brand is not fixable. Home is where I belong, son, back with my family in Key West."

"*I'm* your only family," Wrecker points out.

"Technically, yeah."

"Pump the brakes, Dad."

"You and me can go out in your boat together, like we did the other day."

"You never even touched a fishing rod."

"I'll sell my Gibson and take fly-casting lessons."

"Do *not* sell your guitar, Dad."

A car that Wrecker doesn't recognize pulls up to the curb and beeps. It's a candy-red Porsche with tinted windows—not exactly low-key transportation.

"My ride's here," Wrecker says to his father.

"But it's so late, Eight. What kinds of friends are you making these days?"

"Bye, Dad."

Wrecker climbs in, and Silver Mustache pulls out into traffic. He claims the sports car belongs to an old college fraternity brother.

Sure, Wrecker thinks, *Crooked State University.*

"Wow, a four-door Porsche," he says.

"I know, right? What's the point?" The smuggler laughs. "We're on the same wavelength, you and me."

Doubtful, Wrecker thinks.

"This baby's a blast to drive, though," Silver Mustache says, "once you get off the island and the road opens up."

He seems to be in a good mood, considering that five thousand of his illegal vax cards are in police custody and the story was big enough to make the TV news in Miami. Wrecker decides not to wait for Silver Mustache to bring up the subject.

"Where have you been?" he asks. "Everyone's talkin' about those pizza boxes."

"Yeah, I know. Seemed like a good time to go hang in Nassau for a couple days. Thanks for your genius intel about the shrimp boat, by the way."

"Like I said, my friend heard it at a bar."

Silver Mustache snorts. "Absolutely no help whatsoever."

"So, what do you think really happened?" Wrecker wants to be sure the smuggler doesn't view him as a suspect.

"My guess, some dumb yokel was out fishin' and found the packages floating. He stashed 'em somewhere, then cooked up that shrimper story to see if there was any blowback. Once the dude heard whose load it was, he dumped the boxes at the cop shop."

Wrecker says, "Word is the FBI took the case."

"Wooo. I'm shakin' in my shoes."

"Still, it's the FBI."

"Valdez, you watch too much television."

I watch hardly any, Wrecker thinks.

Silver Mustache is staying below the speed limit, unusual behavior for anyone at the wheel of a red Porsche. Clearly he doesn't want to give the police a reason to pull him over.

"When's the last run?" Wrecker asks.

"Tomorrow night. Clear your calendar."

"I'm supposed to work till seven."

"We'll be leaving port earlier than that. Better call in sick."

"But what if—"

"Call in sick, Valdez. Tell 'em you got the 'rona."

"No, then they'll make me stay out a week," Wrecker says. "I need the money."

"You'll be well paid for your time on the water. *Overpaid*, in fact. End of discussion, amigo."

They're on the Overseas Highway, waiting at the last traffic signal on Stock Island. The instant the light turns green, Silver Mustache stomps the accelerator and the Porsche rockets forward, pinning Wrecker to his seat.

Seventy, eighty, ninety, a hundred . . .

Blowing past every car, truck, and SUV all the way to the naval air station on Boca Chica, where Silver Mustache whips a sliding U-turn across the grass median.

"Fast, fine, and furious," he says, grinning in the dashboard lights. "That would be perfect for *my* tombstone, heh?"

It takes miles for Wrecker's heartbeat to slow to normal. By then they're back in Key West, tooling down Truman at thirty miles an hour. The only other life on the streets is cops, cats, Uber drivers, and a few tanked tourists on mopeds.

"The weather looks decent for our run," Silver Mustache remarks. "Scattered showers but nothing biblical."

"Is it Boca Grande again?"

"Sometimes Rodrigo likes to switch things up. But since I'm the one buyin' gas for the boat, you don't need to worry about that."

"I'm not worried," Wrecker says, the biggest possible lie.

Silver Mustache shakes his head. "You with the mental GPS in your head."

"Just drop me at the end of my street."

"Of course. We don't want to wake your stepsister."

Wrecker stays cool. "I've got a question. It's personal."

He can see that Suzanne's house is dark; she must be in bed. Silver Mustache stops at the corner.

"I'm not telling you my name, bro," he says.

"I honestly don't want to know your name."

"Then what's the question?"

"Did you get the vaccination?" Wrecker asks.

The smuggler's expression says, *Are you freakin' kidding me?*

"I'm not an idiot, kid," he says. "Me and everyone that works for me got the shots. That's a 'corporate mandate' from the CEO, yours truly."

"Who sells fake vax cards for a living."

"It's ironic, I admit. But business is business is business."

Wrecker gets out of the sports car and says, "The virus nearly killed my stepfather."

"Bring your rain gear tomorrow, just in case."

The smuggler points up at the sky and then drives away slowly, not even a squeak from those high-performance tires.

Just like a model citizen, Wrecker thinks.

TWENTY-TWO

He wakes up to the sound of Suzanne hollering his name and knocking on the door. She says his *Princess Pandora* video is burning up the internet—Twitter, Tik-Tok, Instagram, Reddit. The cruise company has hastily issued a statement, falsely blaming the mud plume on "a regrettable engine malfunction."

When a reporter called Suzanne for a response, she said, "The only thing pathological polluters regret is getting caught."

Proudly she thrusts her phone at Wrecker to show him the online tempest.

"Wait till they see the flotilla, Valdez. You'll be there, right?"

"Gotta work, sis."

"Call in sick!"

"You guys are gonna rock it," Wrecker says.

After a quick shower, he drops a text to Willi: Nice work. When did you post all that?

She replies with a winking emoji and: Late last night. Easy peasy

Major viral. Thx again

You The Man, Willi writes back. Vid was awesome

Cruise co. is saying the dolphins were photoshopped

Desperation, dude.

Wrecker wolfs down a cinnamon bagel, steps over the dozing cat, and walks out the door. There he's greeted by the unwelcome sight of Valdez Jones VII, sitting on the front steps with a travel bag and guitar case.

"Oh good," Wrecker says. "More drama."

"I forgot to tell you," Suzanne calls after him. "He's been waiting an hour."

"She was sweet enough to offer me breakfast," his father says, "but I didn't want to go inside until after you and I talked."

Wearing a rumpled T-shirt from a Greek diner in Tarpon Springs, he's still sporting the snakeskin boots but no cowboy hat. His hair is morphing back to its natural crimp and color, no longer weirdly straight and blond-tipped.

After an awkward hug, Wrecker says, "So you were already in town when you called last night."

"Dog Beach. That's where I slept."

"Smells like it."

"Not everybody cleans up after their pets," his father says. "Some people are slobs."

"And this is a shock to you?"

Valdez Seven sniffs his shirt. "I think it's more the seaweed than the dog poop."

"I gotta go to work, Dad."

"I came back home to bury Austin Breakwater. Forever, starting right now." He tugs the boots off and deposits them in the garbage can by the shed.

"You can't stay here. This isn't my house," Wrecker says.

"But Suzanne just told me—"

"You *cannot* stay here. Sorry."

"Guess what, Eight. I took your advice."

"What advice?"

"This morning I started writing a brand-new song—and I mean authentic," says Valdez Seven. "No more lawsuits for me."

A new direction for the wayward musician in his dirty socks and sandy jeans.

"Wanna hear the first verse?" he asks. "It's good, son."

"Play it for me later."

"But for now I can crash here, right? Come on."

Again Wrecker says no. He feels guilty, mean-hearted—the works—but today isn't the day to go soft.

"Motels down here aren't cheap," Valdez Seven is saying. "The 'Tequilaville' money, most of it went to the lawyers."

"Try Stock Island—a place called the Jackfish Inn. By the way, the timing of this grand homecoming—or whatever you're calling it—is terrible."

"Doesn't Suzanne have a futon?"

"Nope," says Wrecker. "Not even a hammock."

*   *   *

After punching in for his shift at Fausto's, Wrecker tells his boss that he needs to leave work early that afternoon to get a tooth yanked. When the boss asks for the dentist's name, Wrecker comes up with "Dr. Franz Boogenleaper," knowing the manager won't even attempt to look up that one to check his alibi.

The locals in the grocery store who aren't griping about the cruise ship are gossiping about the vax-card mystery at the police station. The chief told a neighbor that the Peter Pan's Pan Pizza boxes came from a shipment that was stolen months earlier from a family pizzeria in El Paso, Texas. Detectives have been ordered to find out who pranked Officer Nedrick Nugent—the list of suspects supposedly includes five different citizens who've filed use-of-force complaints against him, plus half a dozen fellow cops who dislike him intensely.

Meanwhile, the FBI has finished interviewing the high-school students who got busted selling bogus CDC cards. Apparently they'll avoid jail time by cooperating and paying a fine. The agents are still on the island, nosing around. Rumor is they're staying at the Hampton Inn near the airport. A butcher at Fausto's claims one of them came into the store and ordered a knockwurst sandwich from the deli.

Wrecker clocks out in the middle of the afternoon. It's breezy and drizzling in the streets of Old Town.

The *Princess Pandora* blasts its horn, summoning its wide-walking passengers. Soon the mammoth liner will be departing—or trying to. Suzanne is still working on last-minute instructions for the flotilla. Blocking the ship from leaving on schedule would cost the cruise company tons of money, and bring lots of embarrassing, unwanted publicity. But Wrecker worries that the weather might discourage some of the protesters with boats from showing up.

He covers his head with one sleeve and jogs through the rain toward Mallory Square. As he passes Willi's house, he pauses to look up at her window. A voice from the speaker box at the gate surprises him:

"Be careful, Wreck."

"You too." He waves and runs on.

Down at the square, Officer Van Zorn and several others are standing around in blaze-orange ponchos watching both the crowd and the puddles get bigger. Most of the protest signs are homemade and hand-lettered:

SMALLER, SAFER SHIPS!

STOP KILLING OUR REEFS!

KEY WEST IS AMERICA, TOO— WHAT HAPPENED TO OUR VOTE?

The demonstrators are energized but peaceful, a mix of flip-flops, Crocs, and designer sneakers. Some carry umbrellas, while others stand bareheaded. A few of them are wearing face masks to avoid catching the latest subvariant.

Together they're practicing a popular sports chant for when the *Princess Pandora* departs: "Na na na na, na na na na, hey, hey, hey, goodbye!"

In the meantime, uniformed guides from the cruise line are trying to herd curious passengers away from the scene and back to the ship.

Van Zorn spots Wrecker and waves him over. He says the chief wouldn't give him the afternoon off to participate in the floating protest.

"How come *you're* not out on the water with the others?" he asks Wrecker.

"I will be."

"My brother's bringing his kids on the catamaran. Wish I could go."

"Where's Nugent?"

"Right where the chief wants him—writing parking tickets," Van Zorn says. "Hey, I watched our security video of that pizza drop-off at the police station. The delivery dude? He had a tarpon gaiter just like yours."

Wrecker's chest tightens. "They sell 'em all over town. Anybody can buy one."

"Okay, let's call it a coincidence." The cop is studying Wrecker's eyes, waiting for a telltale twitch.

"I don't have a car," Wrecker adds, "or even a driver's license."

"Or any friends who drive, right? All of 'em got bikes and mopeds." Van Zorn is smiling, but not really. "The vehicle that brought the pizza boxes was a white Honda Accord with the tag numbers taped over. But here's the funny thing: there was a Conch Republic sticker on the rear bumper. That's what we in our business call a clue."

"You can get those things from any shop on Duval." The hitch in Wrecker's voice makes him sound like a Muppet. He can't believe he and Willi hadn't thought to peel that sticker off Miss Bascomb's car.

In the background, the anti-*Pandora* protesters are warming up, getting louder by the minute: "Na na na na, na na na na, hey, hey, hey, goodbye!"

"We need to talk," Wrecker says to Van Zorn, "but not here."

The officer glances up at the rain clouds. "Sure, let's take a walk."

The thin-haired man working in the sexton's office is ruffled by the paperwork he's been handed.

"Unfortunately, the cemetery closes at seven," he says.

His visitor, who looks like a spray-tanned middle-aged bodybuilder, tells him not to worry. "We'll lock the gate on our way out."

"This normally isn't done at night. Can you come back first thing tomorrow?"

"No, the Vachs family wants Bendito moved as soon as possible," the No-Neck says. "He belongs back in Miami."

"Yes, that's what it says on these transfer documents—"

"Which is all you need to see, right?"

The man in the sexton's office is fidgeting. "Sir, it's just that we don't ever do this after hours. There's no one here to supervise. We have a very small staff."

"This ain't a space launch, mister. We're just loading a coffin in a station wagon."

"A hearse, you mean."

The No-Neck holds up a familiar-looking key. "We'll let ourselves in and let ourselves out. No muss, no fuss. Can you sign the papers now? Please."

Down the street, alone on a bench in the dog park, Willi can hear the rowdy chorus of boat horns all the way from the harbor. She adjusts her Katy Perry wig and patiently waits for the sun to go down. The paperback book that she holds open on her lap is just a prop, her favorite Judy Blume novel, which she read twice three summers ago. The bench offers a good view of the graveyard—the tombs are still slick from the rain, but the clouds are thinning and the air smells fresh.

A middle-aged couple enters the park with a weird doodle mix, which hops up on Willi's lap and starts nipping at the corners of the book.

"Worst dog ever," one of the women mutters, tugging uselessly on the leash.

"Tucker's a rescue," her partner confides to Willi. "Five years old, and he still pees the couch! But we love him, don't we, sweetie?"

"Only when he's sleeping," the other woman says.

A man struggling to control a Great Dane puppy enters the park, distracting the frisky doodle and its owners. Willi closes the book, gets up, and leaves. From the sidewalk she can see the smugglers' mini-mausoleum—the No-Neck Quartet hasn't appeared for guard duty yet. She skateboards down to the place on Frances Street where her ladder is hidden, and where she left tonight's candle and flowers.

She waits for pitch-darkness before climbing the fence and approaching the grave of Manuel Cabeza. A white hearse and a royal-blue pickup are parked bumper to bumper under a streetlight on Olivia. Tinted windows conceal the occupants of both vehicles, but Willi feels the scorch of unfriendly eyes.

Wrecker would totally freak if he knew where she was, but she had to come. It might be the last time ever. She lights the candle and places the flowers—fresh tulips and irises—in an empty mayonnaise jar in front of the Islander's headstone. As she begins to sing, softly, she hears the hearse and the pickup truck start moving toward the entrance of the cemetery.

Willi goes silent. She wishes she'd talked Wrecker out of his wild plan. There's a chance she'll never see him again, and that would suck.

It's also possible that nobody will see *her* again, either, and that would suck, too.

She bends down to blow out the candle before disappearing among the mute crypts and vaults.

The waterfront was lined with demonstrators from the Mallory dock to the private cruise-ship pier. Most were doing the goodbye chant, but some banged cowbells and others blasted air horns. Swarms of noisy seagulls and terns added to the jangled symphony as they wheeled and swooped overhead—the larger the throng of humans, the more dropped food for the birds to snack upon. The setting sun was playing peekaboo in the clouds, and the wind had slacked.

Boats were buzzing all over the harbor, though they looked curiously small—almost like bathtub toys—compared with the towering cruise liner they surrounded as it slowly motored out of port. There were flats skiffs, Jet Skis, houseboats, teak-trimmed sloops, little Sunfish sailboats, a shrimp trawler, go-fasts, commercial dive boats, cabin cruisers, bay boats, sleek offshore sportfishers, pontoon party barges, lobster boats, crabbers, even a couple of private yachts. All except one displayed protest banners and signs or Friends of Blue Waters mast flags stitched with an image of a leaping, teary-eyed dolphin.

Technically it wasn't a blockade, as several Coast Guard vessels were poised to clear a departure path for the *Princess Pandora*. Nonetheless, Suzanne was flying high as she led the flotilla, riding solo in the harness of a brightly striped parasail being towed three hundred feet in the air alongside the cruise liner. Pumping one fist defiantly, she held a bullhorn in her other hand and shouted "Save our reefs!" at the tourists staring from the ship's decks and cabin balconies. Lots of them were taking videos with their phones.

Wrecker clapped and whistled, knowing his stepsister was soaring too high to hear him. Never had he felt more proud of her. He held back the urge to wave because he didn't want her to glance down and see him, since he wasn't in his skiff.

Silver Mustache grunted scornfully as Suzanne sailed past, swinging from the bright billowing chute. "She's gonna croak if she falls," he said to Wrecker.

"She can swim just fine."

"Yeah? How's that work?"

"Push yourself around in a wheelchair for a few years," Wrecker said, "and watch how strong your arms get."

"Don't get pissed, kid. It's a long way down to the water is all I meant."

"She's got a life jacket."

"You couldn't pay me to do that. The rope snaps, the wind shifts, and *splat*—you hit the side of that cruise ship like a grasshopper on a trucker's windshield."

Wrecker didn't want to be around to see the underwater silt volcano when the *Pandora* picked up speed. "Time to go," he said.

Silver Mustache ignored him. For some reason, the smuggler had decided his shiny black tracksuit was smart boating attire in the dead of a Florida summer. Wet moons of sweat bloomed under his arms, and his mustache glistened like a moist gray caterpillar. He was chugging his third bottle of water while marveling at the size of the harbor demonstration.

"I can't believe so many people came out for *this*," he said.

"They live here. They care." Wrecker was on edge, and running out of patience.

Earlier the smuggler had refused to let him attach a Friends of Blue Waters flag to the speedboat. "I stay clear of local politics," he'd said. "First rule of business, bro."

What bull, Wrecker thought.

Suzanne was making a wide turn in her parasail, lining up for another pass along the starboard side of the *Princess Pandora*. Her wheelchair had been safely strapped to the deck of the tow boat, which was bouncing as it crossed its own wake.

"Know what I see when I look at one of these cruise ships? Satisfied customers!" Silver Mustache was saying. "Every single one of those passengers needed a vax card to book that trip, right? I guarantee you some of 'em bought theirs from me."

"The fakes."

"'Authentic reproductions,' let's say." The smuggler lifted his wraparound shades to gloat.

"People still get sick from the virus. People still die," Wrecker said angrily. "What if your mother went on a cruise and caught it from some unvaccinated jerk who got on board using one of your phony cards?"

Silver Mustache cocked his head and eyed Wrecker as if he'd lost his mind. "There is no possible scenario," he said, "where my mom would set foot on one of those ships. She hates buffet lines, she doesn't gamble, and she says salty air makes her hair frizzy."

"I can't believe you think this is funny."

"Grow up, Valdez. People don't buy those vax cards from me, they'll get 'em somewhere else. It's called commerce. Don't tell me that nobody in your righteous family tree ever smuggled anything on or off this island. Key freakin' West? It's tradition here, dude. A legacy, whether you like it or not."

"My great-great-grandfather brought in rum from

Cuba," Wrecker heard himself saying. "But that was during Prohibition, not a pandemic."

"And you seriously don't think the booze he hauled ever killed anybody? Did then. Does now."

Wrecker chewed his lip and looked away, toward the west. "If we don't leave soon," he said to the smuggler, "we'll miss the right tide."

"Then, by all means, vamos ahora."

And so the only nonprotesting boat in the protest flotilla turned and sped out of the harbor, heading for Boca Grande Key.

Where it now lies at anchor, in advance of the *Zoolander*.

TWENTY-THREE

In 1853, a British brigantine ran aground near Boca Grande, setting off a heated race among wreckers a dozen miles away in Key West. A schooner named the *Champion* dispatched a rowboat with ten oarsmen, but they were swiftly passed by a twelve-oared boat from a competing ship, which reached the wreck before anyone else. When the crew members from the *Champion* arrived, the other wreckers wouldn't let them work on the grounded brig. The dispute ended up in front of a judge, who ruled that the *Champion* deserved a share of the salvage settlement.

Wrecker knows the whole story. His great-great-great-great-grandfather, Valdez Jones Jr., was employed on the *Champion*. The schooner's listed captain was a prominent wrecker named John Geiger, though a backup was in charge at the time the British brigantine foundered. Captain Geiger and his wife had nine children, and the home they built on Whitehead Street exists now as the Audubon House, a historic tourist attraction a few blocks from where Willi lives.

Although she's not there now, if she's sticking to the plan.

And Silver Mustache is showing basically zero interest in the history of shipwrecks in the waters of Boca Grande. Wrecker had begun with the tale of the *Bayronto*, a four-hundred-foot freighter hauling wheat from Texas to France. The ship capsized in the Gulf during the 1919 hurricane and floated upside down more than a hundred miles to the island where Wrecker now sits in the driver's seat of an absurd neon-green speedboat.

This time Silver Mustache didn't ask to be dropped off at Ballast Key; he said he wanted to say goodbye to Rodrigo in person, out of respect. Yet to Wrecker he seems nervous, and not as cocky as usual, as if he senses that tonight's deal is riskier than the others.

The Cigarette is anchored a hundred yards from the shore of Boca Grande. In its darkness the island looks raw and unexplored; tomorrow it will be crawling with day-boaters and their kids. Every now and then Wrecker hears a tarpon roll nearby.

Silver Mustache has been in radio contact with Rodrigo, who says he's on the way. It turned into an ideal night for smuggling, the seas empty except for the distant lights of the *Princess Pandora*, steaming toward Jamaica after escaping Suzanne's flotilla.

Celia Cruz is singing softly on the speedboat's speakers. Silver Mustache isn't very talkative, which is fine with Wrecker. He's nervous, too. The first smuggling run had been a surprise; this one, his second and last, is much different. He's had a whole day and night to worry about it.

"When is Mr. Vachs being moved?" he asks Silver Mustache.

"It's happening right now. What do you care?"

"I still don't get why you picked the cemetery, of all places."

"Seemed like a clever spot at the time."

The smoke from the smuggler's cigar hangs over the boat like a foul fog. He props his feet on the cash-packed Yeti cooler that they'll soon be delivering to Rodrigo.

"When you're in a business like mine," the smuggler says, "the biggest problem is finding a safe place to stash the money."

Like an old sneaker, Wrecker thinks, *or a hollow fishing gaff in a sunken shipwreck.*

"The fake tomb wasn't a terrible idea. We used it like a bank," Silver Mustache goes on. "Deposits and withdrawals, whenever we needed. I figured nobody else in their right mind would go prowling in a graveyard at night. Even the macho gorillas who work for me get creeped out big-time. But not you, Valdez. You weren't ever scared of that place, even sometimes when you should've been."

"It was just a job."

"Not a normal one, it wasn't."

"Yeah, but who's normal?" Wrecker has no explanation for his state of calmness when he's at the cemetery, surrounded by the dead.

"Those scumbags who tried breaking into the vault," Silver Mustache says, "they didn't mind being there, either."

"A million-dollar coffin can make a person forget about ghosts and zombies."

"No doubt." The smuggler laughs. "Our organization is having an epic year. Really solid." He's starting to loosen up and brag again. "Our vax cards are selling like lotto tickets. The best counterfeits on the black market, by far—and the ones I'm gonna print, they'll be even better."

"But what happens to your business when the virus is gone?"

Silver Mustache pops opens a beer can. "I'll be retired by then, dude. Livin' my best life."

Wrecker checks the digital clock on the speedboat's instrument panel. Rodrigo is already half an hour late, and the tide won't wait.

"Where is he coming from?" Wrecker asks.

"Another galaxy far, far away."

"Meaning it's none of my business."

"Exactamente." Silver Mustache blows a smoke ring to make it look like a halo over his head. "Dude, quit worryin' about the tides. We got plenty of water."

"I'm not worried."

"Liar."

"Maybe a little bit worried. I feel like that's reasonable."

Silver Mustache says, "Relax, you'll be done soon."

Wrecker isn't thrilled by the smuggler's choice of words. "Done" carries more than one meaning. Between the sharks and the strong currents, Wrecker's body might never be found if something bad happens out here. He remembers the assault rifle that Silver Mustache kept on the purple go-fast, and wonders if the smuggler bought a new one.

"Is there a gun on board?" he asks.

"How would that information be useful to you, Valdez?"

So I can dive off before you shoot me, Wrecker thinks.

Silver Mustache leans forward in his padded chair and turns the dial to silence Celia Cruz.

"Hear that?" he says.

Another boat, running wide open. Gradually it comes into view—a pale sleek form cutting a seam across the flat, black-looking sea. The driver's in total outlaw mode: no running lights, no cockpit lights, no spotlights.

"That's our man," says Silver Mustache.

If I jumped now, I could make it to the island, Wrecker thinks. *They'd never catch me in the mangroves.*

Unfortunately, though, escaping wouldn't let him finish what needs to be finished.

The *Zoolander* slows down as it approaches the lee

shore of the island. Instead of dropping anchor, Rodrigo idles directly toward the speedboat. Silver Mustache tells Wrecker to hang a couple of rubber bumpers over the side. When the big Hatteras pulls up close, Rodrigo's men tie the boats snug together. No dinghy needed tonight.

Wrecker pulls a mahi-mahi sun mask over his face (he'd ditched the tarpon-scale gaiter after his conversation with Officer Van Zorn). Rodrigo, also masked, steps aboard and bro-hugs Silver Mustache.

"How come you brought junior again?" he asks, eyeing Wrecker.

"Because he's a born night driver, that's why," Silver Mustache replies. "He can run these flats with both eyes closed. Also? I don't want to be the one behind the wheel if we get stopped. I'm just innocent old Uncle Mo-Mo."

"Yeah, good luck with *that* story." Rodrigo turns to Wrecker. "I forget your name."

"It's Charles."

"Charles what?"

"Breakwater," Wrecker says.

"Like the singer?"

Wrecker is beyond stunned. "Yeah. He's my dad."

"That's dope! I friggin' love 'Tequilaville,'" Rodrigo says.

"Sure. Okay."

"Yo, boys!" Silver Mustache cuts in. "Let's hurry

up and do this thing. Take the cooler, Rodrigo. It's full of everyone's favorite."

Rodrigo hoists the Yeti and passes it to his crew on the *Zoolander*.

"Count it," he tells the guy with the stupid butterfly gaiter, the one who made fun of Wrecker on the last drop.

Silver Mustache and Rodrigo drink beers and talk baseball while they wait. The lookout posted in the *Zoolander*'s flybridge calls down to report a freighter in West Channel. It's so far away that nobody else can see it.

"Night-vision binoculars," Rodrigo explains. "Same kind as the SEAL teams use."

Butterfly Face reappears at the gunwale of the Hatteras. "Count's good. The money's all there," he says.

Rodrigo orders him and the others to transfer the wrapped pizza boxes to the Cigarette boat. Like last time, they don't ask Wrecker to help, which is fine; he'd rather not leave his DNA on the evidence.

Looking out across the endless Gulf, he thinks about all the dangerous nights endured by the early Valdez Joneses, starting with the first. This trip to Boca Grande is a leisure cruise compared with what the real wreckers faced, usually in howling winds and ripping seas.

There's no cell service this far from Key West, but Wrecker checks his phone anyway: zero bars. He wishes he could text Willi. It's important that she remembers everything he told her to do. Life-or-death important.

A young loggerhead surfaces, exhaling like an industrial steam valve. The sound startles Butterfly Face, who gropes for something in the back of his waistband. Wrecker grabs the man's wrist.

"Dude, it's just a turtle," he says.

Butterfly Face yanks his arm away. Rodrigo and Silver Mustache crack up laughing. Wrecker can't wait for this to be over. The tide is literally running out.

As the last of the packages are stowed in the speedboat, Rodrigo says, "That's it. One hundred boxes even. You wanna count 'em?"

Silver Mustache, who was silently counting the whole time, says no. "I trust you like a brother."

"A hundred thousand clean cards."

"And they'll all be sold by the weekend."

"Love it." Rodrigo slaps Wrecker on the shoulder. "Drive safe, junior. That's precious cargo you got there."

"Slam dunk," Wrecker says.

Butterfly Face's mask puckers at his mouth. "Sabelotodo!"

Silver Mustache does the translation for Wrecker: "He thinks you're a smartass."

"What's the Spanish word for a man who's scared of turtles?"

"Zip it, kid," Silver Mustache says.

He shakes Rodrigo's hand and tells him it's been cool doing business together.

"See you next time," Rodrigo says.

"No next time, amigo. This is my last run." Of course Silver Mustache doesn't mention that he's going to start printing his own counterfeit vax cards. "I'm gettin' too old for this kind of action," he says.

"What happens to junior?" Rodrigo asks.

"That's up to him."

"So he's available? I mean, if he's as good as you say."

"Put this kid in the right boat," Silver Mustache says, "and there's not a cop on the water that could catch him."

Wrecker can't believe what he's hearing. "No, I'm done, too," he cuts in firmly. "School starts up again in a couple weeks."

"School? *School?*"

All of them laugh—Silver Mustache, Rodrigo, Butterfly Face, and the other men on the *Zoolander*. Everyone except the guy up on the flybridge; his night-vision binoculars are fixed on a slow, low-flying aircraft.

"Let's roll!" he shouts down to the others.

"Coast Guard?"

"Don't know, jefe."

"Navy?"

"I can't tell."

Within seconds, the ropes are untied and both boats are under way, speeding in opposite directions. The plane that the men were watching continues moving due north, toward the amber glow of Miami; clearly it doesn't belong to the Coast Guard or navy.

Silver Mustache disappears into the go-fast's cabin, leaving Wrecker alone at the helm and in fear that the smuggler will return with a gun.

Every minute drags by like an hour. Wrecker feels that if something's going to happen, it will be here and now—miles from Key West, with no witnesses. He keeps one hand clenched on the wheel, the other clamped to the throttle levers. Even his kneecaps are trembling, a weird sensation. The GPS screens are turned off because he doesn't want Silver Mustache to see how far off course he's steering.

The stern would be the best place to jump from; if Wrecker went straight over the side at this speed, he could get sucked under the hull and chopped into slaw by the propellers. No, a long leap from one of the tall outboards would be the safest exit. After that: go deep and hold your breath as long as you can.

At least I've got the dive gene, Wrecker thinks.

When Silver Mustache finally emerges from the cabin, he's holding a champagne bottle, not a rifle.

"This ain't for you, kid," he says, raising his voice over the engine noise. "You're the designated driver!"

He pops the cork and takes a swig. Wrecker's knees stop shaking.

"I don't want to work for Rodrigo," he shouts.

"Ha! You oughta be flattered he asked."

"I'm finished with all this."

"Not quite, Valdez. Once we're back on the island, then, yeah, you're officially allowed to retire."

Quizzically Silver Mustache taps a forefinger on one of the blank GPS screens. Wrecker lies and says there's a loose wire. The smuggler reaches behind the devices and starts tinkering with the connections. Wrecker checks the speedometer: forty-two miles per hour. The lovely lights of Key West aren't far away.

Between gulps of champagne, Silver Mustache locates the power button on one of the GPS units. Instantly the map screen lights up, revealing that Wrecker isn't following the straight green line back to the harbor. Not even close.

"Where the hell are you going?" the smuggler yells.

"Home."

"WHAT ARE YOU DOING?"

"Hold on."

What Wrecker is doing is driving the speedboat solidly, purposely aground. Plugging it, as they say.

He hits the kill switch and power-trim buttons simultaneously, tilting the lower units of the motors so that the props won't chew up the seagrass and coral bank. The Cigarette coasts silently until it basically runs out of water.

Clueless, Silver Mustache had ignored Wrecker's advice about holding on. The impact throws the smuggler and his champagne to the deck. The bottle doesn't break, but what's left of the bubbly fluid spills out.

Silver Mustache gets up rubbing his neck and bellowing curses. Wrecker pretends to be surprised by what happened, and fakes an apology that Silver Mustache probably can't hear over his ranting.

Actually, it was a nifty bit of nighttime navigating. Wrecker beached the speedboat exactly where he wanted, on just the right tide, and made it look like a dumb mistake. With the water dropping fast, the knee-deep bank will soon be bone dry. The go-fast isn't going anywhere.

"This is, like, the worst-ever déjà vu," Silver Mustache groans, worn out by his own tantrum. "By the way, you're not gettin' paid a nickel for this run."

Wrecker shrugs. "I can't believe we got so far off course."

"Not *we*, junior. *You*. Just shut up and tell me how long we gotta wait till it gets deep enough to float off."

"Four or five hours. Maybe more."

"Wrong answer, bro. I'm not spendin' the night out here again."

They step out in the shallows and try to push the

Cigarette, which, of course, won't budge. Panting and sweaty, they use a small dive ladder on the stern to re-board the boat. It's a struggle for Silver Mustache, his injured leg still tender. He is also seething because he just ruined an eight-hundred-dollar pair of calfskin loafers.

Which only a fool would wear on a smuggling run, Wrecker thinks.

He picks up the air horn and blasts it three times, telling Silver Mustache that he sees the lights of another boat in the channel, which is true.

"Maybe they can pull us back to deep water," Wrecker says.

"You better hope and pray that happens."

Silver Mustache waves a spotlight to hail the other craft, which turns and approaches slowly. It's a light-colored skiff with an old outboard engine. The only person aboard is a slender driver wearing what looks like, from a distance, snow-skiing goggles.

"Yo, can you tow us off this flat?" Silver Mustache calls out. "I'll pay good money."

"My boat's not big enough to pull yours!"

"Is that a girl? It sounds like a girl," Silver Mustache says to Wrecker. "What's she doing way out here all alone?"

"You better call Sea Tug," she shouts.

"What?"

"CALL SEA TUG!"

"No way," the smuggler grouses.

Wrecker finds the loose end of the bow rope and uses a bend knot to attach a second, longer rope. Then he steps out of the speedboat and begins wading across the flat toward the channel edge where the skiff floats, motor idling.

"Let me go talk to her," he says over his shoulder to Silver Mustache.

"Tell her I'll pay five hundred bucks."

"Yup. I remember."

"And don't say anything about the load, Valdez."

Duh, Wrecker thinks.

The water feels silky warm against his ankles, and the current is strong. In the darkness Wrecker can't see anything beneath the surface, so he shuffles his feet as he goes—it's the best way to avoid stepping down on a sleeping stingray.

"What's the tide doing now?" the smuggler yells.

"Running out," Wrecker calls back. *Just like your luck.*

The bottom is uneven, as soft as quicksand in some places and crunchy with small shells and corals in others. Wrecker's glad he wore thick-soled sneakers. Silver Mustache keeps the boat's light aimed at the back of his head, which is annoying.

Willi brought a light, too.

"Fancy meeting you here," she says when Wrecker reaches the edge.

"Nice work, Captain."

"A nearsighted chimpanzee could work one of these things." Willi holds up the handheld GPS. "The numbers you gave me were dead-on."

"Keep your voice low," Wrecker says.

Willi waves at Silver Mustache aboard the grounded Cigarette. He doesn't wave back.

"Your friend's a grump," she says. "You ready, Wreck?"

"So ready. You've got no idea."

She noses the bow of the skiff closer. Wrecker steps aboard and ties the go-fast's extended rope to the small steel eye on the skiff's transom.

"We good?" Silver Mustache yells out.

"Golden!" Wrecker calls backs.

There is zero chance—less than zero, actually—that his skiff will be able to move the hulking Cigarette even a millimeter. The stranded smuggler is counting on a miracle that defies Newton's laws of motion. The smuggler who pays no attention to the tide charts.

Willi scoots over to let Wrecker take the tiller. When he twists the throttle, the skiff surges forward and the slack goes out of the towrope. At the other end, clueless Silver Mustache cheers to himself.

Not realizing that Wrecker, before wading off, had purposely loosened the bow knot, leaving the Cigarette high and soon-to-be dry.

And leaving the smuggler to stare helplessly at his departing rope, attached to an infuriating little boat that's definitely *not* coming back for him. He grabs a gun from a hatch and starts firing madly, wildly, at the fading sight of Valdez the traitor.

TWENTY-FOUR

Wrecker and Willi duck below the gunwale when they see the muzzle flashes. Bullets whistle past and kick up small round splashes in the channel as the skiff races away.

Willi waits until they're far out of range—and the gunfire ends—before reaching back to pull in the long trailing rope. She's wearing a navy watch cap and a hoodie with a Gators logo—but no shoes, in case she'd have to swim.

"Well, that was something new and different," she says breathlessly.

Wrecker is shaken, too. "The guy totally lost it. What a lunatic."

But thinking: *I'm the one who's crazy. We could've died.*

"Ever been shot at before?" Willi asks. "I believe it's a first for me."

"Totally my fault. I'm sorry."

"Oh, please. Don't you think I knew what I was getting into?"

"No, I'm really, *really* sorry."

"Shut up," Willi says. "I mean it."

Wrecker feels clear-eyed and free sitting beside her, shoulder to shoulder, skimming across satin waters.

An armed Coast Guard response vessel barrels by the skiff going the opposite direction. Lights flashing, the high-powered chase boat is likely heading to a latitude and longitude point that was called in by a young female citizen who politely declined to give her name.

"What else did you tell them?" Wrecker asks Willi.

"I stuck to our script: Suspicious vessel aground. Possible smugglers."

"What if they trace the cell number?"

"Then they'll have a pleasant but very confusing conversation with Miss Bascomb. I borrowed her phone to make the call. It'll be back in her handbag by the time she wakes up."

"You're pretty good at this."

"You want me to turn on the spotlight?"

"No, I'm fine." Wrecker is navigating by the lights of Key West.

"Oh, now you can see in the dark," Willi says. "So, you're like a cheetah, right?"

"Very much like a cheetah, only faster."

"Seriously, dude, aren't you worried?"

"Only an idiot wouldn't be worried," Wrecker says. "And scared, possibly."

"Not as scared as I was ten minutes ago."

"That man's gonna come after you hard, Wreck."

"Not unless he talks his way out of this."

"Is there cell service out there? What if he calls his goons?"

"He won't be calling anybody." Wrecker reaches into a pocket and pulls out the smartphone that Silver Mustache had carelessly left in a cupholder on the Cigarette.

"Dawg!" Willi says. "You're pretty good at this, too."

"I also yanked the cable out of his marine radio."

"Aren't you the slippery one? For once I am actually—"

"Don't say it."

"Impressed. Oh yes."

Wrecker's eyes remain locked on the water ahead; channel-marker posts are fairly easy to spot at night, so he's mainly watching for loose debris. Striking an object even as small as a coconut could break the motor's propeller.

Willi sneaks an arm around his waist and says, "Wouldn't it be awesome if we just kept going?"

"You mean, like, to the Bahamas? We don't have enough gas to get halfway across the Gulf Stream."

"God, you're killing the vibe, bro. I'm not talkin' about right this minute. I'm talkin' about you and me after this part is over. I hope *we* keep going, Wreck."

"Me too," he says, wishing he was the one who said it first.

"I don't ever want to leave Key West. I want to be here when Jesus rolls up on that Jet Ski."

"Wearing a life jacket, let's hope."

"Totally! He's all about setting a good example."

"Willi, look, there's a chopper coming—more Coasties."

"Guess your shady pal in the speedboat couldn't come up with a story they believed. A bad voyage for him tonight."

"It's about to get way worse," Wrecker says, smiling. "And I've told you like a hundred times, the man is *not* my friend."

The white hearse and royal-blue pickup truck got pulled over at mile marker nine on the Overseas Highway. It was a major show of force: city cops, sheriff's deputies, state troopers, even a pair of FBI agents who happened to be in town investigating counterfeit vaccine cards.

Officer Van Zorn was the one who'd gotten the tip and then told his lieutenant, who organized the stakeout at the cemetery. The decision was made not to do the bust there, out of respect for the dead. Also, several of the officers stated they would be uncomfortable in a graveyard after dark.

Road stops were easier, anyway.

The No-Neck Quartet had split into pairs for the

ride to Miami: two of them in the pickup, two of them in the hearse. They all carried loaded guns but also grasped the stupidity of starting a shoot-out; they were outrageously outnumbered. As soon as the convoy of blue lights appeared behind them, one of the goons tried to call Silver Mustache. The phone was answered by an unfamiliar female voice.

"Peter Pan's Pan Pizza," it said. "Can I take your order?"

Confused, the No-Neck immediately hung up. The police directed him and his muscular companions to exit their vehicles, raise their hands, and line up along the side of the highway, clear of the traffic. The men had dressed identically for the mission: black T-shirts, black jeans, and black sneakers. To Van Zorn they looked like a modern dance troupe on steroids. Passing motorists found them a peculiar sight in the headlights, even for the Keys. Some honked their horns, thinking it was a movie shoot.

The No-Necks were shown a search warrant and asked to open the casket of Bendito Vachs. In unison they said no. Their wrists were so large that the arresting officers had to use jumbo zip ties instead of standard handcuffs. The cops promptly confiscated the suspects' firearms, phones, and wallets.

Van Zorn and the others donned rubber crime-scene gloves before hoisting the evidence out of the hearse. The cedar coffin was brand-new, the first one having been gored by a crowbar, according to Van Zorn's tipster, who'd also provided a photo of the money stacked inside. Once the casket lid was open, every law-enforcement officer on the scene wanted a selfie. None of them—not even the FBI agents—had seen so much cash in one container.

"Who does this belong to?" Van Zorn asked the No-Necks.

The tallest responded in a dull tone on behalf of the quartet: "We don't know anything about that. We thought we were moving a legit dead body."

"And you need semi-automatic weapons for that job?"

"We want to call our lawyer. Now."

"You can do that at the jail," Van Zorn said, "when we're finished booking you geniuses."

Each of the No-Necks was transported separately. Van Zorn selected their tallish spokesman to ride in the back of his patrol car.

"Where's your boss tonight?" Van Zorn asked. "He'll be seriously pissed off about you losing all that dough."

"I don't have a boss. I'm an independent contractor."

The big man's chin stayed on his chest during the ride to the jail. He looked up only once, when Van Zorn pointed to a Coast Guard helicopter in flight.

"That means a boat's in trouble somewhere," Van Zorn said.

"Boo-hoo," the No-Neck mumbled sullenly.

Neither of them knew it, but the Coast Guard chopper was flying to specific GPS coordinates provided by one of the agency's patrol vessels on the scene. The location was a shallow tidal bank a few miles to the west, between Man Key and Woman Key.

It was there that Silver Mustache was desperately trying to talk his way out of trouble, one lame lie tumbling into another. The first challenge was scrambling to explain all the packages that he'd tossed out of the beached speedboat after being abandoned by the young mutineer and cell-phone thief. The kid's name would not be shared with the authorities because the smuggler planned to deal with him personally, back on dry land.

Unfortunately, the final silvery fingers of tide had trickled out before Silver Mustache was done ditching the load. Now the flat was exposed, lumpy and ripe-smelling and littered with blue-wrapped pizza boxes—exactly one hundred of them, according to the Coast Guard petty officers who did the counting. They were wearing black masks and night-raid outfits, and did not give their names to the smuggler.

"Those boxes aren't mine!" he protested. "They were here when I ran aground."

"Sir, we need to search your vessel," one of the Coasties said.

They found the gun right away because it was stowed in the only hatch that was locked. Silver Mustache had claimed he lost the key, but a Coast Guardsman simply popped it open with a screwdriver.

"Sir, is this weapon registered?" he asked, holding up the rifle.

"Never seen it before," Silver Mustache replied.

"Of course not. The evil gun fairy must have snuck aboard and hid it here."

And that's how it went. Not good. They also found the spent shell casings from the bullets the smuggler had fired at the skiff. His cigar box, it turned out, was not the shrewdest of hiding places.

When asked to explain why he was carrying a fake police badge and three different driver's licenses (with three different names but the same photograph), Silver Mustache said he was working undercover for the CIA. The Coasties didn't buy that bull, either. They scoffed behind their masks and put him in handcuffs even before cutting open the first blue package. Once they laid eyes on the phony vaccine cards, they called for a chopper with a rescue bucket.

Slumped in the front of the patrol boat, Silver Mustache grimly watched the pizza boxes disappear into the belly of the helicopter. Every time the bucket was lowered for more, he cursed bitterly under his breath. The chopper's rotors were deafening, and its blazing spotlight hurt his eyes.

"What about my boat?" he asked one of the Coast Guardsmen.

"We'll leave someone out here to drive it back after the tide comes up."

"Then what?"

"Then it's officially the property of the U.S. government."

"Are you freakin' serious?" Silver Mustache bleated.

"It looks like a super-cool ride, except for the color. Was it your idea to paint it that particular shade of green?"

"Ask my lawyer."

"Orange would look better," the Coastie mused. "Blood orange."

"Whatever."

"I like the name, though. Why isn't it painted on the stern?"

"What name?" Silver Mustache growled.

"*Last Laugh.*"

"Oh no."

"The caller told us. The one who gave us your GPS numbers," the Coastie explained. "The motor vessel *Last Laugh*, she said. That's the name, right?"

Silver Mustache lowered his head.

"Sure," he said miserably. "Why not."

Wrecker's bicycle is at the dock, where Willi left it.

After tying off the skiff, they ride straight to the cemetery, Willi perched on the handlebars. Cautiously they scout the place from the outside, first along Frances Street and then halfway down Angela. There's no sign of the No-Neck Quartet.

As Wrecker unlocks the main gate, Willi pinches his arm. "Are you gonna tell me what we're doing here? I'm really tired of asking," she says. "Actually, I'm tired, period."

He takes her hand and leads her down one of the graveyard's mini-avenues to the Catholic section, where the smugglers built the vault for their cash. The door to the stone crypt stands open, and the coffin is gone.

"Adios, Bendito," Willi says. "I guess they snatched the money and ran."

"Not far."

"Wreck, *what* are you talking about?"

"I didn't exactly tell you the whole plan," he says, "in case it fell apart."

"Fine. I hate you. The snubbing starts now."

"Okay, but first we need to swing by the police station."

"Do we?" Willi says.

"Won't take long."

"You're never going to have a real girlfriend. You know that, right? Your idea of a date is ridiculous."

The phone in Wrecker's front pocket starts ringing— not his phone, but the one belonging to Silver Mustache. According to the caller ID, an individual called "Range Bull" is on the other end.

Wrecker hands the phone to Willi. "Go for it," he says.

She breaks into a grin and taps the answer button.

"Peter Pan's Pan Pizza," she says cheerfully. "Can I take your order?"

At the police department they find Suzanne in the lobby. She got busted for dive-bombing the *Princess Pandora* in the parasail. Disturbing the peace, culpable negligence, a couple of other charges. She's not spending the night in jail because Roger made a call to his commissioner friend, Riggins the golfer.

"I got a little crazed out there, but it was worth it," Suzanne says to Wrecker. "I buzzed that spiral water flume on the top deck. You should've seen their faces!"

"Sis, this is my friend Willi."

"Ah, so you're the one. Excellent!"

"And you're the famous Key West Kite Woman," Willi says. "You were all over the internet today. Very cool."

Suzanne grins. "I like this girl," she says to Wrecker. "But I'm worn out and sunburned and I want to go home now."

Willi holds the door for her. Wrecker says he'll catch up in a minute, and walks over to speak with the desk officer.

Van Zorn comes out to the lobby right away and leads Wrecker to an interview room that smells like Lysol and sardines.

"Busy, busy night," Van Zorn says. "Thanks to your tip."

"Does that mean you caught 'em?"

"Oh yeah."

"How much was in the coffin?"

"One point six million, at least. We're still counting."

"Sweet," Wrecker says.

"Biggest cash takedown in Key West history. I might actually score a promotion out of this bust, so thanks again. Who knows, maybe I can return the favor someday."

"You definitely can."

"Aw, here we go. I knew it." Van Zorn gives Wrecker the look.

"It's Officer Nugent," Wrecker says.

"What about him?"

"You know." Wrecker jerks his thumb over his shoulder, like a baseball umpire calling a third strike. "If you get promoted is all I'm saying."

"Oh, he'll be gone," Van Zorn promises. "That creep is already at the top of my list. He'll be seeking employment elsewhere, hopefully in a different profession."

"One more thing."

"Don't push it."

"I heard there was a big Coast Guard bust tonight near Woman Key."

"Indeed there was." Van Zorn looks intrigued. "A hundred thousand counterfeit vax cards. The nitwit smuggler ran his Cigarette boat hard aground in the dark."

Wrecker sets Silver Mustache's phone on the table. "This belongs to the nitwit. If you cross-check the numbers on his speed dial—"

"Thanks, Magnum P.I. We know how cell phones work."

"You aren't going to ask where I got it?"

"Nope. I'm also not going to ask how you got mixed up in this outlaw circus, or how you made both parts of the case come together at the same time, on the same night. It'll be easier for both of us if we agree that we're not having this conversation."

Wrecker leans closer, drops his voice to a whisper. "He's a bad guy. If he gets out, he'll be hunting for me and my family."

"If he gets out, which I doubt will happen, he'll have some much badder bad guys hunting for *him*. That was an expensive deal he screwed up. His peeps got seriously burned, and they ain't happy." Van Zorn holds up the cell phone. "Yo, Mr. Jones, look what we found on that speedboat. The Coasties must've missed it on their first search."

"Why, it's the smuggler's Samsung!" says Wrecker.

"Can you believe it?" Van Zorn winks and nods toward the door. "If you were officially here, I'd tell you to go home now."

"If I was officially here, I'd already be gone."

TWENTY-FIVE

Sunday brunch on the outside deck with the Dunglers—shrimp-and-pasta salad. Wrecker arrives a few minutes late and is surprised to see Valdez Jones VII at the table.

Everyone's talking about the sensational bust of the counterfeit-vaccination-card smugglers. Key West has been invaded by TV news crews that are camped in front of the police station, where the chief and Officer Van Zorn have been giving interviews all morning. A video clip featuring the cash-stuffed coffin of the fictional Bendito Vachs was released to all interested media, including the major cable networks. Four suspects had been nabbed transporting the loot up the Overseas Highway in a funeral hearse. Meanwhile the Coast Guard caught the gang's ringleader dumping a load of bogus vaccine cards after he ran his high-powered speedboat up on the flats between Man Key and Woman Key.

The man had been carrying a phony police badge and several fake IDs but was quickly identified by his fingerprints. His real name is Marco David Quantraine, age fifty-one, and he owns a criminal record stretching back to his teenage years. The numerous mug shots posted online show the man with and without a thick mustache, which was once jet black. He's a fugitive from felony fraud charges in Colorado, and according to the FBI, he purchased his powerboats using pandemic relief money that he'd scammed from the government. Mr. Quantraine is facing many, many years in federal prison, where cigars aren't allowed.

Wrecker listens intently and acts like it's all big news to him. Briefly he makes eye contact with his father, who shrugs as if to confirm he's there mainly for a free meal. The salad is excellent, and Wrecker's mother proudly offers second helpings. Her Nicole Kidman eyes are less alarming than before; they've moved closer together since the swelling from the surgery has gone down.

"It was Roger's idea to invite your father today," Wrecker's mom tells him.

"That was really nice of him."

"I mean, come on, we're all grown-ups here."

Well, that's a stretch, Wrecker thinks.

Seated at the head of the table, Roger looks better than he has in weeks. He taps a fork on a glass to signal an important announcement. His voice is still weak, and everyone stops chewing in order to hear him clearly.

"Carole and I received an excellent offer on the house," he says, "and we're going to take it—"

"Hold on, Dad," Suzanne interrupts. "When did you put this place up for sale?"

"We didn't!" chirps Wrecker's mother. "Some rich stranger just knocked on the door. Isn't that wild? He deals cryptocurrency in Hong Kong."

"But don't worry," Roger adds, rubbing two fingers together. "He's paying us in good old-fashioned U.S. dollars."

Wrecker's not surprised by the sudden cash offer. It's happening all over town; Suzanne says the real-estate market is nuts.

"So, bottom line," Roger goes on, "Carole and I are moving to Pebble Beach. The Monterey Peninsula—well, that's my idea of heaven. No grass weevils to munch the fairways, either!"

"What happened to North Carolina?" Suzanne asks.

"The weather in the mountains is too iffy during the winter. We don't do snow," Carole explains. "Also, the spa situation isn't fabulous."

She turns to Wrecker. "Of course, we'd like for you to come with us, Valdez. Our agent raves about the salmon fishing."

For help Wrecker glances over at Suzanne, who doesn't miss a beat. "Carole, don't you think Valdez should stay in Key West until he finishes high school?"

Roger is quick to agree. "His grades are good. All his friends are here."

All one of them, Wrecker thinks.

But the truth is that wild mustangs couldn't drag him to California. It's not as if he won't miss his mother, but he'd be heartbroken if he had to leave the island.

"I'll come visit on holidays, Mom. Suzanne, too."

"You will both fall in love with the place! Head over heels. You won't ever want to leave."

Carole was the only reason Roger moved to Key West, so maybe it's her turn to go somewhere for him. Especially now that her flaky first husband is back in town—why would Roger want to deal with that?

"This decision might seem a bit impulsive," he says to the family, "but I did a lot of serious thinking while I was sick. The most valuable thing we've all got is time, right? Wasting it is the big mistake most people make."

"He's right. Trust me." It's Valdez Seven, joining the conversation while gnawing on a shrimp. "The clock is ticking for all of us," he says.

Pearls of wisdom, Wrecker thinks, *from the wandering wordsmith.*

The title of his new song is a mouthful: "A Ballad at the Tomb of the *Isaac Allerton.*"

It tells the story of a young wrecker named Valdez, who risks his life free diving on the sunken merchant ship, trying to find a silver locket that had been dropped by a passenger while she was being rescued. The locket holds a small rosy conch pearl that was given to the woman by her husband, who remains missing at sea.

Not surprisingly, Wrecker's father got a few historical details wrong. Nobody died when the *Isaac Allerton* went down in that big August hurricane; the crew and passengers escaped in longboats and were picked up the next day. Also, the sinking at Washerwoman Shoals happened in 1856, not 1859, but Valdez Jones VII says he needed a year that rhymed with the word "fine."

> *She mourned the loss of a man so fine*
> *That a savage storm had swept away*
> *In the summer of eighteen fifty-nine*
> *The necklace he gave on their wedding day*
> *Now deep in the broken timbers lay . . .*

On and on it goes for nine verses, and the best thing Wrecker can say about the song is that his father definitely wrote every word himself, for a change. It's meant to be a tribute to the era of the wrecking trade, a proud nod to his ancestors, which means Seven must have trekked to the library for some actual research.

"It's a good tune, Dad," Wrecker says during a much-needed break.

"I think so, too! This is the first time I've done it from start to finish. You can never go wrong in the key of C."

"The crowd was into it, too."

Wrecker is being kind. "A Ballad at the Tomb of the *Isaac Allerton*" had slogged on for thirteen and a half minutes, so most of the audience drifted away to watch the tiki-torch jugglers or the break-dancing parakeets. That's how it goes at Mallory Square.

Even Valdez Seven's loyal former bandmate, Rickenbacker Ricky, lasted only five verses before unplugging his guitar and taking a bow.

Wrecker's father is there because Suzanne had, out of sympathy, invited him to perform at a Friends of Blue Waters rally. Tomorrow a 180,000-ton cruise ship called the *Vixen of the Tropics* will enter the Port of Key West, dredging half a milky mile of mud behind it. Suzanne is staging another protest flotilla—the lawyer she's dating advised her to stop using the word "blockade"—and again she'll lead the charge from high in a colorful parasail. This afternoon's rally is raising money to gas up the local boats.

Suzanne made the former Austin Breakwater promise to play one—and only one—of his original songs; the rest of the set list is cover versions of hits by popular artists.

"Should I do 'Cheeseburger in Paradise'?" Valdez Seven whispers to Wrecker. "Or will they kill me?"

"They'll probably kill you if you don't."

"Yo, scope out my new flip-flops. Pink flamingos on the soles!"

"It's a start," Wrecker says.

"I honestly don't miss those skeevy old cowboy boots."

"Nobody does."

"Hey, wanna grab dinner tonight?"

"Breakfast tomorrow, Dad. Harpoon Harry's."

"Great. I'm buying!" Valdez Seven picks up his guitar and goes back to work.

Wrecker feels a sharp tap on the top of his head. It's Officer Nedrick Nugent sporting a blaze-orange traffic vest that looks about three sizes too small. No mask, no gun, same lousy attitude.

"Look who's here. The wiseass fence jumper," he says to Wrecker. "Why are you walkin' around with a fishing gaff in your hands? Did you steal it?"

"Oh. This?"

"And your clothes are wet."

"I was diving a wreck," Wrecker says. "That's where I got the gaff."

"Liar."

"Well, it's the truth."

"Some drunk tourist is gonna impale himself on that thing!"

"Take it easy. I'll leave now."

"Yeah, you will," Nugent says.

"But only because this time you didn't call me 'boy.'"

"What?"

"Hey, where's the best place around here to grab a pizza? I heard you're the expert."

Nugent walks off puzzled and fuming. Wrecker darts into a restroom at the Whitehead Street aquarium and takes the gaff apart. He taps the hollow shaft against the wall tiles until all twenty of the rolled-up fifty-dollar bills fall out. Just to be sure, he counts them twice.

After wadding the cash into a damp pocket, he screws the gaff back together and returns to the rally. He makes sure Suzanne isn't looking when he crams the money into the collection jar. He was lucky to recover it from the sunken barge with no further bloodshed; the short-tempered, long-toothed eel had evidently found another lair. Wrecker's dive had been quick and easy. After docking his skiff, he rode his bike straight to Mallory Square.

The crowd is a low-key mix of cruise-ship protesters and curious tourists. A Friends of Blue Waters pennant flaps on the seatback of Suzanne's wheelchair as she rolls through the square. Meanwhile, Wrecker's father is singing a Bob Dylan number that's even longer than the *Isaac Allerton* ballad. Every time people think the song is over, their applause is cut short by Valdez Seven starting another verse.

At least they're not booing, Wrecker thinks.

Suzanne rolls up and asks about the deep-sea gaff. Wrecker tells her about his afternoon barge dive but not the cash.

"And you couldn't stop by the house afterward," she says, "and put on some dry clothes?"

"I didn't want to miss Dad's set."

"The truth is I've seen worse excuses for a singer."

"He's not hideous," Wrecker agrees, tapping the gaff hook on his handlebars in time to the music.

"Our donation jar's almost full, Valdez. Major bank for the flotilla."

"What time is that ship supposed to get here tomorrow?"

"Ten-thirty," Suzanne says. "You're coming, right?"

"Definitely. Fausto's gave me the morning off."

"*Vixen of the Tropics.* Who dreams up these hokey names?"

"Where do I get one of those Blue Waters flags?"

"Take mine, I have a vanful." Suzanne removes the pennant from her wheelchair and hands it to Wrecker, who ties it to the hook end of the fish gaff.

"I've got to ask you something," he says, "and you need to be straight with me."

"Make it quick. I have to go help Dr. Troxel find his checkbook."

"It's about Mom and Roger moving to California."

"You should definitely stay here with me," Suzanne says. "Was that your question?"

"Yeah, but I feel like a leech."

"Keep talking that way and I'll knock your dumb butt off that bike."

"It's not like I want to leave Key West, but—"

"Then stay. End of discussion. How do you think your girlfriend would vote on this?"

"Thanks, sis."

"But maybe fold your own laundry from now on."

"Deal," he says.

They notice the crowd part for Officer Nugent, stomping red-faced in their direction. He's not thrilled to see Wrecker back at the scene.

"Go home and feed the Deacon," Suzanne says, turning her chair. "Let me deal with this bozo."

As Wrecker pedals away, he waves the flag-bearing gaff high over his head.

Not far from the courthouse on Whitehead Street stands the Cornish Memorial African Methodist Episcopal Zion Church. It was named for Andrew "Sandy" Cornish, who was born into slavery in Maryland. He was hired out to a railroad construction company down in Florida, and he eventually saved enough money to buy emancipation papers for himself and his wife, Lillah. Unfortunately, those documents—the only legal proof of his freedom—were destroyed in a fire. Slave traders from New Orleans later found Cornish and snatched him.

Somehow he was able to escape, vowing to never again be owned by another man. One day, as a stunned throng watched, he pulled a knife and stabbed himself in the leg, cut the muscle in one of his ankles, and chopped off a finger. Those self-inflicted injuries made Cornish worthless to the slave trade, which was his intention. He and his wife bought a farm in Key West, where he became an important civic figure and religious leader. When he passed away in the late 1860s, he was buried in the town cemetery.

Yet at some point, Cornish's grave marker disappeared. It wasn't replaced, and over time the location of his body was lost. Finally, nearly a hundred and fifty years after his death, a plaque honoring Cornish was placed on Clara Street in the cemetery. That's where Wrecker meets up with Willi after dinner.

She knows the whole story. "I wrote a paper on Mr. Cornish for AP English. Those were the pre-Klan days in Key West, obviously."

Both of them came in dark clothes: Wrecker wearing clean jeans and a long-sleeved cotton T-shirt, Willi in her black mourning dress and lacy veil. She brought a dozen fresh roses and a tapered candle that's supposed to smell like coconuts.

"Where's the wig?" Wrecker asks.

"Dumpster."

"It was time."

Walking to the Islander's grave, they pass the former resting place of Sarah Chillingwood. Someone else is now buried in the plot: Daniel "Waxley" Baxter, a local street performer. According to the shiny new marker, which hasn't yet been tainted by iguanas, Baxter lived to be ninety-five. A weatherproof photograph set in the polished granite shows a gray-bearded, normal-looking man with a cat in each arm. One of the pets is dressed up as Benjamin Franklin, complete with bifocal eyeglasses, and the other has been costumed as Dolly Parton, the legendary country singer.

STOP STARING, says the inscription on Baxter's stone.

"He used to come in the store every day for fresh salmon," Wrecker says. "Those cats of his had it good."

"I'm sure they've already moved on. That's what cats do." Willi brushes a mosquito off her veil. "What's wrong with us, Wreck? We stroll through this place like we're in Central Park, but it's basically twenty acres of death."

"I'm a big fan of quiet," Wrecker says. "But you're right. Neither of us is on the normal spectrum."

"Ever wonder why we don't believe in ghosts or spirits?"

"The first time I saw you here, I wasn't so sure."

At Manuel Cabeza's grave, Wrecker lights the scented candle and Willi arranges the roses. They talk about Angela, long passed by now. Willi says she never found a single picture of the woman in old documents and newspapers.

"Everything I read said she was beautiful, but that's all. Then, after El Isleño was killed, it's like she vanished into thin air."

"Probably chased out of town," Wrecker says.

"After she put a hex on the place."

"Who knows if that's even true." Wrecker believes in karma, not curses.

"Yo, what was the name of your great-great-grandfather's boat? The bootlegger dude."

"It was called the *Rum Punch*. He wasn't exactly shy about his profession."

"Well, guess who built the keel on that boat," Willi says. "My great-great-grandfather, the ace ship carpenter and lifelong Klansman."

"Swanson Paul?"

"I found the work order in one of Mom's secret boxes. It was signed by Mr. Valdez Jones IV. You can have it if you want."

Wrecker says no thanks. "Where's your great-great-grandfather buried?"

"Don't know. Don't care," says Willi.

She closes her eyes and sings. It's the only sound in the graveyard.

La tragedia, la vergüenza
Los corazones llorosos deben preguntarse por qué
Y espero que los arcoíris iluminen el cielo

Afterward they walk to the Catholic section to see the now-vacant vault that Silver Mustache and his gang had used as a bank. It's still cordoned off as a crime scene. Willi pulls out a Sharpie, ducks under the yellow tape, and writes NOT REALLY above the words BENDITO VACHS.

A police car rolls slowly down Olivia Street, the door-mounted spotlight sweeping the cemetery grounds. Wrecker and Willi take cover behind a double headstone belonging to a recently departed couple named Garcia, married for forty-seven years.

Willi says she's leaving for Bermuda with the parental units in a few days—mandatory family time before the start of soccer practice, and then school. Wrecker offers to take care of the Islander's burial site while she's gone.

"Actually, I think I'm done," Willi says.

"I promise not to sing."

"Good, because that would literally disturb the peace."

"But seriously, this is it?" Wrecker says. "You're *done* done?"

"Not in my heart, never. But I can't spend the rest of my life singing to a tombstone. Besides, one of these nights the cops are bound to catch me out here—"

"Catch *us,* you mean."

"It's time to dial down the drama in Willi World." She takes off her veil. "I'll just bring flowers on his birthday, like normal mourners do."

"What about Swanson Paul?"

"Who?"

"Exactly."

"What could I possibly find out about the man that would cancel out what he and his mob did to El Isleño? Nothing," Willi says. "Looking backward gets exhausting, Wreck. I've got other things I want to do. Actual ideas."

Once the patrol car is out of sight, they leave the cemetery. The night air lies warm and heavy, and Margaret Street smells like magnolias. Wrecker walks his bicycle alongside Willi, who's slow-coasting in her graveyard dress aboard the electric skateboard. A scrawny dog with a blinking LED collar lopes down the sidewalk chewing the remains of a Panama hat. The road is quiet except for a small pink-trimmed Conch house, where laughter and music spill from the open windows.

"Eighties rock," Willi whispers, leaning close. "Yikes."

Wrecker asks if she wants to go out on the skiff tomorrow.

"Only if you admit it's a date," she says.

"Another one of those mega–cruise ships is docking here. Suzanne's rebooting the flotilla."

"So you're asking me out on a date disguised as demonstrating for a good cause?"

Wrecker raises his hands in mock surrender. "You're right. It's all part of my brilliant master plan."

"I'll go," Willi says, "but only on one condition."

A simple yes or no would be so refreshing, he thinks.

"Afterwards you take me free diving," she says.

"Seriously?"

"On a real shipwreck, but not too deep!"

"I can make that happen," Wrecker says.

When they get to the corner at Southard, Willi picks up her board and says, "I'm going this way. See ya in the morning."

"Ten sharp at the dock."

She stands there, arms folded, as if she's expecting something. Wrecker makes a brave guess and kisses her cheek.

"Not bad for a loner," she says. "Let's call this progress."

"Or just a nice moment under the Iguana Tree." He points up at the high branches.

"Sooo romantic. Good night, Ichabod. Good night, Wreck."

Off she glides on her skateboard, impossible not to watch. Halfway down the block, she spins around and calls out: "Yo, what's the dress code for a protest flotilla?"

Wrecker, laughing, hops on his bike.

ACKNOWLEDGMENTS

I am most grateful for the assistance of David Sloan, Fred and Rita Troxel, Arlo Haskell, and Nancy Klingener in the Florida Keys. Two very helpful books were *The Wreckers*, volume 3 of *The Florida Keys*, by John Viele, and *The Young Wrecker on the Florida Reef* by Richard Meade Bache.

ABOUT THE AUTHOR

CARL HIAASEN was born and raised in Florida, where he still lives. His books include the Newbery Honor winner *Hoot*, as well as *Flush, Scat, Chomp, Skink—No Surrender*, and *Squirm*. Hiaasen wrote a column for the *Miami Herald* for many years and is the author of several bestselling books for adults, including *Squeeze Me, Assume the Worst: The Graduation Speech You'll Never Hear*, and *Bad Monkey*, which is currently being developed for television by Apple TV.

carlhiaasen.com